Under Roman Skies

This is a work of fiction. Names, characters, events and incidents are the product of the author's imagination. Any resemblance to actual persons, living or dead, or actual events is purely incidental.

Be Patient and tough;
Someday this pain will be useful to you

Ovid

Chapter 1

The best days are the sunny ones, of which this was no exception. It was hot and the sun baked the cobbles of the roads and the sand of the pathways, it baked the houses and had already caused two fires in as many weeks, thankfully not serious fires, which was why nobody much cared at the moment because the air was alive with excitement, it hummed and bustled and seeped into the skin making the brains of most, dizzy and mad. Sage walked down almost deserted streets and back alleys relishing the silence, the emptiness that came with the two-week long tournament that sucked the population into the huge Colosseum. She held her breath as she took a side street, being careful not to slip off the stepping stones placed to protect one's feet from the perpetual sludge of chamber pots that festered underfoot. Here the sun did not penetrate the ground to dry it up, for the housing was closely packed. Emerging onto a main street, she walked under a viaduct where a few beggars had sought the shade, a huge roar erupted from the great arena, momentarily breaking into the silence of the world outside. Sage smiled, for today with the sun she felt as light as air, as though this truly was the greatest city in all the world. Which of course it was, for didn't they say that all roads led to Rome? This was why, they had the greatest trading routes, businesses and nothing beat Rome when it came to Charioteers and the famous Gladiators. Another tremendous roar floated across the city, louder now that Sage was closer, her heart sped up a little as she paused to look up at the vast concrete structure with its many arches over three levels. All along the top stood the women and children watching the fighting below. A good view if not a little distant, Sage always thought, far enough away not to care when a

3

blade cut flesh, though in this tournament killing blows were banned. This tournament was for showing off the local and distant Gladiatorial schools, of which Rome itself had four. Everyone who was anyone was here, for here names were made, Gladiators could earn their freedom from the emperor, women swooned and chose their favourites for the bed chambers. Sage knew in nine months a surge of unclaimed babies would be left in the streets to die, babies that husbands had doubts about. For whilst it was common for men and women to have affairs, it was done as discretely as possible, but it was husbands who had the rights over accepting a new born, so if there were doubts, the new born were abandoned. Even prostitutes used arches with rags to hide them away, sex wasn't something Romans advertised. The wealthier women craved for the love of a Gladiator, their sweat was deemed an aphrodisiac, so Gladiators did well from their profession; it was all part of the madness of the tournament. So was the betting, men were made rich if they were favoured by the Gods, or as was more often the case, broken by the crippling losses of everything they had. Youth would drink and fight in the evenings, sometimes just to show off in front of young women, it all made Sage a little giddy, life was always a bit more dangerous when the tournaments were on.

Somewhere on the top row was her Mistress, Heva Decimus, who was the sister of the emperor's wife. Sage was her personal slave and was treated well by her and her husband. Having been born into slavery and losing her mother at an early age, Sage had been given a position in the Decimus family, and had worked her way up to being a personal slave, this was a position of great trust, something Sage took very seriously. She found the entrance she had exited from earlier and now began to climb the many steps to the top, listening to the cheers, shouts and applause of the crowd within. As she ambled passed the rows of arches, booing began, signalling that a favourite had just lost, in other times, that loss would have been his life. Sage shuddered, she had no qualms about this kind of tournament, but when men killed each other for sport, she would not attend, nor would a great many other citizens, partly because, like Sage they disliked the killing, but mostly because the price of entry went up so much the average citizen couldn't afford to attend.

Finally in the open air of the top row of the Colosseum, the suns heat hit Sage as she emerged from the shade of the corridors, she wove her way past women, children and slaves to find Heva Decimus shouting and cheering herself hoarse. Sage smiled at the woman in her white toga, her black hair pinned about her with ringlets swinging in the breeze; she turned at that moment and saw Sage approaching. "Sage! He won! He

4

won!" She shouted, excitement pouring from her very veins, her face flushed. Sage laughed, "of course Mistress, it would be unfortunate if he failed!" They laughed, but relief was etched onto Heva's face, an expression Sage did not miss. For a few days Mistress Heva had shown a particular interest in one of the Gladiators, she tried to be casual about her enquiries, but her questions did not fool Sage, her Mistress was playing with fire, for the Gladiator she so revered was the most famous Gladiator of them all, and he was also the current favourite of her sister, Aquilina, who was well known for the possessiveness of her lovers. Sage hoped this would not end badly, but rarely did things end well when Aquilina was involved. "Did you bring the basket?" Heva asked, Sage smiled and swung the food into view. "I am ravished, we can eat now his fight is over for a bit."

Sage was sure her mistress was blushing, but it might have been the midday sun. They both ate enthusiastically, while Heva told her slave how the first bout had gone. "I must confess, such grace is seldom seen on a battlefield, they duck and dive Sage, then attack with their swords, it is quite the dance!" Sage smiled; her mistress was so full of the euphoria that infected all present; it was a joy to see. "When is his next bout?" She asked glancing down at the arena so far below them.

"I am not sure, but we have the Essedari next."

Sage grinned, for she was fond of the chariot fighters with their slave or willing volunteer drivers, she marvelled at the way they leapt from their chariots with a manica to protect one arm, a small shield and a sword, how nimble they were. How magnificent their horses, swathed in a sheen of sweat, eyes wild with the excitement. The crowd roared with glee as the chariots thundered into the arena racing in opposite directions, the riders aiming a long spear to jab at his opponent. After a few rounds the riders jumped off and used a short sword to battle each other. Sage watched transfixed, her bread hardening in the sun. From the top most part of the Colosseum she could not see the fighters' faces or expressions and their grunts and shouts were hardly heard over the roar of the crowd, but her body twitched with involuntary sympathy which made her mistress laugh at her. "Sage, you look like you're dancing." She teased. When the charioteers left the arena, the Mirmillones returned though not the gladiator mistress Heva wanted to see, still the fighting proved to be entertaining and dramatic. They took water from the water carrier, they munched at the bread and cheese, and drank wine when the water carrier wasn't around to serve them. The sun moved across the sky and finally the most famous Gladiator returned to the arena to the standing crowd who cheered so loudly Sage thought she'd go deaf. He needed no introduction his fame was obvious, but still the chant went up "Robaratus! Robaratus!" He held his arms in the air and nodded his gratitude to them all, upon his face he wore a golden mask so that none could see him, he was a Mirmillon. He looked magnificent from his attire alone, his massive shield, short sword, bare torso revealing his muscular back, it was not surprising he was so popular, for even up here, Sage could see his was built like a bear, powerful muscles tensed and relaxed as he moved with snake like grace. His roar was intimidating and echoed around the arena, making Sage glad she was so far away. It was no wonder women loved this man, he oozed sex appeal, had confidence in abundance and according to Sage's friend, was just as good in the bedroom. April was the slave of Aquilina, the Emperor's wife, and very little escaped her ears and eyes. Sage often wondered how many secrets her friend carried of the first family of Rome. Heva was leaning against the rail, craning her neck to get a better look at this famous Gladiator, who stopped in front of their side of the arena, his eyes searching the crowd, his head up seemingly looking straight at them, he roared at them and the crowd cheered back noisily, he roared again, making Sage cringe at the sheer volume he could muster. After a moment, he stepped back and turned to face the arena. A Retiarii armed with a trident, dagger and net entered, to the joy of the crowd, who cheered loudly. "Velox! Velox!" They chanted as the Retiarii strode confidently around the arena, with the watchful eye of the famous Mirmillon, Robaratus. "Do you not think him magnificent Sage?" Heva's face was indeed flushed, her eyes wide with excitement. Sage smiled and nodded. "Indeed Mistress, a most formidable foe for Robaratus" Heva pulled a face, "I meant Robaratus!" She said, Sage smiled.

"Velox may be famous and to some good looking, but his face is scarred, whereas I have seen Robaratus' face and it is beautiful."

Sage quashed a sudden wave of fear. "Some say Mistress that scars make the man!" She ventured, and got a loud laugh from Heva in return. "I prefer a man who is strong and handsome, like my husband."

Nothing more could be said as the two fighters were circling each other, with the judge and his long stick walking around them at a safe distance away. Velox made the first lunge, a test, Robaratus stepped back arms wide as he turned to the crowd momentarily taking his attention away from his opponent, who lunged with his dagger trying to get around the huge shield, one of them shouted as Robaratus leapt forward and sideward barging into Velox, sending him staggering backwards. Robaratus strode forward, Velox threw his net aiming at the other's feet, Robaratus jumped and avoided being tripped to the cheers of the crowd, and so they danced back and forth. Swords clashed and echoed around the colosseum; their shouts

6

could be heard in the hush as all waited with baited breath for a strike. When Robaratus charged with his shield, which was nearly as tall as Sage, the crowd erupted with cheers, and when Velox crouched and twisted away, everyone cheered again, though some hissed disapproval. The fight lasted a long time, sheens of sweat shone on both fighters making Sage wonder if the cool afternoon breeze was touching the fighters below, it was certainly one of the advantages of being so high up, the rest of the crowd were covered by vast sheets whose shadows did not touch the arena at all, leaving the contestants exposed to the heat and easily visible. Suddenly Robaratus barrelled forward pushing with his powerful legs shoving Velox backwards at such a pace he almost fell over, as Velox twisted to escape the push, Robaratus spun around his shield cutting his blade across the other's back. Velox fell to the sandy floor. The crowd erupted, Heva jumped up and down ecstatically, Sage stared at the bleeding Velox, she felt faint at the thought he was so badly wounded, her mistress's reaction to the strike was equally appalling to Sage, to cheer for a man to cut another was not a game to Sage. Velox raised his index finger indicating he could no longer go on. The judge stepped in with his long stick keeping Robaratus away from Velox as they waited on the Editor, who waited on the Emperor, who waited on the crowd, who screamed and shouted their many views. In the end it was the single cry of *mitte* that decided the Emperor, for Velox was a popular Gladiator and everyone wanted to see him spared. So, it was with this one universal cry that the Editor acknowledged the Emperor and Robaratus stepped back with a nod to his opponent. Several slaves appeared and helped the injured man away, while Robaratus soaked up the roaring enthusiasm of the crowd. Sage couldn't bring herself to like him, he was a showman and had earned every cheer he now got, but he killed men, sliced men, and bathed in the glory that was life or death. In some distant way it was hard not to admire such a powerful man, but she was still glad to be far away from his overbearing, bear like presence. Sage found herself shaking her head sadly, she would never understand why people thrilled for such raw violence; she would always prefer the charioteers.

The day was over and as fast as the stadium had filled, so it emptied, with the prostitutes in their rented cubicles under the Colosseum fornices. *This being just the start of the evening.* Sage thought as they filed past the grunting and groaning couples. They found Decimus walking slowly deep in conversation with another man. When he had finished talking the two men nodded to each other and Decimus turned to his wife Heva and Sage, offering his arm to his wife his smile wide. "Did you enjoy today?" He asked with gentleness. She enthusiastically gave her response, as she told him about all the best bits she had enjoyed, Sage followed a step behind, eyes down as was her custom, as she listened to her mistress talk. To her husband she likely sounded like an excited fan of the games, but Sage knew every gushing word of praise for Robaratus was an obvious declaration of her, more than a fan, interest. Decimus and Heva were well liked and considered one of the most popular couples in Rome, their affairs were always discrete, making some wonder if either really had them. Sage often wondered why they bothered, they were so content with each other, she hardly understood why they needed other partners, yet this was Rome and Romans needed other partners. A nudge at her elbow brought her out of her wanderings. "Are you going to the evening meal?" April walked alongside Sage, her face almost beetroot colour from the sun. Sage shrugged. April had a round face and tanned skin, at least it would be after today's sun, Aquilina taunted her by saying she was dirty; the mud would never wash off it peeled instead. "I hear a certain Gladiator will be there." April sang. Sage nudged her hard shushing as she did.

"Tell me you haven't said anything to your Mistress?"

April rolled her eyes. "I like my life" She replied. "I might tease you Sage, but on my honour, I'd not dare say a word to my Mistress. If she suspects anything, she will find out from her many spies, not me."

Sage eyed her for a moment longer, then returned her eyes to the ground. April walked along with them all chatting happily about the contest. "Did you like the Charioteers?" She asked, remembering that Sage had once said she quite admired them. Sage nodded.

"She was dancing with their every move!" Heva shouted over her shoulder, then laughed as Sage blushed. "Do you not have a favourite?" April asked.

"No. I like what they do, not any individual, besides what point is there in a slave liking one such as a Charioteer?" Sage replied her eyes still on the ground. "Everyone should have dreams." April ventured airily.

"I see no point. I am a slave, I live to serve my Mistress, what use have I for dreams when I live mine every day?" Sage smiled. She truly did love her Mistress and her husband and had no other expectation of life.

"That is so shallow Sage. Everyone has a hero! Have you no dreams of a husband?"

Sage sighed and smiled. "April, you know well the answer to that. I have no dreams or expectations of marriage. I would not want to share my husband, and there is not a man on this earth who would keep to one wife only!"

"What are your objections to sharing your husband?" Heva asked. Sage blushed.

"Forgive me Mistress, I had not meant my words to insult you."

"I am not insulted, just curious. I've heard you say this before, but I wonder why?"

Sage chewed her bottom lip. "If a couple are truly happy, why would they want to invite anyone else into that marriage?"

"Arh! Have you not heard that variety is the spice of life?" Decimus asked. "It keeps a marriage alive if a man or woman can find a little something on the side now and then."

"There is no harm in it as long as the married couple still love each other more than their affairs." Heva put in, with a doe eyed look at her husband who smiled kindly down at her. *And when the wife brings forth not his off spring what then of the marriage my Mistress?* Sage thought sadly.

"I am dreaming of Rufus the accountant." April announced proudly. Everyone burst out laughing. "April that surely is dreaming!" Sage giggled. "I see not why. I *am* the Emperors wife's *personal* slave, so I should set my expectations of a husband high." April shot her chin into the air, making Sage giggle again. "Does Rufus know he is destined to become your esteemed husband?"

"Of course not! Where is the fun in courting and flirting if he is told the outcome?" April protested.

"May the Gods have sympathy upon him." Sage giggled.

"Have your opinions of Gladiators changed yet?" April asked her.

"No. I still think theirs is a distasteful sport." Sage wrinkled her nose.

"I love the grace in the way they move, in the power of their arms. I was once allowed to try and lift a sword; I couldn't get it off the ground!" April enthused.

"Does it not bother you that these men kill each other?" Sage asked looking at her friend in earnest.

"Charioteers die too you know." April sounded defensive.

"They die by accident, a misjudged corner, an over lean, a horse colliding with another, they don't actually attempt to kill each other."

"Well Gladiators don't do that much killing anymore." April tried again, sounding more positive.

"So, who is your favourite Gladiator then?" Though Sage was sure she could guess.

"Velox the Retiarii, he is so sexy, naked but for his loin cloth, and all that muscle on such a body! Not to mention that scar running down his face." Aprils' voice deepened as she spoke, which made Sage laugh. "Not the famous Robaratus?"

"Na! Everyone loves him! Besides he wears that golden mask to protect his pretty face. Although I did overhear my mistress saying she was going to give him a golden helmet" April said waving her hand dismissively, but both slaves gave cautious glances at Heva walking in front of them with her arm through her husbands. Sage had no doubt the woman was keenly listening to them chat, as she and her husband had fallen silent. The evening was starting to produce a gentle breeze to cool the stifling heat of the day, the meal would be a good affair given the weather had stayed dry. They arrived at the villa of Decimus and April said her farewells, promising to find Sage later, Sage followed her owners inside and made her way to the dressing room of her mistress, where she waited, eyes down, to attend her needs.

"I am hoping to see Rob tonight." Heva confided as Sage attended to her hair. Sage pulled a face and bit her bottom lip, a movement Heva caught in her mirror. "What is wrong girl?"

"Nothing mistress." Sage replied, her eyes down.

"Are you concerned about Robaratus and I?"

"No mistress, none of my business mistress."

"Don't worry Sage dear. What can Aquilina do to me? I am happily married and every woman flirts, so she cannot get jealous of that." Heva smiled broadly. "Though if he wanted me, I'd not refuse!" Heva laughed in a naughty way. "Think of all that sweat I could collect and how much more insane would my nights be with Decimus!"

"Forgive me mistress, but is there really any truth to that, about Gladiator sweat being an aphrodisiac?"

Heva shrugged. "Well, my sister swears by it."

Sage knew Aquilina would swear anything if it made other women jealous of her.

Chapter 2

Torches flickered in the street and all along the front of the Colosseum, the thick smoke choked passers-by in the still evening air, the scent of oil stung the nostrils, yet did the masses throng towards the arena where the great meal was taking place. Poor and wealthy side by side sharing and laughing together. Stall holders set up their wares along the fornices of the Colosseum, sharing with the prostitutes. Other stall holders had their wares set up along the front of the great building. Pick pockets were few, but still desperate people who saw an opportunity would risk their lives for an *as*. Sage kept one hand firmly on her purse, for the few as she had, she did not wish a pick pocket to benefit from. She wandered from stall to stall but her eyes were not really on the wares before her, but on her Mistress who was walking with her husband and a certain Gladiator, who walked beside them both in light conversation, for a man who could roar like a lion, his voice was remarkably quiet in company. He was indeed built like a bear, even though he wore a toga along with the present company, his arms were easily double the size of Sage's, and when he moved them, she caught the sight of tattoos. He was taller than Decimus and Heva hardly reached his shoulder, it was no wonder he was so desired, a tall man built like that. *Pity the woman he settles to!* Sage thought with a sly smile. "Arh, I have been all over looking for you!"

Sage turned to find April at her side. "How is it you can just appear out of nowhere?" Sage asked her.

"Hardly like that, I have been looking for you, not my concern if you are daydreaming about that rather gorgeous Gladiator."

Sage sneered at her. "You mean that oversized bear, who stands heads above everyone else?"

"The very same one that your Mistress keeps giving sideways glances at."

"And where is your mistress?" Sage asked.

"Currently entertaining Velox, who is somewhat incapable of escaping her attentions." April giggled.

"How is he?" Sage found herself asking, not that she really cared, but she did worry.

11

"Sore. Gladiators do not complain about injuries, they're not soft Sage."

"What do you suppose they are talking about?" Sage wondered; her friend shrugged. "It's not what is being said, more what is not."

When Sage gave her an odd look, April explained. "Look at the body language. Your mistress can't take her eyes off the bear, as you call him, and see how he often looks over her husband's head to look at her, making her blush."

"Meaning what?" Sage was cautious in her question.

"Meaning your mistress is about to dip her toes in hot water. That Gladiator fancies her."

Sage looked at the man called Robaratus, April was right, he did keep looking at Heva. He had the greenest eyes she had ever seen on anyone, making her wonder at his origins. His hair was closely cropped and with his tattoos, he looked terrifying, tribal, a heathen almost, yet his smile was warm, and his white teeth sat well against his sun kissed skin.

"What would Aquilina do to him if she found him out?"

April thought about it. "Depends what she found out. Technically he belongs to the Emperor, so she cannot decide any fate that might be, um fatal!" April smiled. "I don't think *she* can do anything, but her husband can."

"And my mistress? What can Heva do to her?"

"Arh!" April said, opening her arms. "Sisters can be quite spiteful against each other."

"My mistress says Aquilina cannot do anything, she is wife to a popular man and flirting isn't a crime." Sage informed her.

"Well, no, *flirting* isn't a crime. Sleeping with him *is*."

April had become quite serious. "Really Sage, you need to try and stop this. It could destroy Decimus' reputation. Aquilina can have his senator status removed. He could be fined into poverty. Heva would be gossiped about terribly and no one would want to be acquainted with her."

"It's not my place April. If she loves this Gladiator then she will follow her heart and not think of the consequences."

"Then hope she never falls in love with him. If she thinks she can bed him and walk away, she is a foolish woman indeed. Surely, she must know women love him, would leave husbands gladly to be with him? It is a recipe for disaster." April warned.

"I think she just wants his sweat."

April fell about laughing. "Arh Sage! So naïve! Surely you don't buy all that about Gladiator sweat?" When Sage blushed, April laughed even more. She slapped her friend on the shoulder, "You're not the only one!"

The stalls of food were an absolute treat, both women slaves ogled at the many offerings, and refused to pay most of the prices, yet they munched their way through any number of delicacies, April feasted on the many oysters and mussels, regardless of the warning Sage gave about food poisoning. Sows' udders were another favourite to feast upon, along with as many vegetables as one could want, cheeses and stuffed thrushes. Sage didn't miss the huge amount of food the Gladiators ate, any she spotted ate plates full. She found her Mistress and the bear talking quietly by a stall selling wine, her husband some distance away talking to another group of men, Robaratus was talking easily and smiling at Heva, his fingers every now and then brushing hers making her smile broader. He leaned over and spoke into her ear, making her act girlish, and had it not been night time with fire lit torches, Sage would have imagined she was blushing. It was an innocent enough flirtation, but after everything April had said, Sage saw the play in action, the laying down of the pieces that would decide if the bear would get what he wanted in both respects.

"Do you think he really likes her?" She asked her friend. April looked over at the Gladiator. "Nope. Robaratus has no heart, he only cares about what he can get away with. He fancies his chances with your mistress, and given her responses, He will have his fun, then he will walk away." She answered truthfully.

"Then why do this, surely my Mistress will end up hurt?"

"Your Mistress knows how to play the game, Sage. She has done it lots of times. Why do you act like you don't know this?"

Sage shrugged, yet there was something different in the way her Mistress acted this time, it seemed more realistic. When Decimus called them over, she noted how the bear put his hand on Heva's back, a gentle touch that guided her forward, she shivered.

"Awe, how sweet! In a few days she'll be collecting his sweat for her own use with her husband." April teased.

"That's vile, I cannot understand why anyone would want another man's sweat as an aphrodisiac. Just because he is a Gladiator doesn't make him God like! You're right April, it's utterly disgusting."

"Well, it does to the wealthy!" April laughed. "Smart in business and stupid in beliefs."

"Speaking of smart in business, have you seen Rufus?" Sage nudged her friend.

"I have, he is well. I got to say a greeting to him this morning, he was quite taken aback."

"I bet he was!" Sage laughed.

"Small steps my girl, you will see."

"Oh, indeed I will be watching!" Sage assured her and she went back to watching her mistress and the bear. Heva laughed loudly as Robaratus filled her glass. Decimus seemed oblivious to the flirting, often gripping the bear's shoulder and laughing with him. When Decimus excused himself to use the nearby toilets, which were providing relief for many, the bear brushed his fingers through Heva's hair, tucking a stray strand behind her ear. His eyes shone with fake adoration, and he trailed his knuckles down her arm. Heva understood the silent desire and answered in her own way, by admiring his hand, by being forward enough to hold it against her face, making Sage gasp. The bear said something to her and they both walked a short distance into the shade, where they were hidden from nearly everyone, but they were close to Sage now, and she watched with wide eyed horror as the huge man bent down and kissed her mistress on the lips. Sage was agog, unable to blink, Heva had never behaved so obviously before, she even moaned from the contact. The kiss was long and his hands roamed over her back, even onto her backside, and Heva wriggled and moaned even more, her own hands running over the stubble of his head, her mouth hungry for his. Sage wanted to tear herself away, to run away but she was rooted to the spot, her mouth open in shock. She managed finally to pull herself together and look about for Decimus, she saw him dropping his toga down, and smiling at the next person in the queue then he moved away, and headed back towards where he had left his wife. Sage panicked turning back to where Heva and the bear had been, but they were gone, she found them laughing conspiratorially at a food stall, as Decimus strolled up to them. Sage let out a huge sigh of relief. She turned to move and bumped into April who stood with her arms folded over her chest. "Oh dear." She said sincerely. "Sage if this gets out of hand, you will be a homeless slave. No man needs a female personal slave, except for you know what!"

Sage looked at her surprised. "I never thought of that." She admitted.

"I think this is proving to be a most unenjoyable evening."

"Then let us go in search of some fun." April didn't wait for her to respond, she grabbed Sage's arm and tugged her away, dragging her back towards the further side of the long colosseum wall.

The dawn crept slowly across the kitchen floor, where Sage slept in front of the fire place, the brightness illuminated her face making her wince. *A little longer, the birds are not singing yet.* She told herself, but it wasn't long before a thin song drifted into the morning silence, and an answer drifted back, then a whole chorus of bird song chirped into the kitchen silence, making Sage cover her ears as if that act alone would return the night. Sage sat up, she ached all over as she did most mornings, the floor was cold now, the fire needed starting, so she stood and stretched, bones cracking and creaking. She set about her chores, fire wood, sweeping the floor, getting the coin and skipping off to market. It was the ninth day, so a full market would be available, making it extra important to get there early, so she could get the pick of the food on offer. The sun rose steadily and promised another hot and humid day for those fighting in the arena, though she would not watch today, her Mistress did not enjoy hunting entertainment, but her Master loved it, so he would be gone all day. That brought Sage to a standstill. She remembered Heva's behaviour with the bear, and her stomach flipped as she realised Decimus would be out all day. She hurried on to the market finding it already busy with slaves doing as she was, seeking out the best for their owners. Sage was already hot by the time she got back to the villa, she wondered briefly if April had survived the oysters and mussels, which made her smile to herself. Upon returning home, she set the fire and then, seeing cook arrive, she headed to her Mistresses room. Heva was brushing her long hair by the window. "Forgive me Mistress, I was at the market." Sage said running to her side. "I know Sage, I can brush my own hair!" Still, she handed over the brush that her slave might take over.

"Master Decimus will be at the games all day, and I am entertaining Robaratus, to save him from unwanted attentions." She smiled knowingly, and Sage kept her face neutral as was expected. Heva chose to wear a light mauve toga, with white banding at the edges, her beautiful black hair was ringleted and decorated with pearls. If her Mistress was going to be busy with the bear, then Sage had free time, and she had no desire to hang about while her Mistress had her heart broken. So, when the great man arrived talking briefly with Decimus as he rushed to leave for the arena, Sage waited until Heva had given her a nod of dismissal, taking Robaratus's arm and heading off for a walk around the extensive gardens of the villa in which they all lived. Sage headed for the Campus Martius which lay beside the river Tiber, a place that was so vast, it allowed for chariot races and other horse exercises. Many a youth would be found playing ball games or wrestling. Sage loved to sit and watch them all under the hot sun that kissed Rome. Slaves were invisible to Romans, she was never bothered or talked to, and that suited her best, for Sage knew her place in the world, loved her home and her routine. She watched the young men who would soon become businessmen like their fathers, or soldiers, or officers, she pondered if any might become politicians, but all would have but a short time to be free in, before they were expected to choose wives, to create business, to flirt and have affairs. Romans were not prudes when it came to sex, but they were prudes when it came to privacy. No Roman liked to see another naked and, in the act, so-to-speak, yet a few brave young men were bathing naked in the river, much to the enjoyment and perversion of some wealthy women whose gardens happened to overlook just that place. Sage listened to the shouting, splashing, laughter and jeers, she watched with great interest as the young men raced their horses over the charioteers' pitch, at others who practised horsemanship, she watched a couple of young men mending a chariot, pointing and then laughing at some joke.

Sage knew not what awoke her, she didn't remember falling asleep, but the sun had moved around the sky and the shadows were creeping along the grass, she got up and brushed herself down, then headed for home at a brisk walk. Upon arriving at the Villa, everything seemed quiet, she walked into the kitchen to find cook working at the evening meal, she rushed upstairs to her Mistresses room and halted at the sound of giggles and moans. Then a deeper voice spoke in hushed tones, not her Master, but the bear himself. Sage closed her eyes and took a deep breath, he sounded so calm and in control, his moans perfectly orchestrated to some attention Heva was giving him, when she yelped Sage jumped and turned from the door just as her Mistress began to moan and pant loudly. *All a lie for a Gladiators pleasure, Absurd.* Sage slinked away from the bedroom a deep nausea swilling inside her, she returned to the kitchen.
"You might have warned me." She told cook, who looked up at her and shrugged. "He's still 'ere then?" Her tone carried as much distaste as Sage felt.
"Yup."
"Master will be home soon. That'll get 'em out the bed." The slave boy grinned.
"I hope they're out the bed long before Master comes home Puer Decimus." Sage pointed out.
"Too late for that Sage, Master already came home for the midday meal, and found Mistress was still entertaining. He was none too pleased to discover this so." Cook added, then reached to swipe Puer Decimus for laughing, but he jumped to avoid her.
"You mean Master saw them in bed?" Sage asked aghast.
"They'd moved off the bed by then, I don't think he saw anything, but I am quite certain he damn heard her! She don't make that much noise when he does it."
"I knew this would end badly." Sage uttered as she sank into a chair.
"Won't end badly for the Gladiator, he got a day with Aquilina's sister, few can boast having both women!" Puer Decimus cheered from a safe distance.

16

"Master will have something to say when that Robaratus leaves." Cook said in a hushed tone.

Decimus stood at one end of a large room with deep red walls and paintings of Romans in states of embrace, a tiled floor and several torches that flickered their light into the area. Heva stood in front of him, she knew well what he was about to say. "Well?" He asked quietly. She shrugged. "You knew I was entertaining Robaratus."

"Do you sound like that with every affair you have?" He snarled. Heva blushed. "I have no idea." She lied. She had never felt so invigorated with anyone before.

"Flirting is one thing Heva, but he is your sister's favourite fuck right now, do you think your behaviour is appropriate?" He was still snarling, but his temper was controlled.

"He is a Gladiator; he fucks plenty of married women and she doesn't care." Heva retorted, her own voice defensive.

"He belongs to your brother-in-law, how are you ignoring this point?"

"I can't see why it should matter." Heva pointed out in a raised voice.

"It matters." Decimus replied testily. "You will end it now and not see him again."

"I what? I won't!"

"You will Heva. He is bad news." Decimus growled. He had never laid down the law to her before, she ran from the room. Sage followed her up to her bed room.

"How could he be so cruel?" Heva sobbed. Sage said nothing, she felt sorry for Heva, but furious that the Gladiator had caused so much trouble. He knew what he was doing and he knew damn well the trouble it would cause; she could almost picture him sniggering about it.

"He was so virile Sage. I never felt like that before, sp, special, needed, loved." She stammered through her tears. "He knew things I didn't! Oh, Gods, I cannot give him up. I cannot." She sobbed more loudly now, so Sage wrapped her arms about her and Heva turned to cry into her tunic.

"Did you not hear the things said about him mistress?" Sage asked softly. Heva nodded her head.

"Did you not think there might be some truth to those things?"

"Y, yes and no." Heva pulled away from Sage and wiped her eyes. "I was curious. I never expected he would like *me*!"

Sage was surprised to hear that. "Why ever not? You are a beautiful woman mistress."

Heva sobbed a laugh. "You're biased Sage dear."

"Biased or not mistress, you have a solid and wonderful marriage to

17

Decimus, a Gladiator should not spoil that."

"Decimus will get over it, but I shall not be so forgiving. How dare he order me to give up this pleasure." She was sounding angry again and there was nothing Sage could say to change her mind. Decimus had unwittingly challenged her, perhaps the bear would leave her mistress alone now he'd had his fun after all.

Indeed, there was no sign of the Gladiator for two days, and Heva's mood reflected her anxiety. Decimus stayed at home to add to the problem, or maybe he was the problem, for Robaratus had to know he was found out. If Heva wanted to go out, Decimus offered to go with her, so she stayed at home. Sage hated the atmosphere in her loving home, where once everyone was cheerful, now they all tip toed around hoping not to be shouted at. Sage did manage to get out and found April in the shopping district watching men put out another fire the heat had caused.

"Hey Sage. How is your mistress?" April smiled.

"Obviously you know what happened?" Sage looked at her intently.

"Puer has a big mouth." April said still smiling. Sage rolled her eyes.

"That boy is going to cause some trouble if your mistress hears about it." A large piece of wall crashed to the ground making both women jump. "Where is that hideous bear? Too cowardly to show his rotten face again." Sage allowed some of her anger to show.

"He is training most of the time. Fucking the rest. It's what most of them do." April informed her.

"See this why I hate men so much. They have no hearts, not an ounce of caring inside them."

"Sage Gladiators make a good living from their loins and sweat. You forget they pay for it all eventually. Most do not last the three years minimum they might sign up for. Robaratus has survived ten years, which makes him pretty unique."

"He must be as rich as the bloody Emperor then." Sage seethed. April shrugged. "He might be, but it takes two to destroy a marriage, and I saw Heva at the evening meal remember. She wasn't exactly fighting him off or calling for help!"

"Trouble is she says he made her feel loved and she has no intention of giving him up." Sage lowered her eyes; it was depressing to think that one slave could change a woman's thoughts so utterly. April looked at her friend, she felt sorry for her. Sage was such a loyal and innocent woman whose only knowledge of men was what she observed, and now she was seeing how easy it was for a woman's heart to be turned by a little false kindness.

"I am sorry Sage, but if your whole life was a roll of the dice as to whether

18

you lived or died, think how nice it must be to be distracted from that as often as possible. I don't say it is right or wrong, but it is how these men get by. They don't marry very often, they don't have kids very often, because if they die what would become of their wives and off spring? Theirs is not the wonderful life everyone wants to imagine it is." April put her arm around Sage's shoulders as a comfort.

"I'll go with the distraction bit. Judging from the amount of grunting he was doing I'd say he was definitely distracted."

April gave that all of a moment before she burst out laughing, and then Sage found herself joining in. "Bloody men!" They both said together.

It was on her day off as she sat watching the young men race chariots, wrestle and socialise at the Campus Martius, that she was drawn to familiar laughter. Squinting from the sunshine, Sage saw Heva and the bear wandering openly along the grassy field, they were leaving the sacred precincts, arm in arm. Sage was furious, how could her mistress be so foolish, or that idiot man encourage her to be so. She almost wanted to run down to talk to her mistress, but reigned in that thought, this wasn't her marriage, nor her business. She watched as Heva looked adoringly up at the huge bear, his muscular arms flexing as he moved, even his forearms were muscular enough to flex visibly. He wore a toga as Heva did, and every now and again he would stop and tuck a stray curl behind her ear, then bend down and whisper something in her ear that made her giggle. Sage curled her hands into fists, it was embarrassing to see her mistress behave so, and worse, it was in public. Robaratus looked about him, then steered Heva straight towards where Sage was sitting, in the shade of large bushes. Sage was sure they couldn't see her, but she was going to be seen if she didn't find somewhere to hide. She scurried deeper into the undergrowth just as the couple arrived and sat in the shade too close to Sage for comfort. Heva was laughing as the bear trailed kisses down her neck and felt her breast over her tunic. Sage held her breath and sent silent prayers to any God listening in. Soon Heva was moaning and sighing, the bear breathing heavily and grunting just as Heva had her climax. Sage dare not move, dared to hardly breathe as she waited for them to leave but they didn't.

"Rob how is it you know so much?"

There was no reply to that question, just more kissing. Heva sighed. "You know you have my heart, don't you?" Sage caught a glimpse of Heva stroking the man's face. He looked unemotional as she spoke. "I love you, Rob." He made no reply but smiled at her. Sage thought the smile looked sad. His green eyes were sharp and piercing and showed no affection at all. They lay there for some time, before he said "We should go. I don't want Aquilina finding out I am missing."

Heva moaned her objection, but they both stood up. "When can we see each other again?" She asked. Sage saw the desperation in her eyes and the smile on his face. "That depends upon your husband." He said.

"I'll send you a note my love." Heva replied. He kissed her cheek and off they went. Sage stayed put until they were safely away, then she crawled out of the bushes and brushed herself down. Heva had been sending the bear notes, but she had not been asked to deliver any of them, so who had? Worse than that, how often had Heva secretly met with this Gladiator? Sage fumed at not being trusted and at not being smart enough to know what her mistress had been up to.

"Tell me honestly Heva what does Robaratus mean to you? He is a slave, for all he is a Gladiator." Decimus asked into the silence that their meals now became. Heva took her time answering, then sighing heavily she said. "He means nothing my husband."

"Yet you were entertaining him in the Martius today, very openly and many people saw you both." Her husband kept his tone mild. "I did not expect you to entertain him in that way."

Heva hung her head.

"Was there a reason for such openness when you know what Aquilina will do to us when she finds out?"

Heva looked up at him, pausing in her eating. "She won't find out."

Decimus smiled and made a sort of laughing sound without opening his mouth. "You think so many people would not want to tell Aquilina what they saw? Heva and Robaratus arm in arm in public. I expected better of you." His disappointment sounded bitter even to Sage.

"At least he has time for me." Heva retorted defensively.

"He has used you." Decimus told her. "He has been flirting with you to get exactly what you gave him.

"What do I care? He shows such affection and tenderness, an .."

"Enough!" Decimus interrupted her. "I have no wish to know. Gods but you make me sick." He sighed and pushed himself off the lounger he ate from. "You will sleep in the guest room." He added, unaffected by her tears. "Be warned wife, what punishment Aquilina delves out will affect this whole household. I hope you can live with that." He left the room, and Heva collapsed into a torrent of tears.

Chapter 3

Once more Sage found herself hiding behind a pillar as April stood at the front entrance to the Gladiatorial training school, and once more she watched as Robaratus appeared, tall, muscular and intimidating with his arms folded across his broad chest, tattoos down one arm and half his face, his strange green eyes bored into April as she again thrust a piece of folded paper at him. He smiled in a sneering way. He wore a crude groin wrap, and his upper torso was bare showing a sheen of sweat. "It is amusing how Aquilina's personal slave has become a messenger for her sister. I am sure your mistress would be interested to learn of your activities." He mused.

"Do you reply or not?"

"Not." He said turning away, the door slamming behind him. April stepped back to avoid being hit by it, then she returned to where Sage hid. "It's been a week. How much longer is Heva going to keep doing this? It is humiliating."

"I wish she would stop, but she keeps saying she loves him, I wonder her marriage can survive. She cries all the time and I think even she cannot remember for what." Sage heaved a deep sigh.

"Your mistress is so caught up in her own woe she cannot see what she is doing to her marriage." April grumbled. "You'd think she would realise he has moved on; he has other interests now."

"Does Aquilina know?" Sage asked.

"Hades, Sage, if Aquilina knew, you think we'd be standing here passing on stupid messages?"

Sage shrugged; April was right. They trudged back to the villa, and Sage went inside to pass on the usual reply. Heva waited in her room, pacing to and fro. "What news?" she almost begged. Sage felt huge guilt, shaking her head sadly. "I am sorry mistress; he would not take the note nor give a reply."

"I bet my husband has warned him off. I should leave him, go to Rob myself; talk to him. I have coin, we could leave."

"Mistress please stop." Sage interrupted. "Listen to yourself! You cannot love a gladiator more than your own husband!"

"My own husband has shown his true self, he is not the man I thought he was. He has little knowledge, lays down the law to me and excludes me, his wife, from the marital bed. I have no love for him anymore." Heva

21

paced with pent up energy, balling her fists and seething.

"Robaratus has been seen with other women of late, he appears to have moved on." Sage said and was struck by Heva before she even knew what had hit her. She held her stinging cheek in shock.

"Don't you dare speak out of turn with me, nor tell me lies." Heva almost screeched. Sage was dismissed for the day and she gladly left intending to go to the Martius to forget the misery her life had become, all because of a damned gladiator, but half way there April and Rufus crossed her path. April smiled cheekily at Sage and introduced Rufus to her. "Rufus is an accountant to his master." April said grinning. "He has high intentions, don't you?" Rufus looked a little embarrassed and his cheeks took on a rouge tint. "I have hopes." He said modestly.

"Good luck with them." Sage said sincerely, and left, but soon found April catching up to her. "What about Rufus?" Sage asked, looking back, not seeing him. "He is busy, I only caught him on the way to someone else." April told her. "Why are you out and about looking like a rainy day?" Sage burst into tears and told her friend what had happened.

"Sage, I am not delivering any more messages. Your Mistress is making a fool of herself. Aquilina will not be in the least sympathetic to her feelings." Sage understood it completely and nodded her acceptance. "With no one to deliver her messages she might stop." She added hopefully.

"She has to stop, I'd hate to see her like some women, who will take their lives for the love of a gladiator, or be like that other woman who ran off with the ugliest gladiator ever."

"The one with the ever-weeping bloody eye wound?" Sage asked.

"And hideous boil on his nose, that seeped puss all the time."

Sage cringed. "Why would anyone run away with one as ugly as he?"

"Wasn't his face she was in love with!" April winked at her friend and laughed as she blushed.

"April! Is there anything you talk about other than sex?!" Sage couldn't help laughing.

"Arh but I got you to smile again." April hugged her. They walked into the Martius and basked in the warm sunshine, the shouts of young men wrestling in the sun, of the shining horses being put through their paces, with riders and instructors, a ball game was being played and some men were weight lifting, it all looked and sounded so far away from the drama that was unfolding in Sage's life. "I hate that bear." She said softly. April draped her arm about her. "Heva will get over him eventually."

"What the Hades does he do to women to make them behave so insanely?"

"You should know! You were around when he was entertaining your mistress."

"I don't spy on them. You spy on Aquilina, surely it's you who should know?" Sage pointed out.

"I have no clue, although I do know it takes him a long time to get in the mood, so to speak." April and Sage giggled.

"Didn't take him long in the damn bushes last week." Sage said and then realised she hadn't told April that bit of news, and the look on her friend's face was hilarious, so Sage told her how she'd hidden in the bushes, holding her breath for fear of being found out. April laughed and laughed.

"That's brazen, even for the bear!" She admitted.

"Yes, but ever since that day, he has refused to acknowledge her."

"That's because your silly mistress poured her heart out, it stops being fun to gladiators when the women get all sloppy about them."

"So Robaratus isn't unique in that?" Sage asked.

"No. They all like a bit of fun, to them that's all it ever is. Most women never get hung up on sex with a slave, but for some reason Robaratus has a gift our men are not aware of!" April smiled wickedly.

"Hades but I wish none of it had happened." Sage confessed sadly.

Later when Sage got home cook was in a state of panic, telling Sage the Mistress was packing to leave. Sage rushed upstairs wondering how she might prevent her Mistress from making such a dreadful mistake.

"Help me pack." Heva ordered, rushing about the room grabbing togas and shawls.

"Master would not want you to leave." Sage begged, wringing her hands to stop herself from helping or grabbing her Mistress.

"I cannot stay with a man who is so insufferable. He will not talk about things, will not understand, and keeps reminding me how I have never found fault with his bedroom behaviours in the last ten years. I hadn't met Robaratus though, had I?" she paused in her actions, staring out into space. "I have never felt so much emotion, so much passion, patience, attention and love." She looked at Sage, seeing her bewildered expression, she smiled. "Of course, how can you understand? The girl who thinks men are so bad! Perhaps if you were to try it someday, you would change your mind."

The twang of sarcasm wasn't lost on Sage.

"I am not permitted to marry Mistress, without master's consent. I have no desire for casual flings, nor a husband who takes his pleasures away from me."

"Oh, silly girl!" Heva snapped, returning to her packing.

"Where will you go?"

"I will leave Rome. If Robaratus cannot return my feelings, I cannot stay here and see him with another, nor bring myself to imagine him with my sister." Heva shivered her dislike of the thought.

"I beg you to think of the Master, he will be ruined by others mocking him."

Heva stopped for a moment. "Then he should've listened to me."

"I think I have heard enough."

Both women turned to find Decimus standing in the doorway, any emotions he may be feeling were hidden from them, as he slowly took in the scene before him. Togas scattered all over the room, and a trunk half filled. "Really Heva, your behaviour is akin to me announcing that I shall divorce you in favour of marrying Sage."

Sage's eyes grew wide at that.

"Absurd Decimus. Sage has no knowledge of the wonders of a real man, she prefers to remain a spinster all her life. You cannot compare Robaratus to her."

Sage was sure that was meant as an insult, but she was quite happy to not be compared to the bear.

"I merely meant she is a slave, so is that gladiator." Decimus sighed.

"He might be just a slave to you, but he so much more than that to me." Heva snapped.

"Then where is he this amazing man you have lost your wits to. Where is he Heva? Have you hidden him under the bed? In your closet?" He strode across the room to check her closet.

"As if I would bring him here!" Heva retaliated.

"Do you know where he is right now?" Her husband asked. Heva gave no reply as she stood pathetically in her room.

"So, what life do you imagine you will have away from Rome?"

Heva hung her head and soft sobs filled the room. Decimus walked towards her. "We have ten years together Heva, and you would throw them all away because a slave served you better than I could. How shallow that marriage has been if this be true."

Sage kept her eyes on the floor, yet she agreed with everything her master said.

"How can I stay with you, when you know I will be yearning for him?"

"We will remain apart until you come to me to say you are over him." Decimus smiled kindly, but Sage glanced up, she saw the twist of spite in his eyes. Heva looked defeated, she had lost Robaratus and now her husband, banished to the guest room until she could be trusted and then she would have to beg his forgiveness. Sage felt a wave of pity for her, yet her behaviour had caused Decimus much humiliation, she felt sorry for both.

*   *   *

Robaratus, I beg you to answer. I must know how you feel about me, for my heart aches for you. Please reply, if you are unable to write, then speak, for the slave before you is trustworthy.   Heva.

Aquilina laughed cattily. "And did you reply?" She eyed the gladiator in front of her.

"Of course not." He looked less than pleased to be standing before his Mistress. Aquilina laughed again. "I am assuming Heva has no idea she has been found out?"

"I do not think so." Robaratus answered.

"Arh, Robaratus, who'd have thought your disobedience would have brought me so much amusement?"

The gladiator glared at her, whilst he had no care for Heva, he disliked being the puppet in her games, and it annoyed him that he had no clue who had betrayed him.

"I have all her love notes to you my dear. Tell me, was she any good?"

Aquilina's eyes glittered with fun. The gladiator shrugged, to him she'd been easy prey and it had amused him immensely to see her be so willing. He'd had to do Aquilina's spy work for so long, he wanted his own kind of get back at her, and it had been so much fun, fucking them both without either of them knowing about the other. Alas that fun was over when Heva started pouring out her heart to him, it was pathetic almost juvenile and he was glad to ignore her, though he had not quite counted on her persistent sending of notes, firstly through his mistresses' private slave, and then through a boy. His mistake had been to keep the wretched things for they did amuse him to read.

"I see you are weary of my fun, fair enough, time to bring this to an end." Aquilina looked annoyed now, and he felt smug satisfaction to see it, though he knew she couldn't do much to him, he belonged to the Emperor, and he would care nothing at all for the suffering his affair would bring to Heva or her husband.

It was an unfortunate day that Heva chose to visit the baths, some days after realising she had no escape from her husband. He had been amenable to her staying with him, but his coldness towards her was adding to her self-made misery. She had to ask his permission to go anywhere, and was always accompanied by her slave and another who was not seen or known about by Heva, but who watched her from a safe distance. This

25

day she had wanted to wallow in the mineral waters of the baths, to try and let the misery of her life float away for a while. As she entered the waters, Sage stood in the shadows as normal, ready to serve her mistress if called upon. A gaggle of laughter echoed around the baths, and the peace was disturbed by a group of women also arriving to bathe. Heva was astounded to find Aquilina amongst them, but her sister was not at all surprised to see Heva.

"How nice to see you out and about." Aquilina purred. Heva wanted to leave, but she dare not, her sister could not know what ailed her.

"How is that husband of yours?" Aquilina asked as innocently as she could. Heva looked at her suspicious of her behaviour.

"I believe he is fine." She answered.

"Believe? Did you hear that ladies?"

The women all giggled. "Well, I am glad to hear it." Aquilina said warmly. "It's never easy when a man is humiliated, poor Decimus."

Heva turned scarlet.

"Oh, I'm sorry Heva, you know I never discuss anything that isn't common knowledge."

Heva wanted to die. "It wasn't his fault; he shouldn't be punished." She said finding some defiance in herself. Aquilina turned to her friends, "now isn't that so sweet? You cannot deny my sister is a good and loyal wife, she'd never disgrace her husband." They all gave knowing nods and grins. Heva was confused, Aquilina was playing games she had no doubt but what meaning she was hinting at; Heva was no longer sure. Sage chewed her bottom lip to stop herself shouting anything out.

"You should come with us after our bath to watch the gladiators train. I do love to see the sweat on Rob's body." Aquilina shuddered and licked her lips. I have special phials that my friends can use to collect his sweat, though you'd need 1 Aureus for it." The women gasped; it was a small kingdom to most.

"No thanks." Heva said. "I have to be back home."

The look of curious glee on her sister's face made Heva turn away. "Surely you don't need your husband's permission to watch gladiators train?"

Heva knew she was trapped. "It's not that at all. I just have things to do."

"What in all of Rome is more important than seeing men sweat and watch their glorious muscles ripple. You do like to see men make their muscles ripple don't you?" Aquilina looked hungrily at her sister. Heva sighed, it was an opportunity to see Robaratus after all, and her heart begged her to go. "Very well." She capitulated. Sage smothered a whimper of misery, this was going to end so badly, she just knew it. Aquilina swam around with her friends and then got out of the baths. Heva had hoped they might forget about her, but she was wrong. Aquilina reminded her not to dawdle, so she reluctantly followed them. Once they were dried off and perfumed, they all returned to the Gladitorial Training ground. Heva shuffled in last hoping to be unseen, but Aquilina had no such intent for her. Robaratus was called forth and he stood before the women his skin a fine sheen of sweat. He smiled sexily at them. If he saw Heva, he made no acknowledgement to her, and gladly allowed the women to harvest his sweat. Heva watched as he flirted and smiled for all of them. Sage noticed how dead his eyes seemed, another act for the mistress no doubt. Heva joined in, unhappily trying to catch drips into her vile, whilst desperately trying to catch his eye. He ignored her. Aquilina watched with great interest and smiled smartly, watching her sister's heart break and the discomfort of the gladiator was just reward for his betrayal of her orders. Eventually Heva left, unable to suffer the humiliation any longer. Sage met her outside the large wooden gate, tears flowed softly down her face. "He ignored me." She muttered. Sage almost missed hearing her at all. "He was under orders to I expect." She answered. Heva looked over at her. "So, she knows then?"

Sage nodded, Heva sobbed and the gate opened.

"Heva dear, I almost forgot, if your husband needs a loan at all, do ask him to come and talk to us." Aquilina smiled as sweetly as she could. Heva turned to her. "Why would my husband want a loan from you?" She asked accusingly.

"Why we were talking about it in the baths, you know, when you said it wasn't his fault. I understand that and I am sure the investigation will clear him, but even so, it is going to cost him dearly especially after losing those mines. I was just doing the family thing and offering you and him some financial support." She looked at her sister. "Oh, my poor dear Heva. Don't cry. You have a wonderful husband, you are both so famous for your strong relationship, I am sure things will recover in time." She smiled so broadly; Sage thought it might slide off her face entirely. The colour had drained from Heva's face and Aquilina turned triumphantly and closed the gate behind her. Heva looked stunned. "What investigation? What mines?."

*   *   *

Decimus had not been expecting any visitors, he was quite annoyed by the sight of Aquilina, and her Gladiator.

"Welcome to my home Empress, to what do I owe such a visit?" He gave

Robaratus a curious glance, it wasn't normal for gladiators to accompany anyone around, so he had a suspicion this was not going to be pleasant.

"I wish to address your household." Aquilina announced, causing raised eyebrows upon Decimus's face.

"My whole household?" He asked wondering if he'd heard her wrong, but she clarified it for him so clearly, he could not be mistaken a second time. Once all had gathered in the large red room, Aquilina began. "I believe my gladiator has been a very naughty slave. He has ignored my express orders to stay away from my sister. I am here to apologise to you Decimus, the hurt he has caused must be tremendous." She even managed to look humble about it. Robaratus shifted his feet, he had a look of unease about him.

"That is very kind of you." Decimus said into the silence when it dragged out too long.

"It is isn't it? But acceptance wasn't what I was hoping for Decimus. Your wife is equally to blame here. I am sure you can understand my own hurt to think she would throw herself at my slave in such an embarrassing way, and so openly as well."

Decimus frowned and looked at his wife, who stood at the back of the room.

"I have given her a few opportunities to admit her wrongs and apologise for them, yet she hasn't, so I thought perhaps together we might attain something. What do you think?"

Decimus was furious, but kept it in check. Aquilina wanted to openly humiliate Heva in front of the household, in front of slaves. A tic in his jaw twitched as he clenched his teeth together.

"Aquilina, I am quite able to punish my own wife without your help." Decimus growled in warning, but Aquilina just purred and smiled warmly. "I'm sure you can Decimus, but I am entitled to an apology."

Heva walked steadily to the front of the room, her face pale. She made a point of ignoring the bear, who stood in a very expensive looking toga, his eyes focused ahead of him, his face blank of expression. Heva cleared her throat. "I apologise to you Aquilina for having an affair with your slave. It was a foolish endeavour and I have most sincerely learned the error of my ways." Her voice was cold as ice. Sage thought she saw a twitch of amusement on the gladiators' lips. Aquilina smiled. "It's such a pity you couldn't have done this at the time. I am forced to require a bit more than just an apology Heva."

"Aquilina. I caution you against whatever you have in mind. You have caused enough trouble for me already. My wife has suffered plenty, and I really cannot think what else you could want from us." Decimus said through almost clenched teeth.

"Arh, yes. My next action is to do you both a favour of sorts." Aquilina smiled.

"A favour?" Heva asked. "We have no need of favours."

"Oh, but you will my dear. You see Decimus isn't able to retain all his staff, are you dear?"

Decimus now looked thunderous.

"Thing is as you didn't come to me for a loan as I offered, I am going to take it upon myself to do you a favour. You see, I am nothing if not generous, even when insulted!" She let the silence linger like a rain cloud, heavy and dark. "My gladiator needs to have some responsibility, so he can learn the error of his ways, so I have decided to marry him off." The bear's eyes grew wide with shock, clearly she had not informed him of her plans. Heva gasped. Decimus looked worried. "You intend him to marry my wife?" he asked confused. Aquilina laughed. "Gracious no!"

Robaratus almost breathed a sigh of relief, except he couldn't quite imagine who else his mistress might intend for him.

"He shall marry my sister's personal slave. She won't be needing her services any longer with your financial constraints, food is food, and one less mouth to feed is a blessing is it not?"

Heva wailed. Sage collapsed, and Decimus looked lost. Robaratus just looked blank. Aquilina had done it again. She could not punish Decimus more than she had, nor could she get back at Heva personally, being the wife of Decimus prevented that, but to take away her beloved personal slave, was as good as cutting her with a knife. Aquilina smiled triumphantly. Robaratus was looking like thunder. His green eyes positively glowed with rage as he stared at his Mistress in disbelief. His jaw clenched so tight they could hear his teeth grind in the silence, and Aquilina revelled in it all, smiling triumphantly at every shocked face in the room.

"Well, that got your attention didn't it!" She laughed, then turning to her murderous Gladiator, she lost the smile and addressed him personally. "I dislike my slaves to think themselves beyond my notice. I have allowed you far too much freedom when it comes to pleasing women. I am giving you a wife, to remind you of your indiscretions, and I am banishing you both from Rome for a year." She smiled then at him, though Robaratus made no response, showed no emotion, he stood perfectly still, expression passive, eyes coolly calculating the seriousness of his Mistresses intent.

Chapter 4

Sage watched the room blur in and out of focus, as every eye in it turned to her. She instinctively lowered her eyes, at least by staring at the floor, she could hide her emotions. Robaratus carefully followed the gazes of everyone else, but could not see the female slave he was about to marry, she was surrounded by the staff of the household.

"I cannot and do not permit her to marry *him*?" Decimus stated.

"As Empress I overrule you."

"This is outrageous" Decimus repeated.

"It is rather isn't it, but Heva has no use for her, so it makes good sense to marry her off."

Robaratus glared at his Mistress, she had thought of everything and now he was the one being saddled with a responsibility he never wanted. Decimus was speechless and hung his head, beaten.

"Come forward girl." Aquilina ordered. It was only then that Robaratus saw her, a young woman if that, who had auburn hair with glints of copper in it, she was about as tall as his shoulder, thin and she shook violently as she was guided towards him; large tears dripping from her eyes as she sobbed silently. She wore a slave tunic dress to her ankles and as she got closer, he noticed she had freckles on her face. At any other time, Robaratus would've loved those freckles, but today was not such a time. He looked at her with some confusion, for he'd never seen a woman cry at the sight of him. It might have been the situation Gods, but he felt like crying himself, but even so, most women or slaves would be honoured to be his wife and be the envy of every other woman in Rome.

"Aquilina, please don't do this." Heva begged.

"I am doing *you* a favour." Aquilina replied, rolling her eyes.

"She has no knowledge of men." Heva retorted, her sister laughed. "Oh, how fortuitous! Robaratus gets a virgin wife, what fun you will have my darling." She cooed sarcastically at the silent Gladiator. In all the arguments, Robaratus heard only as a distant noise, his head was spinning in confusion and panic, he could no more run than could the girl he was about to be married to, he hated children, he preferred his women to be *women*. He could hardly recall the last time he took a woman's virginity, so few existed in Rome, it was more than just punishment from his mistress, it was punishment from the damn Gods for his carefree attitude, for his

30

popularity, for surviving every damn fight in the arena, Hades, it was punishment for living at all. He ground his teeth in frustration and rage, perhaps it would be better to be tied to a stake and killed by wild beasts, anything than years with a pathetic kid tied to his side. His fingers balled into fists and relaxed, then balled again as he warred with his inner turmoil. Perhaps she would run away if he scared her enough, then they would both be free, but she knew nothing of life, he heard Heva plead that the girl had no knowledge of travelling or places outside Rome, so where might she run to? He wondered. *Has no experience of being a wife, or of men. Knows nothing about running a home, likely she will breed like a rat.* He shivered inwardly at the thought of too many mouths to feed. *I hate kids.* Then again he didn't have to touch her. He could pretend, be nice to her in public sight, and ignore her when they were alone, he could still sleep with whatever woman he pleased, even prostitutes would do the business if he could just get the relief. A small smile teased at the corners of his mouth, perhaps things might not be so bad after all; he was master in his own home, so he would make his own rules.

Sage stood beside the bear, trembling violently, his very presence seemed too large for the room and she felt depleted of air because of it. A priest was standing in front of them both, though she'd no memory of seeing him arrive, yet he stood in his robes of office looking as grim as she felt. He asked her to repeat words, which she managed to do through a trembling voice. Robaratus did his through tight lips, his green eyes boring hatred at Aquilina the whole time. If nothing else he could spend the rest of his life imagining all the ways he could make her suffer. The priest left having watched them both sign an official contract.

"Obviously you won't be able to live in the training grounds anymore, so I have given you a house nearby for a few days. You will leave Rome in three days and travel to your old trainer Albus Juventus, he has need of an extra trainer for his own gladiators." Aquilina smiled at them both. From all the sobbing going on, Sage felt she was attending her own funeral, she never so much as lifted one eye off the floor during her ceremony. She could feel the anger rolling off her new husband and she prayed to any merciful God that he wouldn't take it out on her.

"Every morning you wake Robaratus, may you look upon your wife and be reminded that she is the consequence of breaking my rules. May you also learn that a wife is a responsibility that you now need to respect." She then turned to her sister. "In the year he is banished for, I hope you both find a way to make up. When he returns he will be a reminder to you to keep away from my gladiators." She then gave Robaratus a key and told him where to find their temporary home.

All the way to the new apartment, Robaratus smiled at passers-by, his new wife trailed behind him doing her best to pretend she wasn't really anything to do with him. He was so tall up close, menacing with his muscular frame, and those hypnotic green eyes that held anyone's gaze, even Sage's from a distance. His shaven head of prickly stubble matched his unshaven face, she was relieved not to have to kiss him and be wearing the rash all that stubble would have caused. At times she almost had to jog to keep up with him, watching the way he exerted himself with females made her want to be sick. Once inside the apartment, he slammed the door shut behind them, making Sage jump.

"I am Master of this house." He growled. "As such I will tell you now, you are nothing to me; just a child and I loathe children. I have no interest in virgins, so rest assured, I won't be touching you. Outside, we will have to pretend we like each other, I will not let Aquilina win, but alone you do not exist to me, understand?" He waited but she never raised her eyes from the floor, just nodded her acceptance. He hesitated; she might at least have spouted some hatred back at him; her silence was unnerving. His eyes roamed over her slim form, simple tunic dress, with her long auburn hair and freckles that his fingers longed to touch. Roman women did not find freckles attractive, and thus did all manner of things to hide them, but slaves had no such benefit rights. Robaratus had always thought freckles beautiful, so it was insulting his wife had them. He noted the way her body trembled slightly in his presence, and it hurt his feelings to think she was probably the only woman he'd ever met who feared him, or hated him, or both. When Sage heard his footsteps retreat and a door slam shut, she let out a soft breath of relief. Tears threatened her composure, but fear of him seeing her weak, made her blink them away. She was alone in a room with a fireplace, a table and two chairs, a shelf above the fire which was empty, and a single pot for cooking. At least the fire was ready to be lit, so she did so and sat before it shivering uncontrollably. His words had not cut her as they were meant to, instead she felt relief that he hated her as much as she hated him, she only hoped that being out in public would be a rare affair. She knew not how long she sat there shivering, but as the room darkened, and night crept in, she wondered what she was supposed to do for food, in the end when he showed no signs of leaving what she assumed must be the bedroom, Sage stoked the fire and settled herself down on the warm hard stone floor, and waited for daylight. It'd be a short marriage if she died from starvation perhaps that was his plan.

Robaratus tore his toga off, ripping it to pieces as he allowed his rage to finally run free. Despite his telling himself he could manage this, he could not. He raged at his helplessness, at his own stupidity for thinking

32

he might have some fun with Aquilina's sister, and nothing would come of it. He seethed at her ignorance, which at the time, he'd found quite entertaining, she was so naive. *Yes, and you should've known what would follow, but did you think Robaratus? Of course not, you let your groin rule your common sense. I am giving you a wife to remind you of your indiscretions.* The words cut deeply into his soul. *You cannot take it out on the girl, she is innocent,* a voice whispered to him, *yet she is the only one here, she is my punishment.* His punishment for the rest of his life and he hated her for it.

A persistent knocking at the door had Sage waken in panic, why had no one attended the door?, then she squinted at the strange place she found herself in, memories came rushing back, and she gulped down air to smother the tears of realisation, it was all real. Again the door rapped annoyingly. Sage got up gingerly, she spared a worried glance towards the bedroom door, then she quickly snapped open the front door. April stood on the step about to rap again, nearly using Sage's forehead for her knuckles. "Even married you sleep like a log!" she smiled, but got no smile in return. "Oh, don't worry about the bear, he has long gone to training." She pushed her way into the dark room. "Bloody Hades Sage, it's freezing in here, let's get the fire lit." She began to unload a basket of wood, then she presented Sage with some hard cheese and fresh bread. Looking around her, April nodded. "I didn't think you'd have anything to eat."
"Thanks. So you knew I was getting married." Sage took the food and put it beside the fire. "You can eat in front of me, and no. I had no idea about the marriage, which is why I am here." April replied.
"I have no *as* for food."
"Seems you're not the only one who has no idea about marriage"
April fished in her tunic and found some spare coin for her friend.
"You going to pay for my food for the rest of my life?" Sage asked sadly.
"He will catch on in time." April sounded confident, but Sage didn't share it.
"You look ok." April added after staring at Sage intently.
"Is there any part of being married that says I shouldn't?"
"No, but I feared he might take his anger out on you."
"Perhaps he'd have done us all a kindness if he had." Sage said softly.
"Stop that Sage. You are going to win; no man is going to lay a hand on you unless you want him to of course." She smirked.
"He says I am nothing to him, we must act when in public but alone I don't exist." Sage choked on the last bit.
"Normal marriage then." April asserted. "All marriages are a farce in public, and a sham in private."
"Decimus and Heva were not."

33

April pondered that for a long moment, then shrugged and confirmed that they were now.

"So how was he last night?"

Sage shrugged. "He told me he is Master now, laid down his rules and stomped off to that room over there." She nodded with her head.

"Gosh me! How quickly marriage takes the shine off things, I think you had a point Sage old girl, life sucks when married!"

Sage rolled her eyes. "Now you get it." She sighed.

"Seriously April, I have no clue how to proceed. I had no idea he'd even left the place."

"He will rise at dawn to begin his training. He will come home at sunset when training is done. Or he may not now he's married."

"And what do I do?" Sage asked.

"Good question. I have no idea."

Ferox used two hands to brace his wooden sword against the violence of Robaratus as he smashed against his opponent. Ferox staggered back, sweat pouring down his face, as he regained his balance, Robaratus lunged again, smashing into the heavy wooden sword, then again and again, unable to stop himself from venting a night's frustration and lack of sleep. "Robaratus calm yourself!" But the Gladiator had no ability to find calmness. He hit out again and again, until Ferox staggered back so fiercely he tripped and fell upon his arse. "Cede!" Ferox shouted panting with fear in his eyes. "What in Hades has got into you?"

"Don't pretend you were not told." Robaratus sneered.

"Told what?" Ferox asked genuinely perplexed.

"I was forced into a marriage yesterday."

Ferox looked astonished. "Marriage? To whom?"

"The slave of Heva Decimus." Robaratus threw his own sword violently at the sandy ground.

"Shit." Ferox sympathised, pulling his legs up in front of him. "Aquilina has surpassed herself this time. Death was obviously too good for you." He smirked in an effort to find a bright side, but the bear wasn't in the mood for amusement. "A fucking kid no more than sixteen by the look of her."

"Man, you really did piss her off didn't you." Ferox shook his head sadly.

"And we are leaving Rome tomorrow." Robaratus added snarling.

Ferox frowned. "Leaving? Why?"

"I will be training the slops outside Rome to be at least something of a challenge to you lot, starting at Albus Juventus' place."

"Your first trainer?"

Robaratus nodded.

"And this causes you anger?"

Robaratus slumped. "I should be glad to see him again, and I might have been if I didn't have to explain why I have a child wife trailing after me."

"How long will you be gone for?" Ferox asked

"A year." Robaratus sighed deeply.

"At least you won't be fighting in the arena Rob, you can look forward to a whole year of knowing you will live." Ferox smiled, his friend was luckier than he wanted to admit.

Sage and April wandered round the food stalls, buying nuts, some sausages and a hare, they added plenty of vegetables and herbs to the basket. Sage walked nervously afraid she had a notice stitched to her stating who she was now, but April kept whispering to her to be herself, no one knew Sage, unlike April who everyone knew because she was the Empresses personal slave.

"April! You will know! Is it true that Robaratus is now married?" Sage stiffened and looked at the floor, but April smiled warmly. "I haven't had it confirmed, but I have heard the rumour." She said with confidence. The woman who had spoken was a noble woman, with rich silks for a toga and her hair piled atop her head with ringlets bouncing about her face. "I cannot imagine Robaratus getting married, it has to be a lie! Especially given his wife is said to be a common slave. Imagine that. The most famous gladiator in Rome marrying a common slave, what *was* he thinking?"

Sage shivered involuntarily, this was the real reason why Aquilina was sending them away, she would become a target of hatred to every woman in Rome, and heaven only knew what they'd do to Robaratus, but she had to wonder if she'd be safe anywhere, he *was* the most famous gladiator, which meant anyone anywhere would know him, and eventually her.

"I thought he was having sex with Heva Decimus." Another noble woman said.

"Oh, that's old news! Aquilina found out about that." The first noble woman informed her friend.

"Then what common slave might he have married?" Another noble asked.

"Exactly!" April butted in smiling. "Given that gladiators reputation he probably married a serving girl!" She linked arms with Sage and smartly walked them away from the group of gossips.

"I owe you." Sage said softly once they were clear of flapping ears.

"Thank the Gods you're both leaving tomorrow." April said with a sigh of relief.

"What makes you think life will be any easier anywhere else?" Sage sniffed. April looked at her. "I never thought of that." She admitted. "Gods Sage, this is a bloody nightmare."

Sage nodded. "I have no idea what lies beyond the city, how am I to survive with a man who hates me as much as I hate him?"

"You are better than he is Sage. Think of it as a wonderful opportunity to see what lies in the big wide world and ignore the stupid bear."

Sage admitted to herself that April had a point, no matter the circumstances of her life, it would be an adventure to leave the city, to see the massive tombs of the Appian Way, and inwardly she smiled, determined to make the most of it all.

In the later part of the day, Sage sat on her favourite hill side in the Campus Martius, watching for the last time the charioteers racing their horses, the pounding of the hooves on the dry earth that echoed in her heart. The young hopefuls who would one day be officers, putting their horses through their paces. Her eyes wandered to the wrestlers, shouting and cheering, those playing ball games and the splash of brash young men swimming in the Tiber. "I will miss it all." She whispered to herself. She wandered amongst the shadows of cherry trees that blossomed once a year, and bathed the walkways in a carpet of pink petals when they fell, she said silent farewells to the statues and art work that stood scattered about the Martius. Looking up at the sky she wondered if the clouds she saw here would be the same somewhere else, she didn't know, she'd never had cause to wonder about it. She wandered home slowly looking at all the streets and roads and houses and business that were her world, would it have changed by the time she got back? Perhaps not.

It was late into the night when Sage heard a muffled sound and a soft thud. She woke straining to hear what had woken her. Muffled feet and then the bed as a body slumped onto it. He hadn't been training this late into the night. She smiled to herself, glad that he had found some kind of entertainment to keep him away, or may hap he was just saying his own farewells. Entering and leaving through the window was preferable to disturbing her, so at least he was being considerate even if that wasn't his intent, she almost giggled. It pleased her that he'd missed the evening meal she had cooked, the hare had been wonderful, and she hoped the smell of it made his stomach growl. Sage settled back down upon the stones, her head on her cloak. Robaratus watched the door anticipating her arrival, but she did not enter, so he assumed she was a deep sleeper. He hugged the bottle of wine he'd been drinking, solace for a short time. He noted a faint aroma of food which surprised him, he hadn't imagined she could cook. He lay on his back looking up at the darkness of the ceiling of his room, this was going to be the rest of his life, avoiding the girl in the next room. He found it worrying he couldn't even remember her name. One thing was certain, he couldn't imagine a long life that continued like this, perhaps losing in the arena might be his best hope eventually, until then he would have to bide his time. To her credit, his new wife had kept out of his way, most would have tried to get on his good side, but the thought of seeing her tears again was awkward, he couldn't understand why she was scared of him, perhaps by the morning he would see she had got over that. He groaned at the thought of the long journey ahead, obviously Aquilina had the notion they would have time to talk. Well not if he had any say in it.

Chapter 5

.

    Sage trailed along behind a small wagon where her new husband sat slowly walking two horses along the smooth sandy path, while his wife and other pedestrians walked on the cobbled road. She goggled at the many tombs along the Appian Way, often having to run to catch up with the wagon that never slowed or stopped, Robaratus being completely unaware if she was even still following him, and he didn't care. The sun beat heat and many travellers were sitting resting on the shady side of the street, mopping brows or fanning themselves with ornate fans. Sage had no opportunity to stop and rest, her husband had no intention of waiting for her, so she walked and kept her eye upon the wagon ahead of her. He had risen at dawn and told her they would be leaving as soon as he returned with the wagon, she'd had no opportunity to say goodbye to anyone, feeling like a criminal sneaking away before being discovered. He hadn't told her how far they would be walking, in fact, he'd not spoken another word to her. Sage was determined not to let his glum mood affect her, so she walked absorbing all the strange but beautiful tombs, huge round ones, long oblong ones, tall square towered ones; some with columns and some with ornate Gods and all stretching for leagues.

    By the time the sun was at its hottest, Sage had bloody blisters on her feet, sweat ran freely into her hair, and her legs and back ached abominably, yet still did she push herself forward after the wagon that had gotten too far ahead of her for to jump onto the back of it. Her simple sandals had given up long ago and all she had now were her bare feet, each step had her whimpering with pain, but she dare not stop for fear the bear would start off again without her. The tombs had stopped a while back and now she saw the open fields of farmers, some cattle and other traders going into Rome. The wagon now stood under some trees, allowing the horses some rest. When she finally caught up, she found her husband lying in the shade, fresh as the morning his eyes shut. She stared at him with murder in her heart, but she said nothing. She found a wine flask in the wagon, but it was water she craved for her thirst, the food she had seen him pack was gone and tears of frustration and anger threatened to overwhelm her, save this was obviously what he wanted so she closed her eyes, and breathed in slowly feeling the calm take over. He'd had to water the horses somewhere, so she went in search of water which was closer than she'd thought, a river with clear sparkling water, she almost sobbed as she tore off her tunic and threw herself into the cold clear fluid. Her feet stung but she didn't care, she sunk herself into the cold, letting her hair get thoroughly drenched; it felt wonderful as she gulped large amounts of water to refresh her parched throat. After a good soaking she reluctantly got out, and sat in the sun till her skin dried then she dressed and returned back to the wagon where she crept inside, and curled up on some sacking, having torn rags of linen from her dress to bind her feet with, she passed out. Robaratus waited quite some time before deciding to make a move. He harnessed the horses up and looked into the back of wagon, seeing Sage curled up with bloody bandaged feet, he felt guilty. She was determined, he had to admire that, and she'd not disturbed him when she had caught up. He had no idea if she had eaten or drunk anything, and he really shouldn't have cared, but something in the back of his mind told him she was a brave kid to walk on bloody feet and make no noise.

It was night fall when they ambled into a small village. People at the Inn watched with suspicion as the great Gladiator rode his wagon by them, he kept his eyes forward as he rode out of the village and towards a villa set upon a slight hill. Upon arriving, he stopped the wagon and walked to the villa's front door.

"Robaratus, so it is true then! Aquilina really is sending us her best to teach our own." The owner grinned broadly, and Robaratus returned the smile, then they embraced.

"Albus, it is good to see you again" Robaratus teased, for they'd only seen each other just a week before at the tournament.

"Come in, we are ready to eat, you must be starving." Albus said with a warm smile. Robaratus was inclined to follow but he knew his wife would be discovered soon enough, so best to get this awkward part done with. "I bring my wife with me."

Albus stared blankly. "Forgive me, did you just say your *wife*?"

Robaratus forced a grin. "I did." He turned towards the wagon hoping she would still be asleep, but he was stunned to find her standing beside it, a large shawl about her shoulders, and her head covered. Her eyes were as usual cast down, with her hands clasped in front of her and her feet wrapped in crude linen bandages. Robaratus struggled to recall her name, so referred to her as wife. Sage walked slowly towards the two men, her feet stung and burned with each step but she made no complaint. Her newly plaited hair hung down over one shoulder, making Robaratus have to concede that she had done her best to look respectable and she had surpassed his expectations. As she came to stand beside him, he casually

39

draped his arm across her shoulders, to her weak state it was heavy, and her legs dipped slightly. "Albus, this my wife."

The owner screwed his eyes up. "You were not married last week Robaratus, what happened?"

Robaratus laughed, but before he could think up a suitable lie, a woman came to stand beside Albus. "Robaratus! Well, sometimes your Mistress lives up to her word!"

"Octavia, you are as stunning as ever." The Gladiator grinned, dropping his arm from Sage's shoulders.

"Apparently our Gladiator has married since last week." Albus informed his wife, who looked just as shocked by this as her husband had.

"Well, come inside, you have lots to tell us." She enthused, noting the small woman and her bound feet. Robaratus stepped inside leaving Sage on the threshold, he turned and grabbed her arm when she didn't automatically follow him, his grip hurt but she bit back a cry of pain. They were led to a large open room with lounges set in front of a long table, allowing them a full view of the gardens beyond which were lit by many torches.

"Your wife is very quiet Rob." Octavia observed as she watched the girl with down cast eyes.

"She is very shy." Robaratus offered. "She has never left Rome before. It's all a bit overwhelming is it not my love?" He almost sneered the word.

"It is." She said softly, keeping her eyes down.

"I must confess, I wasn't sure what Aquilina meant when she said you wouldn't be alone" Octavia offered, "but I never imagined you ever being married Rob, what changed your mind?"

Sage wanted to laugh. *Yes* "Rob" *What changed your mind?* She even chanced looking up just to see his face when he lied.

"I um, was having some problems with Aquilina's sister. You know how it is Albus, the ladies," he shrugged and grinned, Albus nodded and smirked. "Your reputation hasn't changed."

"So, to stop the woman from making an ass of herself and her husband, I took a wife, and what-do-you-know, it worked, she was upset but off my back. Trouble is I could hardly leave the wife behind." Robaratus laughed loudly, then put his arm across Sage's shoulders once more. She winced before she could prevent herself. *So that is how you lie your way into women's hearts.* His face was *so* relaxed as the lie fell easily from his lips. "Well, you are a lucky woman indeed." Albus assured her, she gave him a gentle smile, as she looked at him with soft brown eyes. Albus was a round man, round face and round torso, with a happy complexion, his wife by contrast was thin, flat chested with long blond hair and bright blue eyes. "I don't think Rob said what your name was?"

40

"Sage."

Octavia looked at her for a long moment, but Sage had her eyes down.

"Well, you are very welcome here." Octavia said in a kind tone, one that brought tears unbidden to Sage's eyes, they were the first kind words she had heard all day. The rest of the evening went uneventfully, Robaratus and Albus talking about past adventures and theories for training, while the women listened in silence, though Sage was sure Octavia was watching her, assessing the truth of Robaratus's words, she didn't need to look up to know it, she could feel those blue eyes on her. Before they were shown to a guest room, Octavia insisted on looking at Sages' feet. "Whatever happened to your sandals?"

Sage looked uncomfortable, but refused to tell an outright lie. "I wanted to walk and see all the tombs on the Appian Way, my um husband had seen them before and forgot to slow down for me."

"So, you were born into slavery then?" Octavia asked, seeing as they were alone. Sage looked terrified.

"Oh, don't worry, he only looks fierce. Besides, your whole standing is one of a lifelong service, you don't fool anyone Sage, and Rob is an idiot if he thinks lying to us will be easy."

Sage shivered. "I know my place mistress; he already told me he hates me."

"Then why did he marry you?"

Sage looked lost; she'd confided too much to a complete stranger.

Octavia rolled her eyes. "Don't stop now Sage. Why did he marry you?"

Sage sighed. "We was forced. I am his punishment. He has to look at me every day and remember that he broke the Empresses rules about her sister, who was my mistress."

Octavia stared at her, speechless. The silence lingered uncomfortably, before Octavia found her voice. "When did you get married?"

"Two days ago."

Octavia hung her head. "Oh Robaratus, you never learn! He has never wanted to marry, that's why this is such a shock."

Sage smiled. "Funnily enough I never wanted to marry either, so it kind of suits, we ignore each other."

Octavia looked at her sweet smile and wondered if Robaratus would ever see it, or notice how the girl looked so much prettier when she did so, how her eyes widened and almost shone. Feet dressed; they were given a guest room for the night while Albus organised them to have their own small apartment building. The room was a comfortable size with a large bed. Robaratus was obviously unhappy at having to share a room with Sage. He flopped himself onto the bed and glared at her, waiting to see what she would say. Sage made no eye contact, but took her cloak and settled onto the floor in the corner, resting her head of the softer material, she closed her eyes, and having a full stomach for the first time that day, she drifted off to sleep. Robaratus watched her with some disappointment, she was a quiet thing, made no complaints, spoke not at all, asked no questions. He realised with some guilt that she'd slept on the floor in their home in Rome, may be that was all she had known. She confused him and offered him no outlet for his frustration and rage, he lay on his side watching her until his eyes closed.

Sage was aware when dawn arrived, Robaratus got up and dressed, using the chamber pot noisily, he left the room. Sage got up the moment she was alone, and brushed herself down. She'd not heard when Robaratus had got undressed, but the thought made her smile, that he had been quiet enough to let her sleep. She made her way out of the room wandering towards the room where they had eaten the night before. She was relieved to see the slaves waiting on Octavia as she ate delicately. "Arh Sage, come and join me." She was a bright and friendly woman, Sage sat near to her on the edge of a lounger.

"You're not used to eating like this are you?" Octavia offered as she eyed Sage. "First lesson in your new life, is to learn how to fit in. So come lie with me and eat."

Sage made no movement, but kept her eyes down this was not an easy transition to make, but eventually she did as told, waiting for her husband to arrive and scold her, but he didn't.

"Can I ask how you feel about Rob?" The question came out of the blue, but Octavia's voice was so kind, when Sage glanced up, she was met with a sympathetic expression, and those blue eyes shone in a warm and tender way. Sage was speechless, she had no idea what to say, so she chewed at her bottom lip. "I hate him." She said deciding that she cared not what this woman thought of her.

"Well good for you." Octavia said smiling warmly. "I feared you would lie; I much prefer honesty. By the way, you have to be the only woman who'd hate Robaratus, and I think with good reason." Sage looked at the smiling warm face before her.

"I hope Robaratus hasn't hit you, for if he ever does, I will kill him!" She was looking at the bright bruise on Sage's arm where Robaratus had grabbed her the night before. "No, he just grabbed me a bit too tightly." Octavia nodded. "I should explain some things about gladiators. They are best when they are soulless and heartless, which is one reason why Robaratus never wanted marriage. Aquilina knows this, she is trying to break his spirit. A heartless gladiator stands a greater chance of living longer."

This made sense to Sage, she could understand his harsh words to her taken in this context, he couldn't afford to be soft and care, so she wouldn't want him to. Octavia watched Sage understand this and then said.

"Come with me." Octavia got up and Sage followed. They walked outside along a neatly made path edged with small plants, which led towards a closed area, where the sound of shouting from a harsh voice was heard, accompanied by the grunting and shouting of men, and the dull thud of fierce wooden swords. As they walked around a gentle curve in the path, the closed off area became an open arena, small and suitable for training, where two pairs of fighters were using swords and tridents against each other. Beside it was a larger square piece of ground, with groups of men doing different things. Some lifted large stones with loud grunts, others carried smaller stones with their arms locked at their sides, Albus shouting at them to walk faster. Another group sat chatting, while idly watching yet another group wrestle, Robaratus observed and stopped them periodically to adjust how they stood or held each other. Sage was transfixed by it all. Octavia steered her to a small bench some where they could watch the men train.

"Have you ever seen gladiators train?" Octavia asked.

"No." Sage said, quietly.

"Hmm. Robaratus hates being watched, makes him distracted. It has always been my habit to support my husband by sitting here watching him train. I think your husband deserves a little scrutiny."

Sage found herself warming to Octavia, her gentleness and knowledge would certainly help her survive this marriage.

"Do you know where gladiators come from?"

Sage frowned at the floor. "I supposed they were slaves." She said looking up at Octavia, who nodded. "Before they were slaves, they were criminals or soldiers or prisoners of war. Quite a lot of gladiators have families in faraway lands, and the sadness is that those families will never know the fate of their husbands, fathers, brothers and sons." She let that sink in as Sage looked back out at the men training, seeing them with different eyes.

"Am I supposed to ask what Robaratus was?"

"Not if you don't care to know. I am just starting at the beginning."

Sage nodded; she had no care what the bear had been to bring him to the arena.

"If a gladiator is to survive at all, all emotions have to be beaten out of him, a good gladiator is merciless, ruthless, and murderous. He cannot care for his best friend lying on the floor before him bloodied and helpless. Compassion is not going to help you when it is your life or theirs."

Sage kept her eyes upon the training men.

"There is honour in death. Any gladiator will tell you that. If they have fought well, with honour, and given a good performance, then there is no shame in the death that is coming." Octavia spoke with a warmth and conviction that came from many years of knowledge and experience.

"It is a rare thing for a Gladiator to fight to the death nowadays isn't it?" Sage asked without looking at Octavia, but staring beyond the arena.

"Thankfully yes, they cost a fortune to feed. Eat more than the damn horses!" Octavia joked, making Sage smile more confidently. "Besides when a gladiator is killed, the Emperor has to pay a small kingdom in compensation fees to the owner for the loss. It isn't worth it."

Robaratus happened to look up at that point, and scowled at the two women. A cold shiver ran through Sage involuntarily, but Octavia didn't miss it.

"Do you know why they lift those stones?" Octavia continued her education. Sage shook her head. "So they get strong?"

Octavia smiled. "In the arena some fights last a long time, a gladiator can tire very easily, their swords are heavy, shields are heavy, and if they are Mirmillones they can wear body protection, it all adds to the weight. Those helmets are heavy too, especially Robaratus' because it is gold. He is a Mirmillon, which accounts for his height and powerful build."

Sage listened as she looked at Robaratus, as he demonstrated throwing his opponent.

"They train with much heavier swords than the ones they use in the arena, this way they become stronger in the arm that wields the sword."

"Makes sense." Sage smiled softly.

"The stones build endurance. Albus makes them run around with them, or hang off those ledges over there for hours at a time."

"So it's not all about fighting each other?" Sage asked.

"Not at all, though it depends whose training you might be talking about, as each owner differs with techniques."

"And are your gladiators successful?"

"Some. Our best are brought by the Emperor and end up in Rome, like Robaratus did. The Emperor is very generous with his fees but that does not compensate us for having to start from scratch."

"No but it means the Emperor still has the best of the men, and you have none who can beat his, right?" Sage felt proud of herself, as Octavia nodded, smiling.

"Do the men get to choose which type of gladiator they become?"

"Yes, or the trainer will suggest a suitable type. See that man over there, the rather thin one? His name is Violens, because of his stature he is very well suited to being a Retiarii, see he trains with a trident, dagger and net.

He is nimble and fast, using the net to trip his opponent, his trident can jab from a safe distance, but if he ends up in close conflict, he will use the dagger."

"Why has he so little clothing?" Sage asked a tad embarrassed. Octavia laughed. "He needs to be free to move around at speed, plus, he can show off his muscular body to best effect!"

Sage frowned.

"It matters that a gladiator looks good, his sweat is worth a lot of coin if he is popular. So the better he looks the greater his chances of being chosen by the noble women for affairs."

"Have they no notion of how that ruins marriages?" Sage couldn't quite hide her anger.

"Oh, sorry. I must admit, that is not the normal course of things Sage. Robaratus broke the rules did he not?"

Sage nodded. Albus called for the men to halt, it was the hora sexta hour and time to eat.

"Shall we retire to eat ourselves?" Octavia suggested as she stood up.

As Robaratus left the food table, carrying his grains and pulses, with ash drink, he searched for Albus who sat alone not far away. Robaratus joined him. "Have the rules changed now? You no longer eat with the men."

Albus looked up at him. "Not at all, but I wanted a word with you away from flapping ears."

Robaratus sat, he had a good idea what was coming.

"I remember a young man coming here a few years back, filled with anger." Robaratus laughed softly. "I remember him too."

Albus gave him a hard stare. "You haven't changed a bit Rob. Isn't it about time you did some growing up?"

Robaratus paused in his eating. "What are you getting at?" He growled.

"Your bull shit. You think I'd buy that crap you came out with last night?" Albus ignored any expression Robaratus showed, he was busy eating. "I thought you'd know better by now. Want to give me the truth?"

Robaratus wiped sweat that trickled down the side of his face, and sighed. He told Albus what had happened and why he was married so suddenly, when he was done, Albus stopped eating and gave the gladiator a long hard look. Eventually he spoke. "I feel sorry for that girl. You fuck up and that Heva woman fucks up, but what in Hades did that girl do?"

Robaratus clenched his fists on the table, and Albus moved his eyes to fix upon them, making Robaratus relax his hands. "I have to look at her and be reminded she is my punishment for breaking that bitches rules."

Albus shrugged dismissively. "Serves you right, but I say again, what has that girl done to deserve her punishment?"

Robaratus ran his hands through his shaven head stubble. "Nothing." He admitted begrudgingly.

"Exactly." Albus said sternly. "She had a life she likely enjoyed. By the look of her I'd say she was born into slavery, knew nothing else, then one day she is forced to marry a gladiator, what does she know about gladiators or men or marriage?"

Robaratus shrugged, what did he care?

"She is your responsibility now Rob. How long can you go on hating her for being Aquilina's punishment?"

Rob sighed at the old man's scrutiny. "I don't like her. I never wanted to be married. Hell she doesn't even speak!"

Albus laughed. "Ever thought you terrify her?"

"She'd be the only female on this earth that was then." Robaratus huffed.

"How old are you Rob?"

"Thirty-five. I am getting too old to be a gladiator, I feel my bones aching, but I cannot retire either, I tried many times, but Aquilina made it clear she wasn't letting me go."

"I think she is letting you go now. Think about it. She could have punished you, had you whipped, beaten. She could have stopped at punishing Decimus, after all Heva will suffer from the lack of coin, so why did Aquilina marry you off if she just wanted to punish you? She wants you to always remember who you pissed off. She chose the lowest person she could think of, one that would cut her sister as much as you." Albus kept on eating.

"So what? I still don't want a wife."

"I doubt she wanted you for a husband either from the look of terror she has every time you catch her eye."

They ate in silence for a while. "I ask you again Rob, how long can you go on hating her?"

Robaratus wanted to answer for the rest of his life, but he knew that sounded childish, so instead he shrugged.

"Well think about it." Albus grumbled.

Chapter 6

At the evening meal again they lay on loungers to eat. The men talked shop and the women listened. Robaratus turned his icy gaze to his wife, and asked her if she found her day interesting watching him train. Sage kept her eyes downcast at her food, as she nodded politely, which annoyed him, if she could talk to Octavia, why not to him?

"She wasn't really watching you Rob, your delightful wife has taken your rules to heart, she was watching everyone else." Octavia teased.

"And what were you both gossiping about?" He asked with mock interest.

"Gossiping? Certainly not! I was telling your wife about gladiators."

She could see something in Robaratus's face, which was hard to read but it was different from his usual hatred. Albus smiled. "Not all barbarians really! Some come from respectable backgrounds like Rob here, a soldier." He smiled proudly at the bear beside him, Sage kept her eyes on her food she found it hard to believe Robaratus had ever been respectable.

"I am sure my wife would rather be shopping Octavia, perhaps tomorrow you might show her the town. You women love your shopping."

"Arh we might Rob my darling, but your wife has no coin."

Sage blushed at this, Robaratus scowled, of course he would have to support her now, another thing to loathe her for. "I will leave her some coin tomorrow." He muttered, his green glare washing over the small girl hunched down on her lounger.

"I have sorted you some privacy, a small dwelling that used to belong to the stableman, but he sleeps above the hay barn now." Albus smiled warmly. "Eat with us, but if you want your own space, you have it."

Robaratus thanked him and Sage managed a weak smile, she would be glad to sleep by a fire again, the bedroom floor was cold and having Robaratus so close scared her half to death.

The dwelling was much like their home in Rome, just two rooms, and thankfully one had the fire place which had Sage smiling inwardly. Robaratus immediately shut himself in the bedroom, ignoring her completely. Having lit the fire, Sage curled up in front of its warm glow and closed her eyes certain in herself, that the beast in the bedroom would not disturb her peace. In the morning Sage swept the floor at dawn, laid a new fire and then headed up to the villa, where Octavia welcomed her for

47

breakfast. "You have some coin for shopping." She told Sage, who made no gesture at hearing this news, she would not spend the bear's coin, it was blood money as far as she was concerned, besides it didn't take a fool to know how he resented his role, and her spending his coin hard won as it may have been, just made the knife sink deeper, so she would return every last piece of it. Octavia watched her responses, this child bride so closed to everyone, suffering something she wished she could unlock. They travelled into the village, where a market was in place. "They sell wonderful scarves, and tunics." Octavia spoke enthusiastically, but Sage ignored her, barely seeing the items for sale knowing her heart would break at not being able to afford anything. "You really could do with a new tunic and scarf." Octavia pushed gently.

"I like what I have." Sage said near to a whisper.

"May I buy you a gift?" Octavia said brightly, suddenly catching on as to what Sage was doing, but Sage shook her head. "Slaves don" she started, then stopped, looking at her feet now. Octavia eyed her then placed an arm about her shoulders and led her away. She chose a seat in the shade of a large tree. "Slaves do shopping." She told Sage, who nodded at the floor. "Slaves need clothes." Sage stilled. "Slaves need food. You won't always be with us. Are you really going to let him win?" Octavia's voice was a little harsher now. "I know you don't want to trust me Sage, but you cannot allow yourself to starve to death."

"His coin is hard won Mistress; I hate to waste a single *as* of it." Sage made herself sound so sincere, though she cared nothing for Robaratus's blood money, she would let Octavia think what she liked.

"It is a husband's duty to provide for his wife." Octavia said, gladiator's coin was hard won indeed, how could she think Sage was not aware of how precious money would be?

"I am not your Mistress, Sage. You must get used to calling me Octavia. I can also assure you that Rob has plenty of money."

Sage nodded, as she studied the floor.

"I am sure he would not begrudge you a new tunic." She insisted.

"He does though, it was in his tone of voice. I really do not want to spend his coin."

Octavia sighed; she would not push the issue. "I have an idea; I will buy you a new tunic and your husband can pay me back."

Sage shrugged. She really didn't see why it mattered so much, save her only tunic had been ripped to bind her raw feet, it wasn't as though they were entertaining anyone or seeing anyone. Octavia dragged her to a stall where she was fitted for a tunic dress in soft lilac, with a white shawl. "If Robaratus sees you looking more grown up, he might change his attitude

48

a bit."

"It is a kind gesture mistr .. Octavia." Sage said, though it made no impact upon her, a tunic was a tunic to her. Octavia also made sure she had new sandals, stronger than the pair she ruined walking so much. They ate a pulse porridge for the hora sexta meal, washed down with a cool wine. Octavia rattled on through the meal, but Sage was enthralled at the ripples in her wine, only when Octavia asked her something did she realise she hadn't been listening. "I was saying how very hot it is, and I need to buy a new fan."

"I can wait for you in the shade." Sage offered, as the thought of looking at any more stalls had her wilting. Octavia nodded and left the table. Sage watched her go, then got up and wandered over to a side alley, where the buildings were so close together that the sun could not penetrate past the shadow they provided. She admired the clean white washed structures up to three storeys high. The blue, cloudless sky a beautiful back drop for the whiteness, and the orange-coloured clay tiles that edged gracefully over the rooves. Unfortunately the stench of human waste somewhat spoiled the effect, as the sun was unable to dry up the pools of piss that gathered in puddles, under the stepping stones provided to avoid spoiling sandals. She was surprised to find a smallish boulder just inside the alley, perfect for sitting on. Sage wondered how anyone could've moved it there, but upon closer study, she realised the house had been built up to the boulder and in such a way, as to provide a perfect seat for presumably, the owner. She hoped they might not mind her using it now. She wafted her parcel with her new tunic in, to provide a small amount of breeze, but really the air was quite determined not to be stirred, so instead she watched enthralled at the tiny vibrations that made the smallest stones dance. She watched as ants ran about seemingly confused. She became alarmed when a roaring sound started and the people began to look alarmed. Then the earth began to really shake, and splits began to appear in the ground. Sage stood up and looked about her in panic, she had no idea what to do in an earthquake. She watched with dumb fascination as a large split appeared in the perfect whitewashed building opposite her, plaster began to fall from the walls. Sage stumbled her way out of the alley, watching with horror the mayhem before her of terrified humanity, running in all directions, women screaming and children crying. Men shouted and waved pointlessly; nobody was listening; everyone was trying to save themselves. Sage just stood dumbfounded at the confusion. She heard the grating sound of a tile slipping and then felt it hit the back of her head.

Albus and the Gladiators stopped training as soon as the tremors began. "Earthquake!" Violens shouted. Albus immediately called for Robaratus to follow him, and the rest to start running to the village. The men took off, easy for them, as the quake was not strong in their compound. Albus and Robaratus got the horses hitched to the wagons and set off as fast as they dare. The horses were skittish at the grumbling ground that vibrated beneath their hooves, but the two men urged them on carefully, picking up the gladiators as they caught up to them. The wagons were abandoned just outside the village, it was impossible for them to get any closer, given the tide of humanity charging around them. Violens was first to start taking charge, slowing the surge of panicked people, and directing them to safer places. Robaratus and the rest pushed their way through the crowd towards the village. Dust created a confusing, choking fog that disoriented everyone, the thunder of the quake mixed with the thunder of falling buildings, made the screaming people seem silent. The gladiators split up, jumping fissures in the land, and pulling people away from falling debris. It took just moments, but felt like forever, and when it was done the silence was eerie. The dust hung thick in the stubborn still air, and small fires began to crackle enthusiastically, spreading quickly with no water to stop them. Robaratus coughed and choked as he ran towards fallen buildings. He pulled at the surface rubble, tearing at it as though it were sand. He pulled two small children and a woman from the pile they were buried under. Albus was organising a few men to work at passing larger blocks of stone and concrete, so they could access others that were buried.

There was a complete darkness around Sage, a slight weight upon her back, perhaps the local stray dog had got in and decided to sleep against her. She thought she ought to try and sleep some more, it was too early to get up, the dawn chorus had not begun, she still had time for valuable sleep; gladly she drifted off again. Her dreams were confusing, her mistress crying, a tall stranger she had to stand beside and an unknown face half covered in tattoos with sharp green eyes that accused her, though she knew not of what. She had no notion of how long she had slept, but when she awoke the darkness was the same, it was cold now and she shivered badly, the fire had gone out but she was too tired to relight it. The air was thinner and that should have bothered her, but Sage could hardly recognise the warning, she noted how still her kitchen was, none of the usual sounds of the night, it was just very still. She woke several times like this and still her surroundings never changed, she began to realise this wasn't her kitchen after all, and when she concentrated things flashed through her mind, a strange place she had never known, strange people she couldn't put names to, and that horrid face with the angry green eyes. She remembered the blue sky, the oppressive heat and the stones that jumped excitedly on the ground. Still she closed her eyes again and exhausted slept some more.

The gladiators worked with driven energy, pulling away boulders of buildings, huge chunks of walls, and bucket loads of rubble. All the village men who were able, worked endlessly beside them, shouting for silence when calling for survivors, pulling free more dead than living. The aftershocks rumbled along the ground dislodging piles of collapsed homes, adding to the danger but also exposing some of the dead and living. Octavia had been found two days after the quake, she was alone, and had found her way to the edge of a fissure, she was curled up under a pile of dust, her new scarf wrapped about her mouth so she could breathe without getting so much dust in her lungs. She was able to tell Albus and Robaratus where she had left Sage, and both men focused their search around the area Sage had said she might find shade. Albus never said anything to Robaratus; that the gladiator was frantic told the older man that perhaps he cared for the girl more than he had realised. Then it rained, adding to the hazards of rescue, some villagers gave up when the rain became torrential, but not the gladiators, they worked on. Robaratus soaked, pulled at debris, slipping on the muddy ground and dirty water, he refused to stop searching.

It wasn't a good feeling, being cold and wet. Sage opened her eyes. *Wet?* She was cold and wet, so water was getting in, she could feel it trickling down her face now, a small amount found a path onto her lips and she tried to move her tongue to taste it, but the effort was too great. Her throat was parched and raw, her tongue felt swollen and dry, but the moisture was nice. Her kitchen didn't have water flowing in it, she felt confused for many moments, then she realised she was buried and alive. Panic washed over her, adrenaline pumped through her but she was stuck and voiceless. She had no idea how long she had been there, but she could wiggle her toes, and feel her fingers, so she wasn't badly injured. The ground rumbled and the debris about her moved, more water flowed in allowing her to finally unstick her lips enough to get some of it into her mouth, it tasted of blood, likely her own. When eventually the water stopped flowing, she found that something bright and warm touched her cheek. Sunshine. Sage almost whimpered with joy, a fresh warm breeze touched her skin and she breathed it in greedily, making herself cough weakly. A voice she thought she knew shouted something, and then the debris around her was moving, the sunlight was stronger, and it hurt her eyes. Strong hands cradled her face and that voice was speaking kind words to her, it's tone filled with emotion. Sage felt gladness for the sound of another human being, and she tried to smile to show she had heard him. Then there were many male voices all shouting and calling, but if they called to her, Sage was too weak to answer. Then hands were scooped under her and she was being lifted into the air, then crushed against a strong muscular chest. There was cheering so loud she wished they would stop. She was sure she felt pressure upon her head like kisses, but that seemed unlikely, nobody knew her.

Robaratus stood at the end of her bed watching. A strange feeling curling around his stomach and chest, something he couldn't name. He had found her when she coughed. He had been so choke holding her in his arms, seeing her frail body. She should have died, it had been days since the earthquake, there were no survivors left, and yet.. Though she hardly breathed, he watched transfixed at each soft rise and fall of her chest, no other movement came from her, at times her breathing was so shallow, he'd had to lean his face against her lips to feel her breath. He recalled the feeling of her in his arms, as they were taken back to the villa in the wagon, how happy he was to have her back, alive. He had cried then, let all his emotions go just him and her alone, and he vowed softly to never hurt her again. Who was this girl who had been forced to be his wife, who walked miles on bloody feet and made no sound, who slept on the hard floor curled in front a fire long cold, and who had survived being buried alive for days? He couldn't hate her, though he knew not what he felt, it wasn't hate, in a way he admired her, she was frail in build but strong in will, *the heart of a gladiator* he thought. Silently he kept his vigil watching, praying she would live, she deserved that, but what kind of life might he give her, she deserved more than he'd offered so far. Her thin arms were badly scratched and her whole body had been covered in bruises. Robaratus had seldom seen her face, it was always cast down or hidden with a scarf, yet now he could see her soft features, pale skin, with its speckled freckles adding something special to her looks, her soft lips now cracked and raw, he could imagine as full and gently coloured. Her cheeks were still swollen but he knew she was thin, he could imagine those cheek bones high, lending her a noble look, her rich brown hair that once shone like a mirror, he had seen it so many times, yet now it hung limp and straggly, still coated in dust that he had an irritating urge to wash away. That odd feeling crunched his gut, and he closed his eyes against it as a gentle hand touched his arm, he turned to look down at Octavia. "She will live" Her voice whispered softly. He made no answer just looked back at the soft rise and fall of his wife's chest, a breath for life each time she took it.

*　　　*　　　*

It was daytime when Sage let out a whimper. Robaratus was at her side instantly, her pulse was strong, her breathing came in gasps, and a soft moan escaped her lips, he stood back, stepping into Octavia, who looked at him oddly.

"I shouldn't be the first face she sees." He muttered.

"Why not?" Octavia was shocked at him.

"I have been less of a husband to her, and I doubt my face would be a welcome sight." He moved around Octavia to stand at the door. Sage whimpered again and slowly her eyes opened, squinting at the candle light, shielding her eyes with a hand. It was then that Robaratus saw how brown they were, his first ever glimpse of her eyes. Large round brown eyes that roamed the room confused, until they settled upon him, standing at the door with his massive arms wrapped about his chest. Their gazes locked, hers confused, his oddly soft, in a harsh way. *Robaratus.* His strange green eyes burned into her, his face set in a neutral expression, yet she sensed worry, for all it was wrong on a man whose heart was long dead. Sage tried to sit up afraid he would call her weak or lazy, but a firm hand pushed her down, only then did she notice Octavia. "You're going nowhere." Her voice warned. When Sage went to point out Robaratus, she saw he had gone, her heart sank, this was reality; her husband hated her. Octavia turned to see the empty space, she sighed. "He is afraid Sage." She said kindly. "He was frantic to find you, and when he did, he wouldn't let you go. He has sat beside you for days now watching you, talking to you." Sage let her eyes drift towards the door where he had been standing. *Yet he left.* "He is ashamed of himself; he knows you are scared of him and he didn't want you to be afraid now." Octavia explained, almost as though she had read her thoughts. Sage closed her eyes, perhaps he had a point, he did scare her half to death, yet she had seen something like compassion in his eyes.

"It is a miracle you are alive; you are a wonder to us all." Octavia told her as she carefully held her head so she could sip water.

Robaratus came to see her daily. He would ask her if she needed anything, and mostly she didn't. He made sure he was with her at meal times helping to spoon food into her still swollen lips. "Why do you feed me?" She asked once. "It is my duty." He replied in a voice smooth and deep. Sage wanted him to say he had changed his mind about her, but it seemed duty was his motivation now, her hopes died. It was often an

53

awkward silence that filled the room when he was there, and she wished they could talk about things like her other visitors did. When he was near her he smelt of sawdust and pine, never sweat. His touch was gentle which was at odds with his frame and bearishness. "What do you do when you're not here?" She asked him.

"I train." He answered. He knew she was trying to fill the silence, but he still wasn't sure how he felt. She was a child, too young for him, even if he did admire her courage, he could not imagine being a husband to a woman so young. "Sage. I have not been a good husband. I never will be. I will do what I can to make your life easier, but I am a gladiator, in any fight I could lose and you will be without any support. I would not want you to be a widow, but I am a lot older than you. I don't expect you to understand, but I cannot give you what you want. I will never love you."

Sage listened, but she made no response, she just wondered how old he thought she was. He had mentioned her age a few times, making presumptions, but she had never really thought he believed it all until now. She wondered how much older was he? Surely it wouldn't matter, he was a gladiator it wouldn't serve him well to have emotions.

Her recovery was a slow thing, Octavia often told her off for trying to run before she could walk. Robaratus would smirk at her frustrations, it made her heart soar. His face would change from grim to making him look years younger, almost handsome, though she buried that feeling whenever it emerged. His fellow gladiators all encouraged her loudly, when they watched her trying to walk. Albus holding her arms, as one shaky foot moved in front of the other. If she wobbled the men would shout "Woooah!" and she would laugh, losing her balance completely and falling into Albus' arms. She would laugh then. Robaratus found magic in that smile, her face lit up and he encouraged the men to cheer her on, himself included. When she fell and laughed, his own heart soared, for she was showing her true colours daily, and he thought her a brave and admirable spirit. Each evening, he lay beside her and fed her bits of food, even though she would insist she could now feed herself, he still liked pretending he was more of a father figure to her than a husband. Octavia and Albus would tease them both endlessly. Although Sage didn't mind the attention, she couldn't help but think he was more parent than partner, and the issue of their ages bothered her more and more.

Chapter 7

Sage wandered around the grounds, she was recovering well, though she missed seeing April and being in Rome, she watched from a distance as the Gladiators trained, but today she decided she wanted to go further, push herself a little bit more, so she wandered past the training ground, not looking to see if her husband was there, since she had left her sick bed, she only saw him at meal times. Try as she might, she could not fathom his thinking. She admired the umbrella pines that lined the boundaries to the villa and the huge oaks that were dotted here and there, but most prominently planted everywhere were the fig trees, whose fruit she loved. When Sage became tired she realised she had walked too far, and the villa was too far away for her to return to easily, but ahead of her was the dwelling she and Robaratus had been given, so she stumbled her way over to it, her legs cramping and causing her pain all the way. Opening the door she was met with giggles and groaning noises, a deep rumbling tone that told her at least Robaratus was there, though he couldn't be, he should be training, Sage panicked and threw open the bedroom door ready to confront a thief, and saw to her horror, a naked woman sat atop her husband, rocking madly and giggling, throwing her head back. Sage stood aghast, as her husband looked around the writhing woman.
"Fuck" He groaned. Sage mumbled an apology and shut the door, tears seeping down her face she hurt so badly, but she could not stay so she stumbled from their home and tried to make it back to the villa. She realised sadly that if he couldn't be with her, he was bound to go back to what he knew, it had to be easier for him. She wasn't angry with him, it's what she ought to have known he would do, but more she realised, it was her own humiliation of walking in and seeing. Then it occurred to her how angry he was going to be, and the terror of that spurred her on to try and run, but her legs cramped up and she fell to the floor with a loud cry of pain. A few moments later strong arms were gathering her up. "Sage are you alright?" It was Violens. Sage sobbed and sobbed, unable to tell the kind man why. Violens was not handsome as Robaratus was, but he was kind beyond anything Robaratus would ever be. "Here, I will carry you, is that acceptable?"
Sage nodded and she was scooped into his arms, which were deceptively

strong for a man so thin. He carried her with ease as she cried from the pain. He called for Octavia, who rushed out to them. Violens laid her down on a lounger and Octavia began rubbing Sage's legs to ease the cramped muscles. Violens nodded and left them alone.

"You over did it didn't you?" Octavia scalded. She knew cramp had to be painful and was, but Sage was far more distressed than anything even bad cramp would cause, there was something else that distressed her.

At the evening meal Robaratus was silent. It was he who kept his eyes down. Sage hardly ate nor did he. Octavia and Albus exchanged worried looks, but neither broached the subject as to what was going on. They made their excuses having eaten, leaving the gladiator and his wife to talk.

"I am sorry Sage." He said almost immediately. Sage said nothing. "I had no idea you were able to walk so far yet. I would never have done that otherwise."

"What does it matter Robaratus? You are a gladiator; it is in your nature to bed women. As you remind me, you are older than I, and you cannot love me or anyone, so of course you would bed a woman who can meet your needs. You are a man, and do not all men have affairs? It is the reason I never wanted a husband myself. The type of man I want doesn't exist in this age. So I will ask again, what does it matter? We are wed not by choice." Her words were said with such sadness, yet her voice did not break nor waver. He stared at her with confusion, she ought to be furious, upset, in tears! Yet she spoke with a heartbroken honesty that filled his gut with guilt. She had taken everything she had been told about gladiators, especially him, and turned it against him in a way that humbled and humiliated him. "True" Was all he could manage.

"I am the one who is sorry. I never think that you have to go and do those things. I should have asked if I could visit my own home."

His ire exploded and his fist hit the table, smashing the edge clean off. Sage jumped a mile. "Don't you fucking dare make me feel bad. I'll do as I wish, I always have, and I don't need your permission."

Sage nodded. She hadn't meant it the way he'd taken it. She turned and left him alone, she walked away wishing she had never survived being buried alive, what was her life, nothing. She walked alone to the dwelling but she wouldn't enter it, instead she walked to the arena, which was empty and still, there she sat on the ground, back against a building, and she cried softly. How she missed home.

She watched the men train all the following day, she watched the annoyance in her husband's face, and she ignored him, ignored every glare he flashed her way. She studied the men lifting stones, each stone was a different weight it made their stomachs stronger, their backs stronger and their arms stronger, she watched as they walked with stones in each hand and arms locked at their sides, Albus made them go faster further, until they could walk no more, the sweat poured off them, and then he would rest them. She watched her husband do the same exercises, lifting stones far bigger than the other men could, walked farther than the other men did, and even with the sweat pouring over his eyes he kept going pushing himself to a limit he never found. At first she thought he was making a silent point to her, but she soon realised he was making the point to the other men, no matter your limit, you push beyond it, a part of Sage admired him but the part that had been hurt hated his success. She watched them run and do sit ups, press ups, play a ball game they all loved, she watched them rest and then work again, fighting they learned to hold swords of wood far heavier than the sword they would carry in the arena, she watched as Robaratus pointed out when their feet were in the wrong place, when a lunge was a deadly exposure, how to avoid the sun glare from blinding you, she watched it all learning how he thought, how he moved. It was a dance, his turn their turn, his turn their turn, and around they'd spin, dancing jabbing waiting to kill.

Each day she sat and each night she relived every move understanding what it was about, why Robaratus insisted on this step or that lunge, it mattered for balance, for what followed. She made notes for herself on parchment, looking at how the positions mattered.

"We are to have a small friendly tournament with a rival of mine." Albus announced one evening. "I want to see how you all fare."

Robaratus agreed it was the right time for the men to be tested, Sage silently looked forward to seeing this event too. The training ground at the villa was much smaller than the arena, but it still had the same open area unshaded, so the gladiators learned to fight in the same conditions as they would have in Rome. The locals were also invited to come and watch, it helped new gladiators get used to being shouted at. Sage sat at the front with Albus and Octavia, her face covered by her large shawl, Octavia wore a silk shawl of sky blue over a white tunic. Albus wore a toga as his position expected. The sun was ever relentlessly shimmering its heat and before the tournament even started the Gladiators were sweating. The opponents were a fierce looking band of men, not as tall as Robaratus but certainly as muscular, heads shaved, and faces with scars.

"Caesur it is good to see you." Albus greeted the muscular man in an arm grip.

"You have Robaratus! I didn't quite believe that news, well, it should be good to wager some bets this day." Caesar grinned showing two teeth missing.

"He is fond of fighting himself." Octavia whispered to Sage.

The first round began with two fighters who were relatively new, Sage noted that the men were matched almost to their abilities, to make the fight more even. Two Laquearii entered the arena, both had whips and short swords, the whips were loud and intimidating, making Sage blink and jump each time they were lashed, they were able to cause a lot of damage and both Gladiators bore the scars of such menacing weapons. Neither wore a helmet but both had a shield over one shoulder and leather armlets to protect their sword hand. They watched each other intently, walking slowly circling around each other, the opponent occasionally snapping his whip to distract, but Albus's gladiator did not flinch, instead he just walked in careful circles, which Sage realised after a moment, he was counting, his feet did not cross as the other man's did so when that happened, Albus's man lashed his whip out catching his opponent off guard, the whip wrapped about his ankles and he toppled to the ground as Albus's man closed in for the pretend kill, his sword raised, then suddenly his attacker brought his legs up and kicked out, pushing Albus's man away. The crowd cheered with approval, as Albus's man had lost his whip leaving him dangerously exposed given his opponent now had two whips, and he grinned once his feet had untangled. Robaratus sat still as a statue, watching impassively as his fighter looked lost, the snap of the whip and its tip just missed him as he jumped in time to avoid being cut, he ran toward his opponent snatching both arms and pushing him with as much force as he could muster, the man fell backwards, stumbling along as Albus's fighter pushed forward with both speed and strength, Sage grit her teeth and urged the man on silently, while the crowd shouted and screamed with excitement. The gladiator lost his fight with gravity and fell over, dropping a whip as he did so, allowing Albus's man to regain it and lash his opponent then stab him, piercing his hand to the ground. Sage turned away pretending to cough.

"Arh a good bout Albus, but I am certain we will win the next one." Caesar smiled, clapping as he acknowledged the win. The fights went on all the afternoon, with the sun beating down upon those fighting, shade for those watching, with large sheets that kept the place cool. Finally it came to the last bout. A Gladiator named Durus who had won all his bouts was to face Robaratus. Durus was an equally big man, tall and muscular, a Samnite, wearing the same leather strappings as Robaratus, to protect his fighting arm, he also carried a shield, but a standard one, so not as heavy or long as that of Robaratus. Durus also wore a helmet and carried a short sword, to the uninitiated he looked almost the same as Robaratus, and once upon

58

a time Sage would've been one of those uninitiated, but now she knew all the differences between the gladiators. She sat keeping her emotions in check and her face neutral for she was sure he was watching her somewhere. Durus walked into the arena and the crowd cheered loudly, he paced around shaking his arms in the air, showing off his sword and shield. About his groin he wore a groin cloth held in place with a leather wide belt, his helmet was black with a black plume showing he was the bringer of death; he looked menacing. After a while Robaratus came out, he wore much the same protections, though his shield was bigger and ultimately heavier, he wore shorts with leather strip fringes, shin leathers and bare feet, he also waved his sword and shield and he roared. He was a Mirmillon Gladiator and the most exquisite specimen Rome had ever produced. Sage remembered how that roar had reached the very top of the great Colosseum in Rome, how he could out shout even the loudest crowds, and here in a smaller arena, with smaller crowds, his roar deafened them all. It was hard not to feel a smidgen of pride for the man, here Robaratus was in his world, upon his stage, his shaven stubbled head already beaded with sweat, his green eyes a fire of blood lust, his jaw tense, tendons straining accentuating the hollows in his cheeks, he was a God, muscles rippling, his chest breathing hard, his exposed thigh muscles making his legs appear thick as tree trunks, some women swooned, some were screaming and Robaratus smiled a beautiful white smile. Sage felt the sadness wash over her, a smile for them all, let him smile, she was his wife and the thorn in his side, therefore it came as a shock when his eyes dropped to her, fixed her to the spot, her face was covered with her shawl, her hand covered her eyes that she might shield them from the brightness, yet he stared at her and she at him. He wore no expression that she could read, but his stare lingered all the same, she refused to look away, she tilted her chin very slightly upward and then slowly nodded to him, a brief movement that seemed to satisfy him as he then turned and walked to the opposite side of the arena, bending to retrieve his golden helmet, he turned and looked straight at Sage before slowly putting it upon his head, even then she felt his green eyes upon her, though scared she refused to look away, it seemed as though they were in a battle of their own for what purpose she had no idea.

"What was that?" Octavia leaned over to ask.

"No idea." Sage answered shrugging her shoulders, though she was sure Octavia wasn't convinced. The crowd hushed as both men walked into the centre of the arena, as they stood in front of each other Robaratus spoke to his opponent "Fac mihi hodie" He grinned, Durus nodded then the fight was on. Robaratus liked to upset his opponents by saying "Make my day". Durus swiped his blade, Robaratus blocked with his shield, they spent a good while doing this, sometimes rushing, sometimes lunging yet always blocking with shields, Durus sort to trip but it was Robaratus who caught Durus off guard, sending him staggering backwards, Robaratus ran after him cutting his leg, drawing first blood had the crowd cheering loudly. Sage felt a satisfaction in this strike, but she still turned her gaze away, it was important to Robaratus to make the first strike. Durus made no sound or acknowledgment of the injury, blocking his opponents blows as he got his balance back. Robaratus crashed into Durus with his shield, forcing the man to step backwards, Durus roared, slashing with his blade, unable to get around the mighty shield Robaratus used, they beat at each other for a long time to the shouts from the crowd, then the judge intervened separating the men with his stick, so that they began again from a distance, Durus kicked at the larger shield, pushing at Robaratus, who stood solid, his thigh muscles bulging, but his bare feet glued to the sand, Durus ducked and dived around the side of Robaratus, managing to graze the Gladiator along his ribs, a shallow cut, but the crowd roared with joy at an equal strike, blood dribbled down his skin, which seemed to fuel the bear into an annoyed response, he turned his back on Durus and walked away, forcing his opponent to chase after him, he then ducked and spun, kicking Durus on his arse so he landed face down in the sand, Robaratus jumped on his back with a loud roar, claiming the point. He then got off him and waited for Durus to get up. The crowd roared as the Judge kept his stick over the fallen man, Robaratus stood statue still, his sword at his side. Sage squinted her eyes wondering why he waited, this was his chance to end the bout, *but of course, Robaratus is just warming up!* She realised, and a soft smile snagged at her lips. Durus stirred, rolling onto his side, he turned his black masked head to face Robaratus, if he spoke, nobody heard, the crowd were elated, slowly Durus got himself up and stretched, doing so, Robaratus punched his gut, but the gladiator just stood and offered him to do it again to the laughter of the crowd, who were loving the showmanship. Robaratus then head-butted Durus, sending the man backwards again, Robaratus followed him, landing kicks and punches to the man, knocking his shield aside, until Durus ducked away, landing a punch of his own upon Robaratus, who showed no acknowledgment to even feeling it, though he didn't turn in time to stop Durus from jumping upon his back and head butting him over and over against his golden helmet, a trickle of blood being the only sign that Durus was causing any damage. Sage put her hand into a fist. *Fight!* She willed her husband on. Robaratus must have heard her thought as he met the next head butt with one of his own, smashing into the black helmet, blood poured from Durus's face.

"A broken nose" Octavia shouted to Sage. "That'll slow him down." She was excited at the hit, bouncing to her feet and yelling her support. Sage turned away, trying not to gag. As Durus leaned backwards, so Robaratus grabbed his legs which were wrapped about his waist, and refused to let Durus go, running instead as fast as he could jiggling the man as he fought to hang on and get his legs free, when he lost his grip, he had to use his hands to stop himself being bounced upon the sand, the crowd roared, stamped their feet and waved their arms, Sage couldn't tell if they were encouraging or not, then Robaratus let his opponent go, dropping him hard onto the ground, turning and stamping on his shield, which he only just got into place in time. Durus kicked with both his legs missing Robaratus who had jumped into the air, landing with both feet either side of Durus his sword at the man's throat. Durus raised his finger and the crowd screamed with glee. The judge looked to the editor who in this instance was Albus, he played the crowd, waiting as they shouted to him what they wanted. It was a tournament supposedly of a friendly nature, so Albus gave the thumbs up allowing the loser to live. The crowd cheered loudly. Robaratus stepped away, then offered a helping hand to Durus, who was taken away by slaves to the doctors. Now he walked head up to the crowd, as they cheered and chanted his name he roared and shook his arms at them, so they cheered louder. He walked over to Sage as she sat clapping slowly, her shawl about her shoulders, her head up and a smile upon her face, his eyes pierced through the golden helmet holding hers, slowly he removed it, his eyes not shifting as he did so, they stared at each other, she kept the smile upon her face her hands continued to clap slowly, he stared, his eyes roving over her features as she realised it was the first time he had ever really looked at her. She didn't shy away from the intense gaze, for the first time since they had married, she was determined to face him unafraid. She was amazed when a smile slowly spread across his lips, one to match her own, she nodded to him slowly, cautiously, wanting him to know she approved his win. It seemed like forever before Robaratus returned that nod and forced himself to turn away, walking across the arena helmet under his arm, head held high, but not acknowledging the crowd any more, blood trickled down the back of his head. Once inside the arena entrance he turned and looked across the expanse of sand, his eyes locking with hers. Sage shivered inwardly at the thrill that ran through her, then he dipped his head to her and turned, walking away. She understood the lesson. *This is what I am.* She had given him her understanding, and he had thanked her.

At the evening meal, Ceasur sat beside Albus, Durus beside him. "I have to admit, Robaratus is still the best there is." Ceasur joked. Durus looked over at his rival. "I'm catching up." He smiled. Robaratus grinned back, he waved his hand with an oyster in and mocked "Dream on!" They laughed. "I had heard you were married Rob, but frankly I didn't believe it! You must be getting old!" Ceasur teased. "We are all getting old." Robaratus replied, still smiling. "So who is this wife?" Ceasur asked, looking at Sage. Robaratus introduced her.

"You look young for a wife of Rob here, how old are you?" Durus asked. Sage smiled gently; nobody had ever asked her age. "I am twenty-five." She wanted to burst out laughing at the stunned silence. Octavia had dropped her food, Albus was looking at her with a blank stare, but Robaratus was the best of them all. His green eyes wide, his face a picture of disbelief. "Gracious, you look much younger." Durus confessed, smiling at her.

"Everyone makes that assumption." Sage said politely.

"Have you been married for long?" Ceasur asked.

"A few months." Robaratus replied. He was hardly listening. "*As you remind me, you are older than I, and you cannot love me or anyone, so of course you would bed a woman who can meet your needs.*" He wanted to punch something. He had put her down for being younger than he, a child and he had bedded a woman for his pleasure, now Sage would never trust him, her ideal husband didn't exist. His anger burned at him, he said little of nothing for the rest of the evening, but on the walk back to their dwelling, he did speak. "Why did you never speak up when I accused you of being a child?" His voice was soft.

"Same reason that I never spoke up when my mistress got it wrong, or other people. Would you have believed me?" Sage smiled as she looked down at the ground. In truth, he knew he wouldn't.

"I thought you fought well today, everyone did." She wanted to change the subject badly, but Robaratus wasn't going to.

"You will never trust me will you?" He asked. Sage didn't answer, but walked on in silence. He grabbed her arm gently. "Sage?"

She sighed. "You spelt out your position on our wedding day, and so far you have not wavered from it, why would you change now?"

"I didn't know your damn age then." He grumbled.

"Arh yes! My age was the problem, but now it isn't a problem we can just fuck and be married can we?" She looked at him, her eyes filled with anger. He hung his head. "I was hoping we could try again, be friends this time."

"I'm not sure I am old enough for that, doesn't it take some sort of understanding? I don't *care* what you do Robaratus, I am the same as you, I *never* wanted to be married, and for all *my* sins, I certainly never wanted *you!*" She walked off leaving him staring after her dumbfounded.

Sage lit the little fire in the dwelling and folded her cape into a pillow, then she settled on the hard floor, sore still from being buried under rubble, but at least she was back where she felt most right, in front of a warm fire on the floor. She had hated the feeling of the bed. Had she been married to an old man in his fifties, she wouldn't want his gnarled hands on her, so she could understand why Robaratus had not wanted to be with someone he considered a child, but it still stung that the moment he knew her real age, it was fine to just become married and pretend all his nastiness had never happened. *Friends! Who was he kidding?*

Robaratus sat in the arena sulking. He had screwed up royally and his fist pounded the ground in agitation. "If you want to dig a hole to bury yourself in, there are quicker ways than pounding the ground with your fist."

Robaratus looked up to see Durus walking towards him. Well that was all he needed right now, someone to poke the bear. "Takes time to win a woman Rob." Durus said joining him on the ground. Robaratus said nothing, he was well aware of what courting was. "Right now I'd say Aquilina is laughing her toga off!"

"She had no idea either." Robaratus sneered.

"Give the girl time, she will calm down. She seems to me quite observant. I am sure she will see your position eventually."

"She has no reason to. I made it clear on our wedding day I had no interest in her. She walked in on me a few days back in the middle of taking my pleasure."

Durus burst out laughing. "We've all been there." He said eventually. Rob smiled. "I never wanted her to see me like that. I thought her too young, and she is a virgin still, naïve."

"Well she is going to grow up being married to you!" Durus assured him.

"That's just it. I don't want her condemnation. Truth is, I'm sick of living like that."

"Is that something you decided tonight, because you apparently didn't feel like this a few months back?"

Robaratus hung his head, he was confused and angry, and he had no real idea what the hell he felt or what he wanted. Durus stood up. "I'm off to bed. You need to do some serious thinking Rob."

63

Chapter 8

As Sage wandered towards home, a day after the tournament, a sensual aroma of food drifted towards her. There was smoke coming out of the chimney, she was unsure if she would be invading her husband entertaining another, but she was hungry, so she ventured on. Inside Robaratus was hunched over the fire stirring something in a large pot. It smelt divine to Sage, who also noted the table had two spoons upon it and two beakers filled with wine, but the thing that surprised her most, was the small posy of wild flowers that were sitting in a small vase, one she was certain they didn't own. Robaratus turned round to face her. "Arh, food." He pointed to the table, indicating she should sit. Sage was cautious, *why would he be doing this?* She sniffed the wild flowers for something to do while her husband dished up food. He placed the bowl before her and then sat with his own opposite her. "Eat." He instructed. Cautiously she took up the spoon, he looked at her. "It ain't poisoned." He scooped some into his mouth and swallowed so she could see he still lived, then he grinned. "Bet you never thought I could cook eh?" Sage didn't answer, but sipped from her spoon closing her eyes as the flavours washed around her mouth and caressed her tongue, she had no idea he could be such an amazing cook. When she opened her eyes he was studying her again, she managed a small smile and sipped some more. They ate for a while in silence, Sage thought if she was going to be poisoned then she was going to die having had the best meal of her life. Her thoughts were broken into by his rough deep voice. "We should talk." Her eyes did not move from her plate but her hand paused. *So there is an alternative reason for this, I should have guessed.* She waited wondering what he might have to talk about. "Things have changed."
Sage stopped eating, she raised her eyes slowly and found him looking at her. "I am no good at this." He wiped his hand over his face and sighed. "I can flatter a woman, I can flirt, hell I'm good in bed, but marriage? I have no idea how to do this." He sat back in his chair looking at her. *Why don't you just out and say it, you want rid of me.* Sage had no idea what to say to help him.
"Do you hate me?"
Sage blinked. She hadn't expected that, so shook her head swallowing. "I

64

don't know you." She said quietly, wondering if he hated her. He said nothing more for a while, Sage dared not move, she remained in her seat. "I found these." He threw her notes down on the table. "Why do you do it?"

"I wanted to understand, to learn."

He looked at her, her eyes were cast down as usual her face a little flushed at being found out, yet her words were said with sincerity.

"What is it you understand from this?" He asked, his own curiosity peaked. "Actually I have learned quite a lot. The other day, Violens dropped his trident and was unable to use his other hand. I have noticed that the stronger arm, the preferred arm, is slightly longer than the other. I think that puts gladiators at a disadvantage. If your strong arm is made useless, you are defeated. Perhaps gladiators should learn to be equal with both arms?" Her eyes were bright with enthusiasm, and her expression full of excitement. Robaratus was hypnotised. He could never had imagined anyone being so observant or making improvements for gladiatorial training. Sage took his silence as a cue to continue. "I also noted that when a gladiator is cut on his favoured leg, his other is weaker and he has trouble with balance." She paused. "I have made suggestions as to how this might be overcome." She leaned over to pick up her notes and stopped, seeing her husband had not changed his expression, nor moved. "You asked." She said uncomfortably. "I thought you wanted to know." She lowered her eyes again, all the excitement drained from her face.

"Remarkable. You learned all that by watching us?" He asked, his voice a deep rumble. Sage shivered.

"Why do you fear me? I have never hit a woman. I will never hit you." He assured her. Sage glanced up at him and found him looking at her intently. He shook his head at her. "Sage I promise you; you are quite safe from me. I might shout sometimes but I will never raise my hand to you. I am astounded at your thoroughness, and would appreciate some time to study these in detail. Is that acceptable to you?"

Sage smiled and nodded. He gave her a quick smile back.

*   *   *

"Av anover" the drunk said as he pushed another tankard of wine towards Robaratus. "Cheers" The bear growled.

"Wot we cele bating agin?" The drunk asked scowling as he stumbled over his words.

65

"Fucking women" Robaratus replied staring deeply into his drink. The drunk laughed and giggled. "Yea, I likes fucking women." He elbowed the Gladiator as he laughed again.

"No not *fucking* women, just fucking women!" Robaratus said, then grinned. "Well one in par tic lar." He slurred.

"Any un I know?" Asked the drunk hopefully.

"You better not." The bear growled looking at his drinking buddy with blood shot eyes.

"Oh, who then?"

"My wife."

"Arrr, why is it all woz the wif?" The drunk asked. "Bludy wivs drive us men tus the drink." He grinned. "Wish I had a wif now." He said ruefully. Robaratus giggled. "Na you don't." He informed him. "Yus I do. No excuse for bin drunk udder wise." They both giggled.

"What did she do?" The drunk asked.

"Who?"

"Yus wif."

"Oh. Ummm nuffin." Robaratus admitted.

"So wees getting ham, hammered fer nutting?" The drunk belched loudly.

"No. I'm pissed cos I dun deserf her." Robaratus said, adding "Wots your excoose?" he frowned at the drunk as though he'd just seen him, the man shrugged. "No idea, jus hepping a friend out." He slurred, raised his tankard and supped spilling a good deal down his top. Robaratus slapped him hard on the back, making the drunk drop his drink. "Good man. Av an udder." He waved the barmaid over and took another two drinks.

"I always fort my wif was a kid. Did ya know that?" He sloshed his wine round in the tankard.

"Naaa, really?"

"Yup." Robaratus nodded fiercely, and wished he hadn't when the room began to spin.

"How cud you not know?" The drunk squinted at him.

"The Empress made us marry, fucking bitch."

"An udder woman." His drunk buddy added, Robaratus nodded. "She 'ad no right." He moaned.

"Bitch made you wed a kid?"

"Well I thort so, an she must a fort so, but turns out wif is a woman not a kid." Robaratus gave a leery smile.

"You lucky bastard." His drunken friend grinned.

"But I ain't. I am a gladiator. I kill. I flirt an I fuck good," he giggled, "but I never wanted to be marr, marr, id. I don't know luv, never bin in luv, never wanted to be marr, mar, wed." He blinked hard, as tears filled his

66

eyes, though he knew not why. His drunken friend slapped an arm around his shoulders. "I symp thise." He said earnestly. "Dus she luv you?"

"Who?"

"Ya wif man?"

"No, pretty sure she don't."

"So why you sad?"

"I wish she did." They laughed again, but the truth hit Robaratus hard. He wanted her to love him, he wanted her to feel something for him, because he had feelings for her, had found in her a gladiator, a fellow fighter, a survivor.

Sage had spent two days pondering the strange conversation she'd had with her husband, he had said nothing more about her notes, though she had continued to make them. As they didn't have a slave of their own, she had decided to take the bed linen to the river to wash, she hitched the washing bag into her hip again and wiped the sweat from her eyes, another hot day, the river washing area would be busy, she was annoyed she had not set off earlier. The sound of singing, chatter and laughter drifted upon the wind, it teased the branches of the trees and out sang the song of birds, as Sage approached the washing area, she could see just how busy it was, women knelt on the hard rock scrubbing linens, others stood waist deep in the water dunking linen, whilst others helped each other to spread sheets over bushes to dry. Sage sighed, she would have to wait a bit till someone left, so she sat in the shade of a large bush and watched the others work. She must have dosed off because she was awoken by a sharp kick to her foot. Sage jumped and her eyes snapped open. She couldn't see the person standing in front of her, she blocked out the sun, appearing to be a dark presence. "I thought I recognised you. You are the one who keeps hanging round the gladiators." Some of the women now stopped their work to look over to where Sage was sitting. The woman looked over her shoulder to the other women. "You have to wait your turn if you want one of them." She said then laughed, as did those watching. "I bet you got hopes for Robaratus eh? He has to be the best looking, and most famous. Who doesn't want that well hung stallion?" It sounded like all the women burst into coarse laughter. Sage looked away, how humiliating to have strangers tell her what her husband looked like. "He is such a charmer." The other woman continued seeing Sages' discomfort. "He can flirt like none I have ever seen. Ain't half bad in the bed either." Again the others laughed. "I don't think he has any interest in girls though, likes his women to have experience." She winked at Sage who was scarlet. "Wasn't you who burst in on us the other day was it?" The woman asked jovially, but when Sage remained silent and bright red, the woman started to put things together. "You are ain't ya?" She stared hard at Sage. "You barged in on us, you dirty cow." The other women laughed. Sage stood up with difficulty, given the close proximity to the other woman. Once standing she looked to the river, and stooped to pick up her basket. "His seed is on that sheet." The woman cooed with pride. "You poor desperate cow, offering to wash his sheet to be close to his sperma!"

Sage pushed passed her and waded into the water, tipping the sheet and some of his tunics out. She tried to close her ears to all the things the women goaded her with, and the things he did with one in particular. She vowed if she ever washed his things again, she would do so at night when nobody could taunt her. She cried on the way home; it was a good vent of her emotions. Marriage was every bit as horrible as she imagined. The chimney was venting a thin line of smoke as she got nearer to their dwelling, and once more the aroma of herbs teased her senses, making her stomach rumble. She heaved a heavy sigh and marched her way indoors. Robaratus was sitting at the table with her notes, he looked up startled when Sage barged in, and ignoring him, went into his bedroom, throwing the clean sheet on the bed and throwing his clothes there to join it. She sniffed loudly, wiping her face on her sleeve, then turned and walked into a wall of muscle. Strong arms engulfed her and before she could stop herself, she burst into more tears. He said nothing, just rubbed her back, and held her close. It took some time before she pushed away from him. "I am fine now." She sniffed. He moved to one side and let her pass. Awkwardly Sage sat at the table, and her husband served her food. He said nothing until he sat down himself. "Your notes are impressive." He began, not looking at her. Sage stopped eating and looked at him.

"I have shown them to Albus, who agrees with me." He continued. Sage ate cautiously. "We would like to implement them, with your instruction." He looked up at her across the table. Sage nodded.

"I thought you'd be pleased?" He asked.

"I am. Sorry. I am really." Sage muttered.

"Not as pleased as I imagined you would be, so tell me what ails you?" Sage shrugged. "I had a bad day, it's nothing really."

"Nothing makes you throw my things around, nothing has you crying your heart out, and nothing smothers your enthusiasm for gladiatorial training methods?" He looked at her with a worried expression, which ironically made Sage smile. "I really don't want to talk about it." She said.

"If you did something wrong, I am hardly in a position to punish you." He smiled, hoping she would cheer up.

"It is your right as a husband to beat me black and blue if I did something wrong, which I didn't."

68

"Should I remind you that I have already stated I will never raise my hand to you?"

"Then perhaps you should!" Sage snapped unintentionally. "I understand men will fuck any woman willing, but I wish I didn't have to be the one they taunt about how fucking wonderful you are, and all the rest of the disgusting things you do." Unbidden tears filled her eyes again. Robaratus bit his lip, but the smile slipped out regardless.

"I am so glad it amuses you. I hate being married and I hate being married to you!" She sobbed, she got up and left the dwelling, bumping into Albus as she stormed off. "Arr, Sage. I have been thinking about your notes, most impressive by the way. Are you alright?"

Sage inhaled deeply. "I'm fine, I just don't like being laughed at."

Sensing this was a marital tiff, Albus stayed off the subject. "Then walk with me and tell me how to make my gladiators stronger."

*   *   *

It was a few days of intense work talking to and helping the gladiators to understand why the training was changing slightly. They were all sceptical at first, but soon realised just how weak the weaker sides of their bodies were. Albus had them fighting with their weaker arms putting them all at the same disadvantage. After much swearing and frustration, the gladiators were now finding humour in their fights, so Sage had taken some time to herself and she wandered about the fields that surrounded the villa. She passed the treasured grape vines, with their promised harvest bulging in the Roman sunshine, the apple orchards now with some grafts ready to start new trees, but also with an abundance of fruit. There were olives and figs as well as pears and peaches, all had their own kind of aromas that filled her head. The bees hummed a cacophony of sound as they raced from flower to flower covering themselves in nectar. It was a calming, peaceful walk. Such sights and sounds so very different from anything Sage had previously known, she found she much preferred this to the sounds of Rome. She found herself at the walnut orchard, the husks still green, there would be a good harvest again which would make winter an abundant time of year, if other fruits and nuts did as well. "Well what have we here?" A sarcastic female said. Sage turned to find herself facing the same woman who had taunted her at the river. "You know you are trespassing right?"

Sage looked puzzled. "I apologise, I hadn't realised I had walked onto different land. I will leave immediately."

The woman laughed. "I could have you charged under iniuria." She informed Sage, who paled at the thought, then turned to leave, but the woman grabbed her arm tightly. "You told Rob a lie." She said nastily. "He came an' talked to me about leaving you alone."

Sage tried to wriggle free but the woman's grip was too fierce. "You're a little snitch madam, an snitches are not liked around here." The woman stepped closer; Sage noticed her breath stank as she eyed Sage closely. "And because you snitched, he don't wanna see me no more." The slap came out of nowhere, and Sage gasped, holding her sore cheek. "So according to Rob, you're his new little wifey." Another hard slap on the other cheek. Again Sage tried to pull free. "First lesson girl, you don't ever snitch." This time the woman punched Sage in the gut, winding her badly. Sage doubled over coughing. "Secondly yer don't send hubby to sort your problems out." Another fierce punch to her gut. The woman pushed Sage up against a tree. "Thirdly you turn a blind eye to his affairs, it's what wives do." A fist to Sage's jaw had her bite through her lip, making blood flow down her chin. "Fourth. I fucking hate babies." She punched Sages' eye, kicked her shins, and when Sage slipped to the ground curling up, she kicked her back, legs, arms and anywhere she could inflict damage. When she ran out of venom, she left Sage curled up at the base of the walnut tree.

It was a long time before Sage felt strong enough to get up, her lip still bled, her nose bled, her eye was swollen, her face was swollen, and her arms were starting to turn purple as were her legs. She was grateful not to have broken bones, though her ribs wanted to argue the point with her. She walked very slowly home, unable to cry. She had arrived at the training ground when someone yelled her name and a clutter of weapons told her they had abandoned training, as they all rushed over to her. Robaratus was first. Sage looked at him as best she could, he got down on his knees so she could look down at him, his face a picture of concern. "A messige from your whore, not to get you to invled in my prblms." She was swept off her feet into his arms. Saying nothing he walked back to the villa. Octavia came rushing out, as Rob explained what he thought had happened. Octavia looked horrified. When he had laid Sage on a lounge, he turned and he roared. He roared so loudly Sage thought the sound would carry to the village, two leagues away. The other gladiators stood in a line, and Robaratus charged up to them, but they stood firm. "You cannot do anything Rob." Violens informed him. Robaratus roared again, making each gladiator wince with sympathy. Then he smiled, not a happy jovial smile, but a nasty spiteful, vengeful smile, one that made Albus worry.

Rob had a temper. It might take a lot to ignite it, and generally he relied upon it for his survival, but this was the first time Albus had seen him use that smile outside the arena. Albus could almost taste the shit that was coming his way.

Over several days, Robaratus seethed, but bided his time, He focused on Sage, fussing over her as she recovered. Yet again she proved herself to be a tiny gladiator, fighting with a tenacity to prove herself worthy of his admiration. He discovered the whole story in bits, as Sage got better at talking. She had no issue with telling her husband what his behaviour had caused, and reminding him how much she hated being his wife. She was getting sick of being the laughing stock, sick of being talked about and sick of being picked on. Robaratus felt her frustration. He shared it. Twice now he had failed to protect her, and it stuck in his heart like a dagger. She deserved better from him, yet he kept failing. Violens had pointed out to him it was because of his fame and reputation, Sage was always going to be a target. Robaratus knew it, it was why he didn't want a wife, but he was saddled with her and his feelings about it were adding to his frustration. She was a fighter, she was a thinker, and she hated him, he could think of no way to make himself matter to her, but he was going to stop Sage from being the victim of jealous women.

Robaratus waited for the woman to arrive, she was smiling at his invitation to meet again. She stepped into his open arms and they kissed deeply. "Why did you beat my wife up?" He asked kindly still holding her. "I didn't." She lied. He knew it because she hadn't looked at him, but she had tensed just the smallest bit. He squeezed a little harder. She gasped for a breath. "Rob you're hurting me." She wheezed. He kept his grip, she struggled. "Rob let me go." She pleaded. His arms flexed a fraction more and like a constrictor his grip tightened again. Now she panicked. "Rob!" She wheezed, her face scarlet. "I'm sorry". He relaxed a little. "Why did you beat her?" He repeated. "She snitched."

"I'd gladly break your ribs now, had you been a man." He squeezed again to make his point, and she almost passed out.

"Who were the other women who laughed at my wife at the river?" He pushed. She didn't dare lie again; she was still fighting for her breath. She gave names freely. "You will never again make fun of my wife, or touch her in any way. If you do, there will be no hole on this earth that will hide you from me. Do I make myself clear?" He growled so deeply the ground itself might have vibrated. The woman sobbed. By the time you get home your husband will be wanting a word with you. He smiled in a mean way, showing white teeth against his tanned skin.

71

Sure enough Albus was right. First to arrive at his door was the walnut farmer.

"Albus, your gladiator is out of control. He has almost killed my wife and he confessed he has had sex with her. You realise how this makes me look?" Albus kept his face impassive. "I do."

"Then bring the man here to account for himself."

Albus invited the farmer into the villa, where he showed him out the other side and down to the gladiatorial training ground. The gladiators ceased training, standing to stare. Robaratus walked forward.

"Robaratus, a word please." Albus asked.

"We can talk right here." The farmer said through gritted teeth. Robaratus stood still.

"Do you still claim to have had sex with my wife?" The farmer growled.

"Yup." Robaratus replied. The farmer lashed out with his fist, but Robaratus just leaned backwards and avoided the contact. Albus rolled his eyes out of sight of the farmer. "I have divorced my wife because of you, now I want your life."

"Is that all?" Robaratus growled. When the man made no reply, he turned and walked away.

"Albus. I demand compensation." The man raged. Albus shrugged helplessly. "I sympathise, but I am not in a position to appease you. Robaratus is not my slave. He belongs to the Emperor and as such has his complete protection. It is unlikely he would appease you either."

"Why not? He defiled my wife."

"Your wife beat his wife, he had just cause to disclose his own behaviours." The man looked past Albus at the Emperors favourite gladiator. "You'd better watch your back slave, accidents happen." The man threatened. Robaratus smiled back at him. The farmer turned to leave and a chorus of cheering broke out from the rest of the gladiators.

Over the next few days and weeks several other men came to visit Albus, to make complaints about his gladiators, all of whom had been very busy it seemed. Albus worked it out for himself what was going on. Each gladiator had posted a notice claiming a woman, who just happened to be someone who had laughed at Sage, had been unfaithful and it could be proved. Each husband had demanded Albus give compensation, and Albus had repeatedly had to decline, given the declarations were vague and no actual person owned up to them. As much as Albus hated to admit it, Robaratus had compromised his situation with him and would have to go. Men who had no reparation tended to take matters into their own hands, and Albus knew that was just a matter of time.

Chapter 9

Sage was trying her best to uncurl her legs when Robaratus walked in and saw her. She struggled to cover her legs up but he was instantly at her side. "What are you trying to do?" he asked kindly as he pulled the blanket back over her bruises.

"I'm trying to get up. I've been sitting here too long and my legs have stiffened up."

"Trust me." He said slipping a warm hand under one leg, and taking the top part of her leg in the other. Gently he rubbed and pulled at her leg, encouraging the blood flow. Sage watched him curiously. She would never have imagined the bear capable of such tenderness, yet as he worked on her skin, so she felt the benefits, as her leg uncurled with little pain. He then went to work on her other leg. "I have some good points." He smiled up at her. "I can help with aching limbs."

Sage smiled back at him, but said nothing about his skills.

"What is going on Robaratus?"

He paused to look up at her.

"Octavia has been reluctant to talk to me about things, she says I must ask you, so I am."

Robaratus sat back on the floor looking up at her. He sighed deeply.

"We are going to be leaving soon." He said honestly. Sage raised her eyebrows.

"The woman who beat you up got a warning from me, and is now divorced from her husband." Sage screwed her eyes up. "What did you do?" She asked. Robaratus smirked and shrugged. "I might have written to her husband telling him what she and I did."

Sage's eyes grew wide. "He will want your hide for that!" She said.

"Yea, I know. He already asked Albus for it, but I don't belong to Albus. I belong to the Emperor, and the man is a bit pissed about that." He tried his best sympathetic look, but Sage burst out laughing. Robaratus wanted to close his eyes and listen to that happy sound all day long.

"So we have to leave?" Sage said soberly. She liked it here, she didn't want to leave Octavia, or Albus she had grown to like them.

73

"I'm sorry but there is a greater problem. The other gladiators have been leaving notes in the village naming women who have been unfaithful. There have been at least five pissed off husbands that Albus has had to sort out, though there is no evidence that gladiators are to blame, but those were the same women that laughed at you." He left the rest unsaid. Sage stared at him. "Great. I like being here and now I have to move. Where will we go?" She sounded annoyed and Robaratus couldn't really blame her, but he felt sad that again she would blame him for not letting things be, but he couldn't be expected to just ignore her plight, it would only have gotten worse, even if she didn't think so.

"I must talk to Albus before deciding anything." He replied.

*   *   *

To Robaratus' eyes Albus looked old of late, but then worry would do that to a person he presumed, and he had given Albus plenty of worry. The man sat in a chair hands on his large belly, and worry etched into every line of his face. "How is Sage?" He asked in a warm and caring voice.

"She is well enough to move." Robaratus informed him, saving Albus having to tell him why he had been summoned. The older man Smiled sadly. "I take no delight in having to send you both away. I like Sage, so does Octavia. We will miss you both very much." His eyes seemed watery, a rare sight, though Robaratus remembered the last time he left, Albus had watery eyes that day too. He nodded. Albus looked down at his stomach. "I am expecting a runner from Rome any day, with either instructions for your return there or instructions as to where to send you next. Either way I am unwilling to comply." He drummed his fingers on his bulk for a while. "I dislike Aquilina, as you know. If you had already left by the time her runner arrives, I can hardly be blamed if I have no notion of where you went." He shrugged to himself.

"Aquilina will insist you inform her of where I went." Robaratus interjected. Albus looked up at him. "Yes, you're right, she will." He sighed deeply. "Thing is I cannot be blamed if you do not arrive at the destination I send you to. The complaint she will have comes from a posse of angry ex-husbands who are clearly out for revenge, obviously you would take it upon yourself to protect Sage, so you wouldn't tell me what your plans are, and I cannot tell an angry mob what I do not know." He trailed off letting his eyes wander along the tiled floor, as though following an insect. Robaratus smiled. "Have you a destination in mind for us?" He asked.

74

"As a matter of fact I do. Ceasur Brutus has a small villa several miles from here. I rather think you might cause less trouble if I sent you to him. Certainly he will be overjoyed to have a gladiator of your status amongst his men. It might not please Rome, but we do what we can at short notice. I have no notion of when these men will be seeking to attack me and mine, so I must act quickly. This is the best I can manage at short notice." He gave smug smile.

"And if I don't arrive?" Robaratus frowned at him, Albus shrugged. "*I* won't be punished. It will be on your head dear boy!"

Robaratus smiled at being called a boy in his late thirties.

"Just make sure that wherever you might end up, you're indispensable by the time Rome catches up with you." Albus lowered his head and looked up at Robaratus like a wise old man might. The gladiator nodded.

Chapter 10

They talked through the plan on where to go, Sage listened more than anything, she had no notion of life beyond Rome, so it became interesting as Robaratus talked about options and none of them pleased him.

"How can you avoid Aquilina; she will be enraged to lose control of you." Sage pointed out.

"She will be madder at Albus than me, and Albus has already prepared his excuses!" Robaratus smiled. "Aquilina only *thinks* she has eyes everywhere, there are enough people outside of Rome who dislike her; it is really quite easy to disappear." He spoke with confidence, which made Sage wonder what kind of life he may have led to know so much about the world beyond Rome. He turned to face her, asking if she was hungry, when she nodded, he got up to go cook something.

"We will leave at first light. Albus and Octavia will come down before dawn to see us off." He told her. When Sage said nothing back, he looked over his shoulder, she looked so sad. He left his food and squatted down in front of her. "I know you hate me for making us have to leave, but I have a duty as a husband, which I admit I have not been very good at. If I had not done anything things would have got worse. I had to make a stand, to make sure it is understood I won't have anyone making fun of my wife." His eyes implored her to understand. Sage looked down at him, he seemed so vulnerable for a moment. "Thing is, it is always going to be this way. Are you going to fight the whole world because of me?"

He smiled, such a beautiful smile, she was quite taken aback. "I hope not, but if that's what it takes, then that's what I'll do." His eyes remained steady on her, and she felt a soft heat colour her face. "Why? You never wanted a wife. You hate me." She felt confused. Robaratus sighed. "Am I not allowed to change my mind?" He asked slightly annoyed, she shrugged. "Is it because of my age?"

"No. Well a bit. It's because you're smart. You came up with all that thinking about training. I am beyond impressed Sage. You're more than you seem." Again he smiled, leaving her a little breathless this time. He got up and returned to the fire and his cooking. He had changed, he was making an effort to be kind to her, and whilst she was angry with him, she also knew she should give a little back, it would be a lot easier if they could

76

be friends at least.

Before day break Albus and Octavia arrived at the dwelling. Robaratus had gone for the horse and covered arcera they had arrived with. Octavia gave Sage some herbs for healing properties, and a couple of her old togas just so she had a change of clothing. Albus gave her a hug and told her how he would miss her, again his eyes seemed watery. Robaratus arrived, horse in tow.

"Rob, it has been a joy to see you again, to see how you have changed. You have more than earned your title. I shall miss you both, but am grateful to you Sage for the tips on helping my gladiators." Albus then gave Robaratus a purse full of coin. "Take care both of you. May Fortuna ride with you." He and Robaratus gripped arms and Octavia hugged Sage and Rob. Sage was helped on the front of the arcera, Rob jumped up beside her and as the sun broke over the horizon, they moved off.

Sage wasn't as upset as she had been the day before, the thought of seeing more of the country in which she lived was exciting to her, and she sat watching everything with avid interest. Robaratus was glad that she wasn't crying, he said nothing as they moved through the countryside, his mind intent upon his destination, and his eyes and ears watchful of attack. The clouds were gathering above them, and the wind was picking up, Sage hoped it wasn't a bad omen. By late morning the rain started, and Robaratus made for a nearby copse of trees, which offered a small amount of protection for the horse. Sage moved into the back of the arcera, which had a wooden roof. Robaratus joined her, making the space much smaller with his larger build. The rain pounded on the roof, as the skies blessed the ground with much needed water. "At least the olive trees will be grateful." Sage said shivering. Robaratus offered her a blanket, but she still shivered, so he wrapped an arm about her and pulled her closer to him. She was scared at first, but as he showed no signs of taking advantage of her, she began to relax. Robaratus smiled, as he rested his head on hers, the scent of rosemary and mint from her hair assailed his nostrils filling him with a peaceful sensation, soon they were asleep as the rain beat a steady rhythm on the roof.

Sage awoke to the sudden realisation she was asleep against Robaratus. Her instinct was to move away from him quickly, but then she remembered where they were. The rain had stopped, and the wagon was filled with the steady breathing of her husband. She found herself listening to him and feeling the gentle but firm beat of his heart. He was warm against her and his arms rested loosely around her body, protectively. Sage felt a warmth seep into her, it was nice to be held like this. Then the nasty voice in her head wondered if he held other women in this way, and the warmth seeped away, replaced by a cold sadness. She wasn't special to him, just a wife he never wanted, so he was doing his duty by her and she really ought not to read so much into it. She had no idea where they were going or how long it may take to get there, nor how many days or nights they would need to be in such close proximity; she would have to tolerate things until they arrived at their new home, and she could go back to sleeping on the warm stones by a kitchen fire. She sighed and that woke Robaratus up immediately. She slipped away from him and excused herself to slip outside to relieve herself. Robaratus did the same, checking the horse when he returned, it was damp but luckily not soaked. He hitched it up to the arcera and when Sage returned they set of again. The rain had done a good job of soaking the road, and large puddles allowed birds to take opportunistic baths, the fields looked greener and the air seemed fresher. "I love it when it has rained." Robaratus admitted, "everything feels like new again."

Sage looked up at him. "What else do you like?" She asked. He smiled as he looked ahead. "I like the freckles on your face." His grin was wide and he laughed at her expression of surprise. "Freckles are unbecoming." She pointed out.

"True, but just because something is unfashionable, doesn't make it unpleasant." He informed her. For a man with no heart, this surprised Sage too.

"Your turn." He said. Sage had to think. Her life wasn't really about things she liked, though she did have the one favourite thing. "I love the charioteers. I used to watch them on an afternoon sometimes, in the Martius."

"There was a moment in my youth when I fancied being a charioteer. It didn't last long thankfully." He was smiling at the memory.

"What changed your mind?" Sage asked.

"The first death. Poor boy, and that's all he was, lost his balance, forgot to let go of the reigns and tumbled over and over beside the chariot. When he finally got untangled, he was crushed by another's wheels and trampled on by the horses behind that. Then I learned it still took him three days to die poor bastard. Put me right off." His smile had gone, and he shrugged as he realised he had just killed the moment.

"Yet you kill as a gladiator." Sage reminded him.

"I do, and the killing in the arena is quick. Gladiators die with honour if they have fought well to start with."

"I see no honour in killing for entertainment." Sage muttered.

"Nor I." Robaratus agreed. Sage looked up at him in surprise.

"I didn't choose to be a gladiator. Most gladiators do not choose to fight for entertainment. There are a select few who enjoy it, usually soldiers, who only have to survive three years, many don't make it. The rest of us are prisoners of war, criminals, generally bad men, men who are expected to give their lives for their Emperor to pay for their crimes."

Sage almost asked him what his crime had been, but she reminded herself that it really didn't matter, given they were just chatting. Her life was nothing to him, and his nothing to her.

"Anything else you like?" he asked trying to get back on topic.

"Not really, though sleeping on the warm tiles in the kitchen with the smells of the last meal lingering, was always a comfort." She looked down shyly, what did a slave want with fancies? She was happy to have had a home and nice owners. Robaratus watched her from his peripheral vision, she'd had such a simple life, it disheartened him to realise how far apart they really were. The arcera lurched along, dipping dangerously into deep puddles, though the high wheels prevented either passenger from getting wet, the progress was slow. They spoke little, Sage still admiring the world around her, amazed at how large it really was and how few people occupied it. As the day turned towards night, she was wondering where they would be stopping.

"I cannot risk us being seen in a village. I am easily known." Robaratus smiled. "We will stay in the arcera wherever possible."

Sage felt disheartened, she had hoped to see other villages, but with a husband half covered in tattoos, and a name known all over Rome, she understood his desire not to be recognised, that way Aquilina would not know in which direction they had gone. They stopped before dark and Robaratus watered the horse and let it crop the freshened grass, before unpacking cheese and nuts from a parcel Albus had given him. He made a fire to keep them warm, watching Sage all the time unable to read her expressions. "Is it safe to ask where we are going now?"

Robaratus looked up at her. "I am taking you home." He went back to eating. She was about to ask where home might be, but decided if he'd wanted her know that, he'd have told her. "I think I like the stars." Sage said as she looked up at the open sky, and the many millions of twinkling lights. "Me too." He said looking up as well. "I like the peace they bring. The sound of the crickets and the bark of the wolves in the distance."

Sage looked at him. "You must have travelled a lot in your life to know about such things."

"I suppose I did, yes."

"You're lucky. I grew up a slave, I have never had reason to look at the night sky, never heard wolves either." She looked a bit nervous as one barked far away.

"Think of them as dogs." Robaratus said smiling at her.

"Will they come to us?"

"Nope. They are miles away up in the hills. They might have come down to us had we had meat cooking, but as we don't, they won't."

"I wish I had my book of poems by Ovid." Sage said as she watched the fire crackle and spit.

"For a slave you can read and write, that is rare. Who taught you?" Robaratus asked.

"My mother. She died when I was twelve, but she left me her book of Ovid's best poems."

"Do you have a favourite?" He asked.

"Disappointment, makes me smile." Sage admitted.

"But oh, I suppose she was ugly; she wasn't elegant. I hadn't yearned for her often in my prayers. Yet holding her I was limp, and nothing happened at all: I just lay there, a disgraceful load for her bed. I wanted it, she did too; and yet no pleasure came from the part of my sluggish loins that should bring joy." Robaratus recited with dramatic effect, making Sage laugh loudly, clutching her stomach and wiping her eyes. "I never heard anyone repeat it before!" She laughed.

"Believe me it is every man's worst fear." He laughed with her.

"Has it ever happened to you?" She asked without thinking.

"Which part, the ugly or the limpness?"

Sage blushed, "any of it?"

"Ugly definitely. Most women are ugly to me, limpness I have managed to avoid by thinking of anything but the task in hand, or not as the case may be!" He chuckled. Again Sage blushed and was glad of the cover of the fire to hide it. "Wait! Wait! Wait!" she suddenly said, her eyes huge. "You're a gladiator, how can most women be ugly to you?"

Robaratus smiled. "At first, I admit it was fun. I have been doing this shit for ten years, comes a time it is no longer fun. I get some relief I suppose, but honestly, Aquilina used me to spy on her friends, it was rarely my choice, mostly hers, and there was no fun in that. That's partly why I disobeyed her and fucked her sister. I wanted her to know how it felt to be ignored." His green eyes settled on Sage, who looked crestfallen.

"Sorry. I couldn't know how that would turn out." He said softly, the guilt heavy with every word. "Perhaps there is a silver lining to that, I am seeing the world beyond Rome I would never have seen any of this otherwise." She gave him an encouraging look.

"You hate me for this." He reminded her kindly. Sage shrugged. "Am I not allowed to change my mind?" She quoted words he had spoken to her once, then she smiled. Robaratus paused in his stare, then he hmphed a laugh.

They retired to the arcera, lying down was just as cramped. Sage was shy and very self-conscious of her naivety, but she let Robaratus make best use of the cramped space, by snuggling into her back, resting his arm over her waist. She could smell pine and sawdust on him still, it was comforting, and she smiled as she relived their talk about Ovid, she had never confessed to anyone that she loved his poems, and to think her husband knew of them too, and could make her laugh. She giggled.

"What makes you laugh?" His deep voice rumbled.

"Your knowledge of Ovid." She giggled again. Robaratus didn't understand, but let it go, he was tired and the scent of rosemary and mint was filling his mind, relaxing him into sleep.

When morning came, Sage woke with the sudden realisation she was hugging Robaratus. Somehow they had turned over in the night and it was her arm draped around his waist. She took a moment to enjoy the feel of his solidness, the soft rise and fall of his chest, and the wonderful aroma that was masculine and *him*. When he stirred she scooted away feeling every ounce of her shyness return. He made no mention of it, but left to sort the horse out.

"We will need to stop for supplies." He said when they were well on their way. "I will drop you outside a town and you can get the provisions, then meet me back where I drop you off."

Sage was nervous about shopping on her own in a strange town, but Robaratus assured her she would be fine if she acted as a slave did. They arrived at the town of Chiusi late morning, Robaratus drove the arcera as close to the gates as he dare, Sage jumped down and set off into the town, hiding mostly amongst a group of merchants that entered with her. She followed them, keeping her shawl over her head, and her *as* inside her toga tunic, it was a market day, and the place was packed with people, so she fitted in perfectly. She perused the stalls in the same way she had in Rome, finding she quite liked the cheeses, peaches and fig jam. She brought all and some fresh bread, adding some cured meat. The streets were as narrow here as in Rome, and all were cobbled. The buildings stood three storeys high, and added a brilliant dazzle to a sunny day, being mostly white washed or cream, with the red roman tiles that added colour. It felt odd being out and about without Robaratus, and she missed his company, perhaps it was a foolish thought, but she didn't have to tell him. He had become more handsome since he had let his hair grow, he looked less fearsome, though he shaved his face with his blade Sage found herself liking him a little bit more. When she was done, Sage left to meet Robaratus at the gate. When she arrived, he was chatting to a man, she held her breath, then approached with caution. Robaratus had covered his head, hiding his tattoos, he was nodding as the man spoke. Once he spotted Sage he excused himself, and moved the arcera to where she was standing.

"I thought the idea was to avoid risk?" She said climbing up to the seat. He smiled. "We were talking about a local event at the garrison, a demonstration of soldiers' skills, it might have been interesting to go to, but we won't be here."

"Do you think he recognised you?" She asked, worriedly.

"I doubt it, he was a retired soldier, owns an inn now and I was well covered up, as you see." He still was. They drove past the town, around its impressive walls and back onto the main road that led away. Sage told him about her shopping trip and the food she had managed to purchase. Once more he talked about Ovid and recited other poems he could recall.

"How is it a man such as you likes poetry?" Sage asked, given most gladiators were either illiterate or at least able to read and write.

"I had a good education." He replied with a shrug, which led Sage to realise he'd had some standing in society at one time.

"That doesn't explain why you like poetry." She reminded him.

"I hated it at the time, because I was made to commit it to memory." He laughed. "I confess it has come in useful over the years, especially for myself. Whenever I hurt physically or emotionally I remember Ovid's words. *Be patient and tough; someday this pain will be useful to you.* Those words kept me sane."

Sage stared at him, how un-bear like that confession was, he had just confessed his own vulnerabilities and fears. *He is human after all.*

Chapter 11

Home turned out to be a several days journey from where Albus lived. They had avoided the main road for the most part, as Robaratus wanted them to be unnoticed, so they had taken lanes and muddy tracks, which hampered their pace. Sage didn't care, she and Robaratus were alone, enjoying each other's company. She watched butterflies dipping and diving around them, slaves in fields working on crops, farmers' families on smaller holdings, cattle grazed, goats bleated, chickens screeched and all the while the sun beat down, baking the mud. At night they would lie together, snuggled close for warmth as the nights were cold. Sage had recovered well from her beating; she did the shopping for food and Robaratus cooked it. They travelled safely enough, not followed so long as Robaratus stayed away from the villages. "Is your home much further away?" She asked one morning as the wagon wobbled and creaked its way north.
"I have high hopes we might reach it today if the Gods are willing." He smiled at her.
Sage felt glad that their journey was almost over but she felt a twinge of regret as well, soon she would have to share her husband with others again, and she had got used to having him all to herself.
"I know our destination is a secret, but are we staying with your family?" She played with the edges of her shawl nervously.
"What makes you think our destination is a secret?" He looked at her in surprise.
"You never said where we were going."
"You never asked!" he retorted smiling. "I am hoping that we might be possible to stay with my parents, though I have not seen them in many years, I have no idea if they are still alive." He looked at her with as much reassurance as he could muster given his own doubt about the situation.
Sage eyed him. "What if they are, um dead?" She asked softly, he shrugged and grinned. "Then we will have to find another place to stay. I will think on that once we know."
"What are they like?" Sage asked.
"I can tell you what I remember but as I said, it's been a long time, they will be much older by now and changed no doubt."
He watched her wide eyes that made his heart soar. "Well my Papa was a

83

blacksmith, made the weapons sharper for the soldiers, made the rims for the carts, and any other odd metal work that folks required. Prongs for hay forks and the like. He took over the business from his father, but I had no desires to stay in one place and spend my life hammering metal. It must have broken his heart to have one son and that son to want something more." He sighed as he considered his life.

"Do you regret your choice?" Sage asked intrigued. He laughed half-heartedly. "Hind sight is a bitter thing." He spoke with sadness. "In some ways no, I have learned much from my life, but in other ways, I would not choose it again. Too many men I loved died for what? Glory. Rome. Entertainment? I know not what and their blood seems wasted to me." There was a hardness in his eyes, a bitterness to his voice that made Sage sadder for him than she'd ever thought possible. *The great bear has a heart April, can you imagine?*

"What did your Papa say when you told him what you wanted to be?"

Robaratus smiled at the memory. "He laughed."

"If not a Blacksmith then what do you think you can become Rob?" His father looked at him with dark eyes.

"I aim to become a soldier." Robaratus replied, sticking his chin out in a determined way. His father studied him for a long moment, then burst out laughing, clutching his sides as tears of mirth seeped from his eyes. "A soldier! Well good luck on that score my boy. You who cannot leave your bed before the midday meal? Who drinks too much? Who cannot keep his prick in his pants, wants to be a soldier?" The father started to laugh all over again.

"I can be disciplined. I am bored here father; I need to do this." The young man argued. His father raised his arms in supplication. "I do not intend to hinder you boy, but should you fail, you must come home and do your duty to me."

"And that is how I became a soldier."

"How did your mother take the news?"

"Like any other, she cried." He dropped his head then, looking at the floor as the horses plodded forward.

"I'm sorry Robaratus, I should not have brought back such sorrow." Sage placed her hand upon his forearm.

"The memory is sad indeed, but I was an ambitious fool back then, with great dreams of becoming a Centurion, to have a small legion of my own, to be able to have my own rules for those men." He smirked.

"Tell me about your mother?"

He shrugged. "My Mama was beautiful. She had long black hair and

sparkling brown eyes and the kindest heart of anyone I've ever known."
Sage felt a twinge of envy, but the pride in Robaratus was unmistakable.
"So why did you never go back to visit them?"
"I did once, when I had made Optio. I was the youngest soldier to achieve
this." His eyes stared into space as he recalled that short time in his life.

*"We will have a celebration, everyone will attend." His mother declared, her
eyes brimming with yet unshed tears of pride. His father also stood tall and proud. "I
am more than impressed you have done so well my boy. What next do you aim to
become?"*
"Quite obviously a Centurion" The young Robaratus replied grinning.
*The celebration was indeed a huge affair, seemingly the whole populace had turned out
to see the youngest Optio ever, and the girls were falling at his feet, Robaratus was the
most popular man in town. Banners waved in the summer breeze, ale flowed like river
water, as did the wine, there was a bear dancing and the local Gladiators put on a show
for him of bloody murder, three men gave their lives that day in honour of Robaratus,
who cheered loudly at the slaughter.*

Suddenly Robaratus turned his head away to wipe errant tears from his
eyes. He had gloried in those deaths as an ignorant soldier who saw only
heroism in such wasted lives. Sage began to wonder if returning home had
been such a good idea.
"And now you are one of them." She observed sadly. "Do you know how
your parents took that news?"
Did he know? Oh yes he knew!

*"A note for you Robaratus." His trainer handed over a script for the gladiator
to read.*
*"We are informed of your disgrace. We are shunned by our neighbours and I have lost
many customers from the news. Your mother cries endlessly, her heart is now weak. The
Baccarius boy has broken his engagement to your sister, who is now ruined and can only
face a loveless future as a priestess in one of the temples. My heart is broken Robby,
how could you be so selfish, how could you not think of the consequences. I disown you."
It was signed by his father. Robaratus had kept that note for many years, it had to still
be somewhere in his belongings back in Rome, he had made himself read it every day
of his life to remind himself of what he had done, what his family had lost because of
him. It had broken him to learn how serious those consequences had been, yet he lived,
each fight more anger poured from him and the Gods damned him to live, to suffer, to
watch others die, to be the one who took their lives in the name of heroism, of glory, of
entertainment.*

"I sent home my earnings. He wrote me once more when I became famous in Rome. Told me he was glad I lived, but he hated my coin, it was blood money to him. He never sent it back, and I have no idea what he did with it if anything. I don't imagine he was ever proud of me not even for becoming a famous gladiator."

"Then why did you think returning home was a good idea?" Sage asked near panic in her voice. He shrugged. "We are all of us much older now, may be time has healed some of the wounds. I would see my parents one more time if I could. Perhaps they won't be so angry if they know about you." He looked over at Sage and gave her a sad smile.

"Oh Robaratus! What if they hate me? I am nothing after all, just a common slave, they might have found forgiveness had you married a worthwhile woman."

"Why can't you be a worthwhile woman?" He retorted, an edge to his voice.

"You know full well what I mean. Had you married a farmer's daughter or something, would have been better than a slave."

"I am nothing more than you are." He reminded her. "Fame does not change the fact I am a slave also."

"I know, but you have always risen in your life, to become more than you were, now you are married to a slave, hardly going upwards is it?" she gave him a meek smile, he understood what she meant, but she was wrong. He wrapped an arm about her. "Sage, becoming a gladiator is not moving upwards! It was that or instant death. You are the most suitable wife I could have ended up with. You are beautiful, and smart with it, you understand me so much more than I understand myself. In sooth, there is no one more suitable than you to be my wife. I don't care how that came about, I'm just grateful it did." He looked at her a moment longer, seeing the tears brim in her eyes, then he bent over and kissed the top of her head. It was the first time he had shown any real emotion towards her, she wondered if it been because they'd only had each other to talk to, which made her wonder if it would last. *He said I was beautiful*, she smiled inwardly.

They travelled a half day longer before Robaratus pointed out the trail of smoke on the horizon. "That is where we are going." He said. Sage squinted to see anything other than smoke, but sometime later as the smoke became roof tops and the walls to a city emerged from the heat haze, she could see the soldiers walking the walls and the huge gates that gave entry to the citizens. "What urbs is that?"

"Firenze."

As they drew closer, Sage saw the many watch towers along the wall, the religious icons and shrines along the way, and once they had crossed the bridge over the river, Robaratus slowed the arcera as they approached the many tombs, and as he searched, Sage had a chance to admire the inscriptions of those within. Finally Robaratus stopped in front of a large tomb. Sage read the carved words.

DM FEROX THE RETIARII
Twice victor. Gave his life for the glory of Robaratus youngest Optio of Rome.

DM CALCLUS THE MIRMILLON
Five times victor. Gave his life for the glory of Robaratus youngest Optio of Rome.

DM VIGOR THE RETIATII
Five times victor, three draws. Gave his life for the glory of Robaratus youngest Optio of Rome.

All died heroes of Firenze.

She watched as her husband wiped tears from his face, she found herself swallowing the lump in her throat, but still her own tears ran shamelessly down her cheeks. She reached out and laid her hand upon his arm as it brushed across his tears, then he was bending down upon her shoulder, holding her tight as he sobbed his grief and shame. Sage said nothing, but stood holding him as he clutched her close, soaking her tunic, each wracking sob shuddering through her, as she silently cried with him. He was broken in that place, in that moment and she was all he had to cling to, she who understood him, she who had suffered because of him, how he could never learn from his mistakes. Robaratus sobbed and sobbed, while Sage stood still and held him close. They stood there for a long time while the great bear unburdened his soul. Sage realised she was probably the only person he had ever shared this guilt with, it was in one way an honour yet it felt like the worst kind of secret to be sharing in. Sage had been shocked by his break down, she had never imagined this huge man to be so broken inside, nor that he would turn to her when he bared his soul.

"They never knew what happened to you. They gave their lives with honour Robaratus. That you became one of them and you are famous, and adored is still a justification for their sacrifice. Find pride in yourself for their memories sake." Her words were spoken softly, with such tenderness his heart broke all over again. Sage wiped his tears away with her shawl, his dark lashes soaked, looked beautiful, his great chest heaved from the wracking sobs, his muscles bulging from the effort of trying to control his breathing. He looked into her radiant eyes filled with tears, yet so bright they could shame the stars, her look was filled with belief, a belief in him he realised. She had not laughed at him, nor scolded him, she had not turned her back on him, all of which he deserved, instead Sage who had been the victim of his behaviour had held him, wiped his tears away and found the words that both broke him and freed him. He didn't deserve her, but she was beautiful and in that moment he had never ached for her more. He bent down and let his lips trembling still, softly touch hers, it was meant as a thank you, given he didn't trust his voice, yet when she did not refuse him nor shy away, his hand caressed her hair, ever soft and shining, and his lips pressed harder, finding succour in her response, the way her arms wrapped around his great neck, and clutched at his hair which he had let grow during their journey, her kiss seemed to tell him she was there, she would catch him when he fell, when he stumbled, and he clung to her now as her lips parted and their tongues touched, he moaned from ardent need, the realisation that he had feelings for her overwhelmed him, he hadn't imagined a kiss she gave could feel that good, or that his body would betray him so easily. His need pressed against her, and for the first time since she married him, she knew she wanted this, wanted him, would accept him for who he was and what he was, her great bear.

Chapter 12

They stayed at an Inn that evening, though it was noisy from traders and locals, they were both exhausted and fell into sleep easily. Sage felt sad that after their kiss he had said nothing, just held her close and eventually they had walked away. He had made no attempt to kiss her again, and she felt too embarrassed to ask him if she had offended him, so said nothing. He lay behind her as he always did, close and protective, his arm draped about her, she smiled to herself as her eyes dropped in relaxed comfort, she found it hard to imagine sleeping without him now.

The morning found them rising early, Robaratus was off sorting a meal for them while Sage washed her face and arms in the cold-water bucket, she dragged a wooden comb through her hair and braided it over one shoulder, then draped her shawl over her head. Despite what Robaratus said about her looks, it was hard to break the habit of a life time, so she covered her head and kept her face down as she descended down the narrow stairs. Having eaten Robaratus collected the horses and arcera and they travelled across the bridge over the river Arno to the tombs, where they stopped and laid some wild flowers upon the tomb of the three Gladiators. Robaratus stood in front of it alone, Sage stood a few steps back to allow him his prayers for such honoured men, this time there were no tears, as they climbed back onto the wagon and headed for the great gates of the southern side of the city. Once through the inner court they exited into the bright sunshine of Firenze, where the noise of the city greeted them. They were on the main street which buzzed with the sound of people shouting their wares, shop fronts with dwellings above, where merchants shouted to the passers-by, a jeweller, a potter, cloth merchants and silk merchants, carpenters and painters, plasterers, brick makers and finally at a cross roads opposite two inner watch towers stood the blacksmith. Robaratus slowed the horses and leaned over at the stocky man who stood with sweat and soot on his face, hammering metal. The man paused in his work and looked at Robaratus. "Ho friend, do you know where the smith is that once owned this place?" He asked. "He lives in the north western corner past the viaduct." The big man replied then returned to his hammering. Robaratus moved the wagon forward. "Seems my father sold the business." His voice rang flat and sad, the truth of his choices in life hitting him hard. They turned down by the watch towers and headed for the viaduct at the end of the road, seeing the vast structure that carried water to the populace, made Sage think of the viaduct in Rome, which the homeless sheltered under in the rain and from the sun. A pang of homesickness hit her and she swallowed the lump that claimed to choke her. They passed underneath it to a cluster of houses that stood opposite a green, here Robaratus stopped the wagon. "Wait here, while I find out where they live." He clutched her hand and squeezed it, to give her reassurance, it had been his first physical contact that day.

*   *   *

In the dimness of the small room, an elderly woman took a clay mug and poured some wine into it, as she turned the light from the doorway extinguished and a huge man stood there blocking out all the light. She blinked twice, adjusting her eyes to the darkness. "Mama." A deep voice rumbled to her, the mug fell from her hands and shattered on the floor. "Robaratus?" She whispered, then filling her lungs, and still frozen to the spot, she called "Maximus! Maximus come quickly."
Robaratus entered the room, the ceiling just high enough for him to stand up though his growing hair brushed the plaster work. His mother had aged terribly since he had last seen her, now her long black hair was white and thin, her skin wrinkled from the years of sunshine, her eyes had shrunken into her skull making them small and beady, his heart contracted at the sight of her. Then his father entered the room, and stood stock still. "By the Gods, what mishap brings you back to us boy?" His voice was deep and rough, almost like his sons'.
"Maximus how could you? Our boy is home, thank the Gods, he lives." His mother said reaching out for her son, who still did not move. His father hung his head for a moment, then walked towards his son. "It takes some courage to come back here. Why?" The older man was small next to his son, who was already a good head above the average Roman in height, and twice as broad. His father's hands were gnarled and scared from his years hammering metal, his skin a dirty bronze, but his eyes still sparkled with malice.
"I am here for a last visit." Robaratus said.
"Last?" His mother asked, her voice trembling.
"We are none of us young any more mama. I am in my thirties, I cannot expect to win many more bouts in the arena, I will be bettered and my life taken, to die a hero of Rome." His voice carried no pride, just the defeated

90

acceptance of the inevitable. His father looked at him then, studying the man before him, his height, frame and the tiredness about his eyes that spoke of too many horrors.

"Aye. It has been a long sentence you have served." His father looked suddenly sad. "Come in Rob, stay as long as you wish." He said as he reached for his only lad and embraced him in a bear hug of his own, for frail as the old man looked, he had strength yet in those thin arms.

Robaratus clutched his parents in a one huge embrace, tears welled in his eyes, but he blinked them back. "I am not alone." He told them when they relinquished him. "I bring with me a wife."

His mother gasped; her eyes wide. "A wife? Where is she?"

His father looked astounded. "What madness made you marry? You're a gladiator, what will she do when you're killed?"

"Maximus Ectorius!" His mother screeched. His father grinned, then slapped his son hard on the shoulder.

"Tis a story to be told." Robaratus informed them.

"Let us meet her then?" His mother urged.

Sage sat patiently on the wagon, and after a while of baking quietly, she got herself down, and stood on the shady side, fanning herself with her shawl. She watched an elderly couple exit a small dwelling along with a giant, making her smile, next to his parents, he really was enormous. He walked them over to the wagon, a look of fear on his face, until he saw her standing on the shady side. He cursed himself silently for leaving her in the sun. "Mama, papa, this is Sage, my wife. Sage my parents. Maximus and Iola Ectorius." Sage looked at her husband. "You have a last name?" she frowned. When they were married no last name had been mentioned. "As a slave of the Emperor, I have his last name if any is needed." Robaratus explained. Sage looked at his parents. "It is a pleasure to meet you Mistress Ectorius, Master Ectorius." She nodded her head as was polite to do. Robaratus felt his heart twist again, these were her parents now, yet as a slave they couldn't be. His mother stepped over to her and studied her face, a small breeze tugged at her shawl revealing her dark hair, and the freckles upon her skin. "What trade were you from girl to marry my son?" She asked, and the tone of hope wasn't missed by Sage. She glanced up at Robaratus before answering. "A slave."

The disappointment was clearly apparent before Iola Ectorius hid it. "I see," she said, clearly not seeing at all by the tone of her.

"As I said tis a tale to be told." Robaratus reminded his mother, who just nodded dumbly. They followed the elderly couple into the dwelling. "I think your parents are disappointed that you did not marry a wealthy woman." Sage whispered to her husband. He squeezed her fingers in his huge hand. "They do not know you yet." He reminded her. Inside Sage had to press her lips together hard to hide the smirk and giggle that threatened to burst from her, to see how tall Robaratus was in that small room. They were invited to sit at a small table. "How long have you been married?" Iola asked. Sage found herself looking at the table top, this was not a story she wanted to hear, nor to see the pity on these strangers faces. "Almost a year." Robaratus offered. *How quickly the time has passed*. Sage thought. Robaratus began to explain how their marriage came about, he managed to put all blame on himself, which was admirable but which also meant that when Sage looked up, she knew she would meet sympathetic eyes, and sympathy wasn't something she wanted, never had.

"You break the rules Rob and another life is ruined. How old do you have to be before you start learning from your endless mistakes?" His father sounded less than impressed. "I have come to learn that Sage is smart and understanding." He offered in her defence.

"She is bound to be a better person than you Rob, but your behaviour took her away from a mistress she loved, and put her with a man who cannot offer her a future. What will happen to her when you die?"

Iola gasped audibly.

"No. He is right." Robaratus said. "I have been considering my options for the weeks we have been travelling. I intend to train myself up here and then return to Rome. I shall ask the Emperor to put me up for one last fight, if I can win, I get my freedom, and then our lives can have a future." Sage's head snapped up, as she looked at him with horror, he smiled at her. His parents said nothing. Sage felt a surge of raw emotions running through her, not least anger that he had not so much as hinted about any of this. She would have endured anything just so he didn't have to go back into the murderous arena, yet she knew he would always have to go back sooner or later, so one more fight, just the one and they could be free, but what was freedom to Sage? She had never known it and never wanted it.

"You can both stay here." Maximus said. He wiped his face with his hand, the worry was clear in every deep groove in his wrinkled skin. "It won't take that long for Aquilina to know where you're hiding."

"If I train with the local gladiators, it will look as though I am doing what she intended me to do."

Maximus screwed up his face, he didn't like the idea of his son teaching anyone to fight to the death, he abhorred gladiators, but there was logic in what his son proposed, and it would give him a valid reason to stay put and train himself as he wished to, if he was seen to be doing what the Empress wanted, she might let him stay. He nodded his acceptance of his son's plan.

92

"Then you will stay in the room upstairs." Iola smiled kindly. "It's the only room with a bed long enough for your legs son." She smiled; Sage smiled too.

"I will go and talk to the trainer at the arena here, see what I can sort out." Robaratus stood up, as did Sage, he walked around the table and planted a soft kiss upon her cheek. "I hope not to be too long." He reassured her, which meant she was stuck with these strangers, which was not good in her eyes at all, she watched her husband abandon her, and felt her heart sink.

"Come Sage, let us sort your room out." Iola prompted kindly. Sage followed her up the narrow stone stairs to a large room with a long bed in it, easily wide enough for two. "Was a time Max and I used this room, he also had long legs!" Iola joked, "but we are too old now to manage the stairs, so we use a room downstairs." At the end of the bed was a large trunk, and into this Iola dived to retrieve sheets and blankets.

"What was your mistress like?" Iola asked as they made up the bed.

"She was kind." Sage answered.

"You were lucky to have such a position, or was it because of who you are?" Iola gave Sage a quick glance.

"Who I am?" Sage stopped what she was doing.

"You think us country folk who live beyond Rome have no knowledge of wise people called Sage?" She smiled indulgently. Sage looked surprised.

"No one has ever let on they know the reason for my name."

"So you are a sage?" Iola asked.

"Passed on from my mother." Sage told her, smiling.

"Does my son know that?"

"I have no idea, though he has never said anything, but then no one ever has."

"Then you can be certain he has no idea. Your mistress might have had an idea, which would account for why she kept you so close."

Sage looked at Iola with suspicion. The older woman laughed. "Relax, child your secret is safe with me."

Sage smiled nervously, it was an old tradition for a sage to pass on their knowledge to their own off spring, and for several generations her family had passed on their secrets, which was one reason why Heva had always said she had an old spirit for one so young.

"I am not so good at being a sage though."

"How so?"

Sage looked bashful and blushed. "I hate the sight of blood." She admitted and then wondered why on earth she would reveal something so personal to a complete stranger. Iola's eyes lit up. "Well that is unfortunate *especially* being married to a gladiator."

"I know." Sage hung her head and spoke softly.

"Let's hope Rob has no need of your skills." Iola smiled. Sage quietly hoped so too, as she had no idea how she would cope if she had to face the kind of wounds gladiators got, she had been lucky her husband had not suffered anything major thus far in their marriage. They finished sorting the room out and returned downstairs.

"I'll get some water in." Maximus informed them as they entered the tiny room once more.

"Can I help you?" Sage asked, thinking she ought to offer herself any way she could to help ease the burden of her presence. He nodded and together they set off.

"Well is only on the green there." Max said as he swung a large bucket in each hand. "It's been a long time since I had any help with the water collection." He grinned showing a few gaps where teeth had been removed. Sage said nothing as they reached the well. "Rob used to help when he was a lad, though the water was a bit further away from the smithy. We have not quite caught up with Rome, not everyone has water indoors."

Sage didn't speak, "Have you always lived in Rome?" he asked.

"Yes. Until I was married I'd never seen beyond Rome."

"I have never been. Do you miss it?"

Sage pondered on that. "Yes sometimes, not so much the place, but I have a friend there and I miss her."

Max nodded as he slung the bucket down the well.

"What do you think of gladiators?"

"I never liked them. I have a passion for charioteers." Sage admitted, which made Maximus laugh gruffly. He heaved on the bucket.

"Still prefer the charioteers?" he asked, chucking the second bucket down the well.

"Yes."

"What is so special about them? I ask because we don't have any here."

"Oh, well, it's the speed. I love the way the horses run, they look so wild, elegant, and their muscles are so incredible. The young men who race, have an equal passion, and it is quite breath taking to see them urging those beasts on." Her face flushed from her enthusiasm as she realised the older man was watching her intently.

"I've heard it said they don't last much more than five races?" Max frowned.

"Sadly their lives are short lived, but I watch them train on the Campus Martius, it is really spell binding to watch." Sage's eyes were staring into nothing as she recalled the sights of the horses, and riders exercising their moves, trots, turns and speed. "Gladiators are Rome's passion but the charioteers are definitely our obsession" She smiled. Maximus found himself glued to that smile, her face dissolved into softness, and youth, she certainly had passion for charioteers. They walked back to the dwelling with the buckets.

Chapter 13

Robaratus returned home before the sun got too low in the sky, he was relieved to see his wife and mother busy cooking together over the fire, Sage was informing Iola about adding herbs to the food. "I saw Robaratus add this once." She was saying.

"Rob always was a good cook." His mother replied. Robaratus grinned. "Seems my wife is giving away my secrets!" He chided playfully, as both women turned to look at him.

"Rob. How did it go?" his mother asked immediately. Sage stirred the pot of stew.

"I was welcomed with open arms. Fame travels apparently. They are quite honoured to have such as I in their midst." He grinned proudly but his father didn't return it.

"The food is ready if you are wanting to eat now?" Sage informed everyone.

"Arh then we shall eat, but first I have brought us some oysters and nuts." Robaratus said, pulling from his tunic said items.

"You spoil us Rob." His mother crooned. They all sat at the table and ate, sharing news and memories. As the meal ended, Robaratus asked. "When were you going to tell me my sister was dead?" The silence was instant and heavy. Sage wanted to leave the room, but dare not.

"You went to the temple?" Max asked. Robaratus nodded.

"She died a long-time back son; we were in no hurry to add to your sorrows." His mother said quickly but the sadness was in her voice.

"How did she die? She was so young."

"She saw her betrothed with another, and the hurt was too much. She took her life." Maximus said. Robaratus got up and left the room, walking outside. Sage watched him go with pity in her heart, he would blame himself again for this loss, she saw that both parents sat with their heads hung, and she wondered what she was supposed to do to ease their pain and grief. *Coming here was not a good idea Robaratus, it has added to your own grief far too much. How many more sorrows can your heart carry?*

*   *   *

Robaratus was throwing stones when Sage found him some time later. There was a cool breeze that was most welcome after the days heat, it teased her shawl and tugged at her hair. She sat beside him watching silently as he threw one after another. "I lied. Most of the Gladiators resent me for being so famous, though they welcomed me to train them. It was the owner Julius Brutus who remembers my past. He quite enjoyed how far I have fallen, and he was quite insistent upon reminding me he lost three of his fighters the day I became an Optio." Another stone whizzed through the air landing close to a previous one. "He was the one who told me about my sister." The next stone was thrown with so much force it shattered upon impact with the earth.

"If we all had the gifts of seers and prophets, then we could all make the right choices in life." Sage mused as though to herself. Robaratus barked a laugh. "How many people have suffered because of your choices?" He asked bitterly. "I was already at the bottom of the pile, so I doubt there were many I could have affected."

"I'm sorry, I shouldn't have said that." He grumbled. "I have to fight Brutus's best tomorrow, just to prove I am worthy of training his slaves." The anger was obvious at the insult. "His best never made it to the final in Rome against me, so what have I to prove here?" Another stone shattered some distance away.

"Do not let anger cloud your vision Robaratus, you will prove yourself worthy of this man, make those lives that were lost count. Be what you are. The best." She reached over and touched his arm gently. His other hand covered hers and he bowed his head, how quickly she could calm him.

"Maybe you're right, his best needs to know what Rome's best is like, to see how much more training they need."

Sage smiled at him, and she welcomed the fact he kept his hand covering hers.

"This bed is too big." Robaratus complained, as they faced each other with two candles flickering beside each of them.

"It is nice to have some room for a change." Sage smiled back at him.

"Are you saying I take up too much bed?" He asked, trying to inflict a serious tone into his voice. Sage giggled softly. "Not at all, but we have been crunched up together in that arcera for so long, for once I can stretch out." She demonstrated this by stretching her legs, arching her back and putting her hands over her head. Robaratus groaned as her chest thrust upward, revealing two hard lumps under her nightdress. Sage collapsed instantly, blushing bright red, she grabbed the covers and hauled them over herself. Her husband laughed softly at her. "Pity I cannot see how red your face is now." He teased.

"Which is another good reason for why this bed is bigger." She replied from under the blanket and sheet.

"I can't go to sleep counting your freckles." He complained.

"I hate to spoil your fun here, but you couldn't count my freckles in the darkness of the arcera and you never have." Sage pointed out, peaking at him over the covers. Robaratus turned onto his back, and a silence fell between them. He watched the ceiling for some time before he finally spoke. "It's lonely over here, how is it on your side?"

Sage burst into laughter, then wriggled over to him, funny how a journey can change how people see each other, once her anger would have prevented this intimacy, but now she was placing her hand upon his firm flat stomach, feeling the muscles in his thigh tense as her leg lightly brushed his skin. He smelt of sawdust and pine, and when she looked up at his face he was smiling softly. *How different you are from the ferocious bear who paces the arena. How beautiful you are when you smile.* Her heart soared to see him relaxed with her, even happy.

In the morning he rose before the sun and leaned over Sage kissing her softly upon her cheek. "Stay in bed, you have no need to be up so early anymore." He whispered to her, then left treading softly upon the stairs so as not to disturb his sleeping parents on the ground floor. Sage rose as soon as she heard the door close, she flung a dress tunic on, grabbed her shawl and raced down the stairs after her husband. She caught up to him just as he was about to start running, he wore two sandbags on his shoulders and two strapped to his waist. "Please be careful today." She said as she hopped about on the cold stones, having forgotten to put her sandals on. He smiled down at her, she had never asked him to be careful before, never shown him that she cared, it felt good to have her care for him he realised, so he smiled, winked at her then set off at a steady pace. Sage watched him go under the viaduct and off down the long road towards the main street. She turned and walked slowly back to the house, where she swept the floor and laid the fire.

Sage and Iola sat at the table sorting food for an evening meal, Robaratus was late back from the arena, and neither woman was about to mention it, for fear of having to face an unpleasant truth, in his mother's case a fear he was injured, in Sage's case a fear he was with another woman, he had not been with another, since she had found him at the dwelling they'd shared where Albus lived. "I never imagined sitting here with Rob's wife." His mother was saying. "I always thought it would be with my daughter while her husband worked."

98

Sage said nothing, but kept busying her fingers with the food.

"I have no idea what personal slaves do, but did you ever prepare the food?" Sage knew she was only being chatty because of her nerves, but she had no desire to talk about a life she would never know again, so she shook her head, feeling a sudden loneliness for all that she had lost.

"I must say, your hands don't look like they suffered too much from harsh work." It was meant as a compliment, but it felt like an accusation, Sage bit her lip to try and calm herself.

"Is something wrong?" Iola asked concerned. Sage shook her head; she was worried as to what her husband was doing. "I am fine." She whispered, as she fiddled with stuffing a hamster for the starters of the meal.

"You can talk to me." Iola offered softly.

"It's nothing, really." Sage tried again.

"You're worrying about Rob aren't you?"

Sage shrugged.

"I know he said neither of you wanted to be married but you both seem happy enough." His mother pushed.

"Of course we are happy enough." Sage said smiling, though it didn't reach her eyes. "We are getting along fine." That wasn't what was worrying her, but she didn't want to voice her real concerns.

"I must confess, I never imagined I'd see him again, once we learned of his disgrace. Gladiators don't live very long." Iola looked so sad. "He had so many dreams, and we had so many hopes for him." Her voice trailed away and she glanced at Sage, her disappointment hidden quickly, but Sage had seen it.

"I suppose even if he'd had a choice I wonder what kind of woman he would've married."

Not one like me. Sage said nothing.

"If he wins his last fight, do you think you would fit into a different kind of social class?"

Sage felt a wave of annoyance, who was this woman to judge her, when she didn't even know her.

"I have had to learn to be a wife. I have had to learn how to live away from my home. I am sure I can learn to be a social person." Sage concentrated on stuffing another hamster.

"I heard once that he was much desired by other women. I hope he has calmed down a bit, the gladiators here are not so amorous, due a lack of noblewomen." Iola smirked. "I would think you would like that."

Sage shrugged. "He is a man he will do what men do."

"Did your mistress give you an education Sage?"

Again Sage wondered why this woman pried into her life, she clearly didn't like her, but she answered anyway. "My mother taught me to read and write." She replied defensively.

"I see." Iola said eyeing her critically. *Yes, you see someone not good enough for your son.* Sage seethed inwardly.

"Excuse me." Sage said and got up leaving the dwelling.

Sage walked towards the city wall uncaring of where she was going, really all she wanted was her old life back, but she was trapped, and her new family didn't like her. Robaratus was talking about a future, that he had never shared the idea of with her, and what had he thought he could do? His only skills were in the arena or the bed. What was her role going to be? His mother had been quick to point that out! *Perhaps I should have told her most wives are kept barefoot and pregnant!* She kicked at a stone. Sage was not a social person, she was a slave and slaves were invisible, silent and blind. She kicked at more loose stones in her frustration, all she wanted to do was yell very loudly and let all this annoyance out. It seemed to her she took one step forward and three backwards. He had turned to her, broken his heart in front of her, kissed her even, yet he had dumped her on his parents, strangers to both of them really, and had been planning a future of freedom without saying what that might entail. She wandered on deep in thought, she decided she had no love for Iola and living under the same roof as her was going to be impossible, but how could she ask Robaratus to leave, these were his parents and he had not seen them for many years.

"You don't watch where you're wandering, Miss, you'll find yerself walking right out the West Gate there."

Sage snapped her head up to see an old beggar woman, sitting by the road side, watching her intently. The gate was indeed only a few strides in front of her. Sage paused then turned away, how easy it would have been to just wander away unnoticed.

"Gotta be man trouble to have a young un like you walking around alone. Ain't safe yer know." The beggar woman reminded her. The woman struggled to her feet. "Let me walk with you home, safer in twos." She grinned a gummy smile. She stank like a piss pot, but her bony fingers were not about to let Sage go, so she turned and walked with the woman. "Sage ain't it? Married to the gladiator Robaratus, just arrived in town." The beggar looked up at Sage's shocked expression, and chuckled. "Ain't that big a place yer know. Besides most everyone recalls Robaratus Ectorius, the most famous and youngest Optio. Arh the young uns he inspired. So sad he threw it all away for the Centurions wife, dirty little bitch." The beggar woman spat on the ground. "Why do you say that?" Sage asked.

100

"Plenty of us think she tricked the young lad, and then arranged for her husband to discover them together. He was ambitious Ectorius, was well on his way to being a Centurion, but then *she* 'appened. Timing was too good, poor lad, he lost it all. Family, friends, respect, career. Had nuffin left. He was put in the arena, they hoped he'd be killed, but he did the killing, and the owner offered him a service. Poor lad. I prayed for him for years."

"He's never said anything about that part of his life." Sage told her.

"Na, doubt he ever would. Corse he mighter never twigged it, but me, I think he did. I think he hated himself for being so easily tricked."

"Why would you pray for him?"

"Wasn't always a beggar." She said sniffing and poking her nose into the air. "Once I was pretty, never could catch his eye, so loved him from afar." Her eyes became rheumy with tears. Sage felt a surge of pity for the beggar, with her silver hair, dirty skin and tattered clothes, she couldn't be nearly as old as she looked.

"What makes you think I care for his history?" Sage asked.

The beggar shrugged. "I don't, but I think you see a cold-hearted man, who kills an enjoys it. I just wanted you ter know he wasn't always like this, once he was a good and kind man, with everything to live for."

"He still is." Sage informed her. The old beggar smiled again. "That makes me happy. There's ope for yer if you can say that about him." She nodded enthusiastically. "But it don't make you happy do it?" She gave Sage a measured look. Sage shrugged. "Who cares what I think? I'm just married to him."

"Arh, bleeding contracts. I ate em!"

Despite herself, Sage grinned, "yea me too."

"I seen happier couples, but your man has a problem with the women right? Hard to trust one who puts it about, though he'd be some kind of strange gladiator if he didn't."

Sage said nothing.

"Arh, hit that nail square on didn' I?" They walked on a bit before the beggar resumed her talk. "If you could choose, right now, what type of man would make a good husband, who'd it be?"

Sage laughed. "One who cared for me and only me."

"You think Robaratus don't?"

"Absolutely not!" Sage said it with such conviction, she almost knocked the beggar woman over.

"If you're only wanting a man to care for yer, then you ain't set your sights right high av ya?"

Sage shrugged. "Setting my sights high or low makes no difference when

101

men are not bound to one woman. I never had any notion of wanting a man in my life, besides we're both slaves, in my situation what sights could I possibly have?" Though saying that reminded her of April who had set her sights considerably higher. Sage wondered how that had gone.

"Robaratus cares about ya, wouldn't av yer around im if he didn't, regardless of what the demon in Rome would say to im."

Sage laughed; she could actually imagine Robaratus defying Aquilina again. "You ever wondered if he is just as blind as you, stumbling around in the dark trying to sort out his feelings an the changes you're putting him through?" The beggar woman looked up at Sage, with an earnest glint in her eyes.

"What changes?" Sage stopped walking and turned to the beggar.

"He closed off his heart so he could be a gladiator. A man can't kill with a conscience. A man with a heart can't sleep with numerous women. He'd end up too broken. This is how your husband survived. First it was anger kept him alive, then being a cold-hearted man, a real mean bastard. Then you came along, tiny thing so quiet and helpless, what was he to do with you?" Sage was about to say something, but the beggar stuck her grubby finger in the air and stilled the words in Sage's throat.

"He tried to employ his usual mind set, and at first of course it worked, kept you at bay, but then that earthquake happened, an he mourned just a bit, which scared him."

"And you know that how?" Sage challenged.

"Even a cold-hearted bastard can mourn another, girl." The beggar told her. "He began to change, that wall he built cracked." She stopped talking and watched Sage's face. She nodded at her. Sage was transfixed.

"I meant how did you know about the earthquake?"

The beggar woman waved her hand. "Everyone heard about it, an' you surviving so long buried, was common news."

"He didn't mourn? I didn't die!"

"He thought you was dead all them days you was buried."

Sage felt a strange oddness to that. Octavia hadn't said he grieved only that he felt guilty."

"He has tried to make amends Sage. He is still trying to make amends, but he is as blind as you are. He's got no idea that you're so scared of being free, you'd run away."

Sage snapped back to the topic in hand. "Huh! I can't run away. I have no notion how to survive." Sage huffed.

"Don't stop yer finking bout it."

They walked along the city wall, then Sage spoke. "I don't know how to trust him. He is still just another man when it comes to having another's wife."

"Was." The beggar corrected.

"Is." Sage insisted. "I caught him in bed with one a few months back." She waved her arm dismissively.

"Yet since that day he has been close by your side." The beggar grinned her gums up at Sage, who smiled at her and nodded. "He only stays loyal because I got beaten up by his whore and he feels guilty."

"You fink he don't hate the sound of himself each time he tries to be nice? He knows you know he treats every woman the same, but it is who he is. It is all that is left of the young man I loved."

Sage felt pity for the beggar, she wished she had known this different Robaratus.

"Why do you have such an interest in us?" Sage said.

"I have watched 'im many years. I see you struggle. I seen the way he looks at yer, you don't see it, yer blind. He ain't never spent so much time with a woman as he 'as you. He listens to yer. He is changing cos of you and that makes me 'appy."

Sage frowned at her, this strange woman knew far more about her and Robaratus than was healthy.

"Arh, ere we are. Home safe an sound."

"Thanks for your company. Why don't you come in, he might be home by now, you could see him again?" Sage so wanted to give the beggar that wish, but the woman smiled sadly and shook her head. "You've quite the heart Sage dear, but no. I'll be on me way. Just mind wot I said."

Sage watched as the beggar old or not limped away, wiping her eyes with her sleeve.

Chapter 14

When Sage entered the home, she knew something wasn't right. No candles lit, no conversation, no people. She called for Maximus, Iola and Robaratus, but none answered her. *Where were they all?* She left the house and only then noticed that the arcera was missing. Her heart sank, and she began to walk, then run down the road, though she had no notion of where she was going, she just hoped she might find them coming back. The light was starting to go out of the sky, like the last vestiges of a flickering candle. Sage ran under the viaduct and down the straight street, passing the watch towers of the inner city, her shawl dropped to her shoulders, and her long auburn hair trailed behind her like dying embers in a molten sky. At the end of the street were the two towers that watched over the main street, it was here that she found the arcera; breathless and tired, she approached it slowly, rubbing the nose of the horse, walking to the back she found it empty. She wondered what it was doing here.

"Looking for something?" A male voice asked her.

"The owner of the arcera." Sage answered.

"Up there." He pointed to the tower. Sage walked passed him and climbed the stairs, she could hear the voices arguing, though she couldn't hear what was being said. They fell silent when she entered the room, everyone turning to look at her. Iola gave her a withering look; Max was pale under his weathered tanned skin.

"Who are you?" A Centurion asked, but before Sage could answer, Iola did it for her. "She's the wife of my son." The sneer was laid bare.

"What has happened?" Sage asked. Iola moved to one side and revealed Robaratus, lying on a wooden bed, blood pooled on the floor, his stomach and arm sliced deeply. Sage paled and a quick acting soldier caught her as she fainted.

Cold air tickled her face, which brought her out of the faint. She could hear the soft clip clop of the horse's hooves on the cobbled stones, as it slowly walked back to the dwelling. She didn't move or show any signs that she was awake, instead she listened. In the back of the wagon, she could hear Iola talking, but it wasn't loud enough for Sage to hear the words, of Robaratus there was no sound. It took an age for them to get home. Maximus drove with such care but made no attempt to wake Sage or speak to her. She wondered what his wife was saying to her son, if they threw Sage out, she'd become like the beggar woman. When at last the wagon arrived, there was much ado at the back and the soft groan of Robaratus nearly broke Sage's heart. When he was next to her he spoke. "Come back and collect my wife." He said in a raspy voice.

"Rob. Look at her son, she is not for you, faints at the sight of blood, what good is she?"

"Enough Mama. I will have my wife with me or you can leave me here right now." He could growl even though he was in pain. Sage watched his hunched form through her lashes. Then another voice, that of a soldier agreed to come and get Sage only then did Robaratus move. It took forever until the man came back, and Sage was trying not to shiver from the chill night air. He grabbed her roughly and somewhat ungracefully heaved her over his shoulder, making her eyes pop wide open, hidden by her long hair. It was the most uncomfortable and undignified way to be carried she could think of. When they reached the narrow stairs of the dwelling, it became obvious as to why he had carried her this way, it was the only way two people could ascend. Once in the bedroom, she was laid carefully onto the bed, though she imagined this was not for her comfort, but more for her husbands.

"She should sleep downstairs." His mother was saying.

"She stays with me." He replied. His mother hmphed. "I will stay also, in case you have need of anything."

"Leave us Mama. My wife will not stay unconscious forever and she can tend me if I need anything."

His mother was about to object again but Maximus spoke authoritatively to her and she left them. As soon as the door shut Sage opened her eyes and found her husband looking down at her. He smiled and chuckled, then winced. "I'm sorry." She whispered.

"I was afraid they had chased you from the home." He spoke softly.

"Where were you Sage?"

I never ask that of you. Sage thought immediately.

"Were you with someone else?" He asked, and she could hear the worry in his tone.

"I was with a beggar woman; she was talking to me about you." Sage said somewhat defensively, though she hadn't meant to be. He tensed.

"What was she saying?"

"Why does it matter? She was harmless."

"It matters because she may have been a spy."

Sage didn't think so, the beggar had not been seeking information but giving it.

105

"She was no spy."

"How do you know?" He insisted. Sage could feel annoyance rising in her. "I know. She was talking about personal things, things I cannot share with you just now." She looked over at him with pleading teary eyes. He looked back at her, his eyes studying her face in the candle light. He nodded. "I believe you, but tell me Sage, would you leave me?"

Sage was so shocked she leapt into a kneeling position, looking straight at him. "No Robaratus. No I would not leave you." She paused then added, "well not unless you told me to go."

His smile was so broad, relief flooded his face.

"Gods, is that what your mother told you?"

He shook his head. "No, it's what I feared when you did not come with them."

Sage felt such sorrow for him, he really had been afraid she had left him, *could the beggar be right?* She wondered. She looked down at his stitched stomach and arm.

"You're not going to faint again are you?" He asked nervously. She shook her head. "What happened?"

"Brutus' men cheat."

Sages' eyes went wide. "Oh Gods." She mumbled. "No wonder they got nowhere in the tournament." She chewed her lip. "What will you say to Brutus?"

"Nothing, words are not required, though he will get the message loud and clear in the morning." He grinned.

"You taught the man a lesson?" She asked. Robaratus nodded his head one way then the other. "You might say that. He's dead."

Sage put her hand to her mouth to smother her gasp.

"I don't like cheats." He said flatly. "Gladiators train with honour, die with honour and fight with honour. It's a code we live by. There is nothing as low as a gladiator who has no honour."

This much Sage could understand, having watched the men train at Albus' place, the code was evident in everything they did."

"Won't Julius Brutus be upset with you?" she asked nervously. Robaratus chuckled. "No. He won't be upset, he'll be murderous. This'll be the fourth gladiator who has died for me. So he could put me in the arena, oh wait! That's where I triumph." Robaratus chuckled and held his stitches as he did so.

"You're not funny!" Sage hissed at him. "He'll be running to Aquilina with complaints and then where will you be?"

"Sage, Sage, calm yourself. I cannot think he can go telling lies to Aquilina, she knows me. I imagine his gladiators are well known to the Emperor, so

106

if anyone faces any punishment it'll be Brutus for allowing this fight to happen, and for me being injured in his care."

Sage was not convinced, but she let it go.

"Come settle with me. I am getting cold, you sitting like that."

She smiled at him and lowered herself down beside him.

"Can I ask you something?" she said after a moment.

"Ask." He rumbled, sounds deep in his chest that made her shiver. He put his good arm about her and hugged her close.

"Would you leave me?" It was only fair to ask, as he'd asked her earlier and if anyone was going to leave anyone, Sage was quite certain it would be him.

"No. Never." He spoke with such clarity and certainty that she had to pull away and look at him, he was looking at her, fully serious. His head bent forward and with much pain, he kissed her forehead. Sage snuggled into him and sighed contentedly. *The beggar was right, he has changed.*

"Blow out the candles and let us get some sleep."

She did as asked and settled down.

"Trust me to get a wife who faints at the sight of blood." He chuckled. "You have to be the only woman alive who is married to a gladiator, and faints at the sight of blood."

The hammering on the door downstairs had Sage stop her work on her husband's wounds. "Sit me up." Robaratus asked, at the noise of people downstairs, then the door was opened so forcibly, Sage wondered if it had come off its hinges. "Where is he?" Shouted Julius Brutus. "Where is that fucking bastard?" Doors were thrown open, then stamping on the stairs, the bedroom door flew open with such violence it hit the wall and rebounded back, almost knocking the intruder off balance.

"You fucking son of a whore" The man screamed. Sage sat on a stool beside the bed, face pale. The intruder was tall and thickly built, his face was scarlet from rage, and his hair was stubble. "You murdering whore. I'll have your head on a fucking pole for this."

He raised his arm to assault Robaratus, but as his arm came down, Robaratus was quicker, snatching it mid thrust, and holding it firm. It was a testament to his great strength, Sage thought, that made him able to hold onto another man's arm so powerfully, especially when that man was almost as powerfully built as Rob was. The two glared at each other, then when Robaratus was sure Brutus wouldn't speak, he did. "I dislike cheats Brutus. No gladiator worth the name uses underhand tactics to win. He got what he deserved."

The man Brutus snatched his arm away. "Who the fuck do you think you are to tell me how to train my gladiators?"

107

"The best fucking fighter in all Rome, is all." Robaratus replied, his voice gravelly and low. Brutus spat at him. "Huh. You're still nothing more than a fucking slave Ectorius."

Robaratus made no reply to that, yet his eyes remained upon Brutus with a steady awareness, like a wild beast summing up its' prey.

"State your intentions." Robaratus said. "I need to rest."

"I'll be sending a fucking report to Rome." Brutus said, still red in the face, but less vividly now. Robaratus barked a laugh. "Good luck with that. I am sure the Emperor is well informed about your gladiators, and I don't imagine he will be best pleased to learn that one of your men cheated in a friendly fight."

The rage seeped away from Julius Brutus leaving him staring at Robaratus with hatred. "You will not be training my men." Brutus turned to leave.

"That's a shame, Rome won't like it that you are refusing to cooperate with the orders of the Empress. I'm not sure what sanctions may be enacted as punishment against you."

"Why you fuc" Brutus lunged at Robaratus, only to come face to face with a dagger point. "I'm hardly breaking open a keg of wine myself. We all have our orders, so let's get on with them."

Once more the two men glared at each other for long moments, before Julius Brutus stepped back, lowered his head, turned and made a speedy exit. Sage let out a shuddering breath. "By the Gods Robaratus." She exclaimed. He lowered the dagger and reached over to her, just as his parents arrived at the bedroom door.

"All is well." He assured their worried expressions.

"I am pleased to hear it. Wish I could say the same for the front door." His father grumbled.

"Why was Julius Brutus so angry?" Iola asked.

"I killed the gladiator who did this to me." Robaratus waved at his stitched stomach and arm. His mother paled alarmingly. *So now she knows what you're capable of.* Sage thought.

Maximus turned his wife and took her down the stairs, looking over his shoulder at his son as he did so. Sage wondered what he was thinking, surely he couldn't blame his son for doing what had to be done? Was he disgusted? Maximus was a gentle man perhaps all this violence was against his own values.

"I never imagined that Brutus would be so powerfully built." Sage said shuddering.

"He used to be a soldier. He likes to think he still is."

"Then how can you train his men the proper way if he is going to tell them to ignore you?"

"Loyalty and trust are earned Sage, which is what I am trying to do with you. It takes time, but I will win, you'll see."

Sage was taken aback at his open confession, she could not say he had her trust, he knew her too well to believe it, so she checked his stitches which had held, and cleaned his wounds again, to keep them infection free.

Robaratus was not one to be kept to a sick bed it turned out. He was up and about after four days of rest, and all the protesting in the world from Sage, and his mother, could not change his mind. He began his regime with simple exercises, rolling his neck, stretching his arms, hissing if his stitches pulled. He stretched his long legs, muscles bunching and relaxing, he did press ups with his good arm only, squats and jumping, and as he improved and his stitches were finally removed, he began to jog.

"Sage come with me." He said one morning, smiling like a small boy about to play a bad trick on a girl. Sage followed him outside with a suspicious look on her face. "Something tells me you're up to no good."

Her husband pointed to a large piece of board he had found. "Sit on it for me." He instructed. Sage frowned, but sat on the board.

"Now hold tight."

Sage watched Robaratus slide into a rope harness he had made, it hung from his shoulders to the board. He was wearing shorts, and was naked from the waist up. Sage found herself transfixed to the muscles in his back as they rippled with his movements. He leaned forward and began to walk, the board moved and Sage let out a loud squeak of surprise. "Are you holding on?" he asked. She looked about her for somewhere to hold onto. "I tied some rope handles for you." He shouted when she didn't reply. "I have them." She replied, and screamed as he suddenly took off at a run, she began to laugh and laugh, till they went over bumps and stones and then she would shriek or yelp from the discomfort. He ran along the wall, and the soldiers on top shouted and whistled and cheered him along. As he ran sweat dribbled down his back, sun tanned and beautiful, small children playing nearby stopped and came running over, to join in the fun. They jumped onto the board and clung to Sage as Robaratus pulled them along. Some of the older boys ran alongside the big bear, and shouted at him to go faster, which he endeavoured to do. Sage shrieked as the pace increased, the children all screamed and laughed, as yet more children arrived to join in. On the way back Robaratus had quite a following, even the guards on the wall were following him whistling and shouting. Finally he came back to the green with the well. He stopped, his huge chest heaved in and out, his face drenched in sweat. His parents stood in the broken doorway, his mother laughing at the sight of them all. His father came over and pulled the bucket up, then threw it over his son, who bellowed at the iciness.

"Do that agin." One of the smaller boys shouted, so Robaratus stood, filled his great lungs with air and roared. Everyone covered their ears. Once Robaratus was rested he looked down at Sage, who had not got up from the board. "Ready for another run?" He asked grinning.

"Gods, my poor arse!" Sage moaned, but she was smiling, she was having so much fun, there was no way a sore arse was putting her off, so she sat tight while some of the children climbed on board, then Robaratus was off, first walking then running, to the cheers screams and whistles of everyone around. He ran up and down the wall all day, stopping only to vary his routine by picking up one boy and sitting him on his broad shoulder, then putting another on the other side. He added a boy to his back and carried another two one in each hand, and he ran short bursts then walked, then ran again. This gave Sage at least a moment to rub her bruised backside, before the board run began again. At the end of the day, some women arrived all to watch and flirt, at the sight of him, Sage felt all the fun drain away from her. She watched as Robaratus poured ice water over himself and drank deeply, wiping his face of sweat. Then without warning one of the women stepped up to him and kissed him on the lips. Sage stood open mouthed for a brief moment, she watched her husband look equally surprised, then he carefully peeled the woman off him.

"I am sorry. I am married now and I am loyal to my wife." He spoke kindly, then walked over to Sage, who was looking down at the ground. "Sage?" She looked up at him, and he could see all the hurt in her face.

He chuckled, which was loud now the crowd had hushed. The woman looked smug. "That was no kiss Sage." He said softly, she looked into his eyes, as he lowered his head and let his lips brush hers, then he pressed a little harder, her lips parted slightly for him and his tongue traced the line of them, she sighed, as he made the kiss much longer, more intimate and deeper than any he had given before. Sage snaked her arms about his neck, clutching at his wet hair, as his arms embraced her his hardness pressed against her stomach, he made no attempt to hide how she affected him, and even as he broke the kiss, he held her tight. "*That* is a kiss." He said in a deep and husky voice. The women sighed except the one who had tried to kiss him. The children cheered and the soldiers whistled. "Do not move. I need some sobering thoughts before I dare let you go." He said quietly into her neck. Sage smiled but stayed put. *You have his heart Sage; you just don't know it.*

Chapter 15

Every day for a week Robaratus did the same routine, Iola had given Sage a cushion to sit on as a joke, to which Sage played along happily, grateful for something soft after a day of being bumped about on hard ground. Every evening Robaratus would stop by the well, take his last cold rinse and wash his face, then at the shouts from the children, he would grin, sweep his wife into his arms and kiss her passionately, to the cheers of all the on lookers. Sage and Robaratus were becoming quite famous in their own right. Each evening they would sit around the table talking about improving his training, much to the initial surprise of his parents. Iola listened to the two of them talking, and she found herself more and more impressed with the way Sage came up with improvements. Sometimes they would talk into the night, but mostly Robaratus would sleep, never when alone did he repeat his affections, or the kiss, which gave Sage more reasons to doubt him. *He plays with my affections, puts on the show for the crowd as he always has. The beggar was wrong.* At the end of the week, Sage had had enough of being battered black and blue, she was fed up of being sore, of hearing the children shout adoration to him, of the women who gave him flirtatious looks of open wanton desire, of her husband being surrounded by admirers, while she stood in the background watching it all.
"Are you ready for the board?" He asked one morning.
"I'll sit it out this run, I am sore all over." She smiled at him, hoping he wouldn't see the hurt in her eyes, but she need not have worried, he just shrugged and loaded more children onto the board instead, then he was off. Sage watched with a heartache, unsure if she was jealous or just sad that he hadn't a clue of how his behaviour had affected her. *He is as blind as you are*, came the beggars soft voice. "No he's not blind, he knows exactly what he's doing." She replied to herself.

*   *   *

Robaratus left early the first morning of the following week. He arrived early at the arena where several men had already begun training. He knew before he could announce his intentions, he first had to win their

111

respect. He'd killed their trainer, now he had to make himself liked, not so easy. He removed his tunic and stood in his shorts, rolling his thick neck allowing his jata locs to swing. His hair being down to his ears, he had twisted it into ropes, jata locs. He shrugged his shoulders and stretched his arms forwards, then upwards over his head. Some of the gladiators started towards him, he ignored them.

"Robaratus, five years ago three men gave their lives in honour of you, now you come here and kill another, what gives you the right to think you can train us?" The man who accused was tall and black skinned, his body shone from oil.

"I have no right, yet the Empress has ordered me to train, so I do as I am bid."

The gladiator laughed. "Did you do as bid when you slept with your centurion's wife?" The men were just starting to laugh when the gladiator flew backwards, falling on his rump. It was Robaratus who smiled at him. "I enjoyed her."

The dark-skinned man spat blood onto the sand.

"For what it's worth, I regret the lives lost in my name. I killed more as a soldier; I regret it all but the worst of it are the lives that are taken in the arena. Your lives. We are all slaves, but if you want to live a little longer, you'll accept my help."

"Fuck you." Another man said spitting at Robaratus's feet. He doubled over when a fist hit his gut, eyes bulging, mouth open, desperate to re-inflate his lungs.

"Anyone else?" Robaratus asked, they took a step back, then the dark-skinned man stood forward and charged into Robaratus, but the big bear knew that move already, he twisted avoiding the blade he knew was there, and wrapped his mighty arm around the dark-skinned man's waist and he squeezed, until the man was gasping for air.

"Now. I can let this dim shit go, or I can keep squeezing until each rib snaps. I can keep going until I snap his spine. It's your choice, and his." Robaratus seemed quite at ease squeezing the life slowly from the man who'd just tried to stab him. The gladiators voted for letting the man go, so Robaratus asked the man himself, who wheezed and nodded ferociously. "Anyone who tries to stab me, will be killed by me. Do we understand each other?" The men mumbled their affirmations. Robaratus applied the pressure to the dark-skinned man again. "I can't hear you?" He shouted. The men shouted back, the dark-skinned man fell to the floor coughing and gasping huge gulps of air.

"Then put all your weapons in a pile there." Robaratus pointed. "A few knives were tossed into a pile. Robaratus grabbed the closest man by the throat. "Seems you give lip service better than you give obedience. Perhaps I need to add another life to the four I already own here?"

Several more knives clattered to the floor. Robaratus knew he didn't have them all, just most. He punched the man for good measure.

"Make a line." He ordered. When they didn't move fast enough he punched them. "Hands in the air" He shouted, making a few cringe. Arms rose and Robaratus searched every single man, and for every blade he found he made that man suffer, and the rest had to do press ups, for every failed press up, they had to stand with their arms in the air, and so it went on, the whole day making them suffer for every failed exercise or punishment. By days end, the men were bloody, bruised and ached like they'd never ached before. They were all glad when Robaratus allowed them to sit for an evening meal, not so happy when he sat with them. He had learned some of their names, the dark-skinned man was called Atrox; he had the greatest hate for Robaratus. As they ate, Robaratus talked to each man as though he had known him for years, he spoke of their weaknesses and how he would work them to become stronger, then he got to Atrox. "You must channel your hatred into energy, make it a power, then some day you will have the right to plunge the blade down my spine into my heart." Robaratus gave the man a steady stare, the two of them locked stares. Atrox had no idea what to make of this failed soldier, this famous gladiator who'd as good as named his own executioner, so he nodded a barely imperceptible movement of his head, and Robaratus responded with his own.

When Robaratus reached home, the sun was sending long rays of orange light over the city walls, he saw it reflected in Sage's hair, as she pulled the bucket up from the well, he ran over to her and wrapped his large arms about her, burying his face into her neck, inhaling her sweet aroma. In fright she dropped the bucket, sending it plummeting down to the bottom again. As she swore, so her husband laughed, then he hauled the bucket back up, swiftly and took it from her. "What did you do today Sage?" He asked, putting the bucket down.

"Nothing. Your parents required no help, so I walked and wasted my day. What can I do Robaratus? I have no mistress to wait on."

He noticed the sad tone to her voice, the way she looked down not up at him. His jubilation died. He had missed her, but he had never thought what she might do with her days.

"I am sorry Sage." He could think of nothing else; he dare not take her to the arena, Atrox was too dangerous.

"How was your day?" Sage asked, not that she cared all that much, but she couldn't stand the silence either, so it was a relief when he started to tell her of his day, minus the worst bits.

"On your own again?"

Sage turned to find a soldier standing on the road a little behind her. She smiled sadly at him. "It must be hard to be the wife of someone like Robaratus Ectorius." He said as he caught up to her. "My name is Victus" He said kindly. He was tall, with broad shoulders, a shaved head that left him with dark stubble. Sage shrugged.

"I heard a rumour you were both forced to marry. Is that true?"

Sage stopped walking. "What business is it of yours?" she asked somewhat annoyed. He shrugged and smiled at her a kind, warm smile. "Absolutely none, but if it were my business, I would wonder how a marriage works when you had no idea what type of person it was you were marrying."

Sage looked at him, he seemed genuinely interested.

"Same as all marriages. We didn't like each other at first, but we are growing together." She said confidently, even if she didn't feel it or believe it, she would pretend it.

Victus walked beside her, "you know I admire that commitment you both have, considering how different you both are."

"How long did it take before you were in love with him?"

Sage tripped over her feet; she had not seen that coming. Her face flushed partly from anger and partly from humiliation.

"I apologise mistress, I did not mean to cause offense. I thought you loved him."

When she looked up at him, he was studying her with soft eyes and a look of something that resembled sympathy.

"I doubt many marriages are built on love." She answered softly.

"Mine will be." He said confidently. They walked on in silence for a long while, Sage itched to find something to say she felt uncomfortable with his company, his odd questions about her marriage.

"Why do you not watch him train anymore?" Victus asked. Sage stopped and looked up at him. "Why do you want to know so much about my marriage? It seems to me you have a very unhealthy interest in us."

Victus laughed softly. "I apologise. I do have an interest. I see a lonely woman walking these streets every day, while her husband is off behind tall walls training men to die. I care for the lonely woman who seems to me, to be shut out again."

Sage studied him, his face appeared sincere, and his words sounded plausible. She had walked every day up and down, miserable unhappy and bored, while her husband trained and told her about his great successes, and every day she had nothing to say to him because her life was empty. Her husband hugged her every evening when he came home, then ignored her till the following evening. He didn't bother to kiss her anymore, what was the point, when there were no crowds to whistle and cheer.

"Why would you care for me? There are plenty of lonely women around." Sage challenged him.

"Perhaps, but none walk these streets every day, nor are they married to the most famous gladiator and nor are they as unloved, unappreciated as you seem to be."

Despite her resolve, Sage felt the tears blur her vision, Victus had only just met her yet he had found her most vulnerable emotions.

"You should know that Robaratus and I are committed to our marriage." She said with as much sincerity as she could muster.

"You have a lot of faith in a man who is used to having a lot of women." Victus pointed out. Sage smiled. "That was his past Victus. Do not presume to know my husband."

Victus nodded to her and they carried on walking until they came upon his watch tower.

"I must bid you farewell at this point mistress, but I should like to walk with you again if you'd let me?"

Sage shrugged; some company was better than none. She spent the rest of her day sitting outside the city walls by the river, it was peaceful there, and nobody cared who she was. In the evening Robaratus came home, and told her his news. At first she had listened but as the days had worn on, she found herself caring less and less. It was as though Robaratus only lived for one thing, and as his gladiators trained so they became more loyal, more willing to accept that they had improved, were stronger and had more vitality and endurance. Robaratus was justifiably proud of himself and of his men. Whatever thin thread that had held her to him was so fragile it had almost snapped, they were strangers again, she realised.

The next morning after her husband had left for the arena, Sage walked to the river again. She was sure she didn't want to meet Victus, it had been nice but seeing him again would give him the wrong idea, and Sage wasn't about to be disloyal to her marriage, but as she approached the gate out of the city, a lad came running to her giving her a note. Sage looked at it.

I thought of you all day yesterday.

She was about to ask the boy from whom it came, but he'd gone. Sage smiled to herself, *it had to be Victus, how sweet.* She tucked the note into her pocket and walked out of the gate. It played on her mind all day, she had never been thought of before, at least no one had ever told her she was worth thinking of, so it was something special to Sage to know that someone, even if it was only Victus, had thought about her not just for a

115

moment, but all day. That thought made her smile every time she thought about it. The following day another note was delivered to her.

I dreamt about you last night.

Sage laughed lightly. She sat by the river reading both her notes over and over. *So Victus dreams about me. How sweet.* She mused. Yet from one meeting he had opened his heart to her. Sage could hear the warning bells, but she was sure she had read him right, he was being kind, nothing more, so she allowed herself the luxury of being flattered by his kindness. The next day came another note.

I miss you.

Sage felt guilty, so she headed back to the city to find Victus and at least thank him for making her smile again. Strangely he was waiting for her outside his tower. His face split into a huge grin when he saw her, and he walked to her with confidence. "Mistress, I thought you might be annoyed with me." He said. Sage smiled at him. "I should be. You are kind if the notes come from you, but Victus, I am married for good or ill, I'll not break my promise to stand beside him."

Victus didn't seem put off. "I have no wish to come between you, but to share my thoughts for you, to let you know that I admire you, yours is a lonely life mistress, I only wish to make it brighter."

"And you do." Sage smiled at him. She had been right; he *was* being kind. He was a handsome man closer to her own age than Robaratus was, and it would be so easy to feel flattered and genuinely loved by such a young man, but Sage had not spent her life watching the heart breaks of others to not know flirtations when she saw them. Yet Victus was the first man who had ever flirted with her and her own heart couldn't deny the addiction of it.

"Where do you go mistress, for you haven't been past my tower in some three days?"

"I walk by the river; it is quiet there and private."

"Might I ask if you think of me?" Victus said sheepishly. Sage felt the egg shells she was walking on immediately. *Tread carefully.*

"I wonder if you're mad or have a death wish." She mused. "Do you know what Robaratus would do to you if he thought you flirted with me? Do you know what he'd do to me?"

"I care nothing for myself, but if he hurt you, I would kill him."

Sage laughed. "You think others have not said as much?"

"Other men have flirted with you?"

"No! I meant other men have thought to kill my husband. Yet he lives."

"Would you prefer him dead?"

Sage stopped walking and stared at Victus. "How could you say such a thing?"

"Apologies mistress. I see a gladiator, a man whose heart is cold as stone, so they say. I see a beautiful woman who deserves so much more, and might have it if only she could be honest about her situation."

Sage began to walk again, head down as she played with the edges of her shawl. "I have been honest Victus. I may not have known my husband for long, but I have known him far longer than I have you. I will stay with him for good or ill as I have already told you. We may not be happy but we are married and I will do my duty as best I can, even if I must learn it day by day."

Victus admired her all the more for her steadfastness. "I wish you well mistress, I truly do."

Sage wondered what he meant by that, it seemed like he was giving up on her or perhaps he just knew something about Robaratus she didn't. After all, a beggar had claimed she knew his heart, why not a soldier? As it turned out he had not given up, and the notes kept arriving, making Sage smile, lifting her heart in ways she knew Robaratus just never could. He would not send her a single flower, nor a posy of them, he wouldn't write her either, he wasn't romantic because he never wanted a wife, he could flirt and women wanted to bed him for his aphrodisiac sweat, but Robaratus Ectorius had never loved, never lost his heart and soul to any woman. He could demonstrate the difference between a forced kiss and an intended one, and only then where an audience watched. As the weeks passed, Sage found herself looking forward to the notes, the presents, the simple acts of caring that cost only time and imagination. She would walk and talk with Victus, and slowly she opened her heart to him encouraged by his devotion and kindness. Never once did he seek to hold her hand, nor kiss her, never once did he suggest she leave Robaratus, he was just there, with those dark eyes that spoke a thousand words, shared a million feelings, and longed for her, what need he of words when his eyes said so much more.

One evening Robaratus asked his wife to go on a walk with him, which she agreed to with suspicion, for he had not asked her to go for a walk with him for months, but as they walked, he talked of the training, of the men, of the loyalty they were building, and Sage drifted off into her world, as she felt the note in her tunic that told her how her eyes shone like the stars, how beautiful her skin was to caress with his gaze and how the sight of her brightened his days.

"Sage?"

She jumped. "Sorry, I was miles away." She smiled, suddenly it was good to have a secret, to know that she was appreciated even though her husband didn't care.

"Tomorrow?" Robaratus asked.

"What about tomorrow?"

"Were you listening at all?" he asked, slightly annoyed. Sage put her head down, she had not listened, hadn't heard a single word.

"I want you to come to the arena tomorrow." Robaratus repeated. Sudden panic surged inside her, she didn't want to go to the arena.

"Why?" She asked more defensively than she meant.

"Because it is safe now, and I want them to meet you." He was smiling at her, but she looked at him and realised how much of a stranger he had become, just how far they had drifted, he with his passion for fighting, her with her love for walking with a soldier who understood her loneliness.

"I was, um, hoping to go for a walk tomorrow." Sage said, not daring to look at him.

"You have had months of walking. I want you with me, I missed you." Robaratus admitted, but there was no emotion in his voice, it sounded like an order. Sage nodded, her heart heavy, broken.

In bed she shed silent tears, wondering what Victus would think of her, and only then did she realise how much she had fallen for the soldier, she hated herself. *So this is how they worm their way into our hearts and break them, Foolish me for being so weak.* As much as she knew it would hurt her, she would tell Victus their friendship was done with. When morning came, she left with Robaratus and couldn't help but look up at the tower as she passed it, she didn't see Victus, she only hoped one of the guards would tell him. She did her best to focus on the day, meeting powerful men who looked at her with ice cold eyes and stank of sweat. Then there was Atrox a hard gladiator with a look that promised torture, he licked his lips when he saw Sage, sending a shiver down her spine. He fought Robaratus with such savagery that Sage couldn't look, he disliked her husband that much was clear, but she had no idea why. Robaratus seemed to enjoy the viciousness of the spar, he grinned at every slam of the body blows delivered on him, at every clash of steel. Sage felt despair, her husband had become more violent than ever, more ferocious and powerful, and she longed to run from the arena, to cry at the destiny she had been served, or perhaps it was she who had changed, she who longed for a peaceful life of being admired for who she was instead of ignored. On the way home Robaratus asked. "What did you think?"

"You seem to be doing well." She muttered.

"Now give me the truthful version." Robaratus said, intention clear as a bell in his tone. Sage took a deep breath.

"I never want to go back there ever again." Sage said. "You are a strict trainer; I have seen that with Albus's men but now you are a savage. You have changed Robaratus and I don't know you anymore." A long silence followed, and as they passed the watch tower, she snuck a glance up and saw Victus looking down, he made no acknowledgment of her, but she didn't expect him to, he knew now where she would be.

"You have never known me Sage, nor I you." His voice was forced softness, she could tell he was holding in anger but she didn't understand why. "You asked me for truth." She reminded him.

"I did. Do you know why I am training these men so hard? Do you even care?" There was a roughness to his voice that scared her.

"You want your freedom. You're doing it for me." She couldn't hide the flatness in her tone. "I am doing this for us. This is not what you want of me then. Tell me what is it you want of me?"

Now he asks! He never cared for her opinion before, why would he care now? She could only shrug.

"You are a smart woman Sage, so tell me why it is, I consistently fail you?" His voice seemed broken now, and she dared to look up at him, his expression was blank, his eyes waiting for an answer. "I don't think you could understand." She muttered.

"Try me." He growled.

"Why are you asking me all these things? Sage said, panic gripping her heart.

"I am curious. I am ready to die for you, and that is not enough. I want freedom for us, but *that* is not enough, so tell me wife, what in hades do you want from me?" Now his anger spilled out, and Sage shivered, he was terrifying when he was mad, how could she tell him she hated being his wife, hated that he couldn't and never would love her, hated that she would always be second best. How could she tell him that she hated the violence, that he was a monster? How could she tell him she wanted to be held, wanted to feel that she mattered, she wanted him to love her; to look at her the way Victus did, with eyes that adored. They had reached home, and both entered the dwelling where an uncomfortable silence met them. Sage ran upstairs to their room; she really didn't need his parents picking on her either. As she entered the room, she stopped dead in her tracks. Over the bed were the scattered notes, all of them. Sage stared in horror, he'd found them, but how? She turned on her heel and ran down the stairs, to find her husband missing, with her heart in her mouth she ran to the watch tower and stopped dead as Robaratus held Victus by the throat. Victus was laughing. "Who put you up to this?" Robaratus demanded.

"Who'd you think?" Victus answered, laughter in his voice. "It took you long enough murderer. You have been so absorbed in your training, you forgot you had a wife, why wouldn't I take advantage of that?"

Sage stared at him, was he saying he had played her? It sounded like it. "Who. Put. You. Up. To. This?"

"Julius Brutus, who else." Victus rolled his eyes. "It was easy man, she was so needy, so lonely, so fucking begging for it."

Robaratus punched him in the gut, dropping him to the floor. Sage sobbed, hand over her mouth, so they wouldn't notice her. His words of love just words, the flowers, just flowers. She had been so gullible, so ready to want some affection in her life that she had laid herself open for all this to happen, all to laugh at Robaratus, all to laugh at her expense.

"You're a fool gladiator. Your wife is starving for the want of some attention, a little bit of affection, even love, oh wait! You don't know how to love do you? Yet you can't give her what you give so easily to every other fucking woman you've laid." Another punch had Victus wheezing for air. "You think a few words would fool her?" Robaratus shouted. Victus nodded unable to speak, a weak grin on his face.

"Did you touch her?"

Sage gasped; tears spilled down her face.

"No. I wouldn't touch that; she only needed some kindness to make her feel loved. Even you can't bring yourself to fuck her can you?" Victus laughed, until Robaratus belted him senseless, leaving him unconscious in the street. Sage turned and ran, she sobbed and ran and cared not where she ran to, in fact had a cart run her over it'd have been a blessing. How could she ever look her husband in the face again? She felt so utterly humiliated, broken. How did he know Robaratus had not touched her? Was she so repulsive? Had her husband lied when he said he loved her freckles? Was she the reason he had not consummated his marriage. Sage felt sick, how had she missed that obvious fact? He'd always thought of her as a child, maybe he still did. His mother would love to know what she had done and wouldn't she love it? *Sage, was life really so bad? Of course it was and now it was even worse.*

She ran out of energy at the end of the viaduct, where the disowned and lost went, where the homeless and drunks gathered. She hoped they would kill her, or lend her the knife that she could do so herself. She sat alone with her back to the wall.

"So the grass wasn't greener after all." A familiar voice said softly. Sage got up and tried to move away.

"You can run Sage but you can't hide. You have to face him eventually." The beggar woman said kindly. Sage shook her head; her body shook with sobs. She never wanted to look Robaratus in the eyes again, she deserved every condemnation he'd throw at her.

"Of course, I forgot, you don't care about his feelings, that he'll be worried sick about you."

Stupid woman, he'll want to kill me for what I've done.

Sage got up and walked away, she turned towards the gates and walked out of the city. A few days alone would help her to clear her mind. She walked without seeing, too numb to think, but when it grew too dark to see, she found herself at the tombs of the dead. She searched in the darkness for the tombs of the gladiators who'd died for Robaratus, and then she curled up at the foot of the tomb that held their ashes. She did not sleep, she listened to the wind that whistled in and out of the monuments, carrying their words that the living would never fathom. She knew she had to face Robaratus, hard as it would be, but she need say nothing at all if he wanted her gone, she had no right to want his forgiveness, not when everything he had done, he had done for her. *I didn't ask him to, he never asked me what I wanted, not until today. It's too late now, he would never have understood, he isn't the kind of man who can be romantic, what killer could love?*

Although Victus had used her, played on her vulnerability, she still smiled at the notes he had sent, the last one was still in her tunic.

Your eyes are like the stars. Your face a vision that brightens my days.

Fake it may be but no man had ever written anything to Sage, and still she smiled at how it had made her feel, real. Robaratus had never said anything to her that could pass for romantic, he was just a showman. Victus had broken her heart, but only because she had let him into it in the first place. Robaratus couldn't break her heart because he'd never wanted to be there in any case.

Chapter 16

In the morning Sage heard the shuffle of feet nearby. She stood on cold legs that ached. *He couldn't have found me.* Fear rose within her like a monster, but when the feet arrived they belonged to the beggar woman, who was equally startled to find Sage trembling by the tombs.

"What are you doing here?" Sage demanded, annoyed anyone should know where she hid. The beggar woman just stared at her.

"Huh, I could ask you the same thing." She said in her rough voice. She produced a small bunch of flowers from behind her back, and stepped forward, making Sage step aside.

"You know these men?"

The beggar ignored her, wiping down the shelf with her torn sleeve, then wiping her eyes with the same sleeve. She laid the flowers on the shelf and closed her wrinkled eyes, her lips moved silently speaking only to those long departed. Sage watched her feeling like an intruder all over again. She decided to leave when the beggar closed her eyes, this was a personal visit that Sage had no business being part of, so she slipped behind the woman and aimed to leave her to her prayers.

"I am the sister of Calclus, who was a good and promising Mirmillon. Ferox was my promised, a Retiarii. Such a beautiful body he had."

Sage froze where she stood. So this was how the beggar knew so much about gladiators. "I thought you said you loved Robaratus?"

The beggar remained with her back to Sage. "Aye. I did, but you think a soldier would look at a slave?"

Sage stared at her, going cold at her words. "*I wouldn't touch that, even you cannot bring yourself to fuck her.*" Victus' words echoed in her mind.

"I'm so sorry." She whispered, and turned to leave.

"I watched Ferox kill my brother, with tears pouring down his face." The beggar sniffed.

"Why are you telling me this now?" Sage asked, her throat tight from the lump that had stuck there.

"Did you not ask what I was doing here? Did you not ask if I knew these men?" The beggar turned to face Sage. "Twas Julius Brutus as set them good men against each other, all because he couldn't rape me. I stabbed the bastard, in my terror an' fear of 'im. He said I'd pay, and pay I did, and pay I will for the rest of me days."

122

Sage had no words for her, she was numb from the horror and cold and sadness that wracked her whole body, her whole life. She could not imagine the horror for two men, one a brother, one a lover, friends set to kill each other. She could see the heart-break of the lover, the way he must've pleaded for mercy from Brutus, who would've enjoyed dragging out those last moments, then watching as the victor thrust his trident and dagger into his friend. A woman who would have screamed as she lost her sanity, and now existed only for a memory, for a few picked flowers, that would blow away in the wind. Sage sobbed anew; she couldn't help the grief that overwhelmed her.

"Don't waste your tears on me girl. I lost me life the day your husband made Optio. I lost it again the day he became a gladiator." The beggar watched Sage with cold eyes. "Brutus trained them men to be evil, to stab and hack with small knives. I watched my promised and my brother hack, cut an stab each other to pieces, each begging the other to end it. I see it up ere, all the time." She stabbed at her temple with a grubby finger. "One day I will kill that bastard. One day I will be free of the madness he served on me. One day I will come here an sleep my last, layin as close to them as I can."

The beggar had been a slave who loved a soldier, but being smarter than Sage, she had loved him from afar, seen him rise in the ranks and then fall from grace, to become a slave like she was. "Shouldn't you hate Robaratus?" Sage whispered. The beggar smiled her gums. "Aye I hated him for failing. I hated him for wasting their lives. I even saw his condemned fight, I sought satisfaction, instead I saw his desperation and terror. I saw a young man brought down to earth, humiliated, shamed. I saw him cry that day. His first kill in cold blood. I saw how the madness took him, an after that, I heard stories of his life, an I grieved for another man I had loved."

"But he killed as a soldier." Sage said frowning at the beggar. The woman shook her head. "Big difference killing an enemy, to killing a man for entertainment."

Sage bowed her head and began to walk away again.

"I hope you ain't stayin ere long. You're a stain on good men's memories."
"I've tried to understand." Sage protested. "I never liked gladiators. My love was charioteers, but I have tried to learn his way of life. Am I really to blame if I can't? In the name of Cupid, I only wanted some kindness, affection, heaven forbid, someone I could love who could love me back." And there is was out in the open, her deepest confession, she turned and left, to hades with whatever that tragic woman would blame her for next, Sage had had enough of it all.

The life of the beggar haunted Sage as she wandered further away from the city, it had never occurred to her how tragic gladiators' lives were. How cruel that ordinary people got such a kick out of watching men murder each other, even if those men were deemed criminals, nobody deserved that kind of punishment. Which brought her back to Robaratus. She tried to imagine what it must have done to his mind, to be forced to kill another in cold blood. How did anyone survive that insanity? How could anyone survive the people who made it legal? She had heard of gladiators who rebelled, who fought their superiors for change. Some were crucified for their defiance, or tied to a stake in the colosseums and fed to wild beasts. Who ever considered what the women slaves who loved those men went through? The beggar would spend years of what was left of her life grieving, yearning for death, that she might be reunited with the two men she loved most in the world. Then it hit Sage that Robaratus survived through a cold insanity, that it was not he who should show affection, but Sage herself. She might hate what he did, had to do, but the man had never really been loved, needed or honestly cared about. Used, all his life used. Used as a soldier to kill enemies, but that was his choice, it wasn't his choice to kill in cold blood, over and over, nor to be adored by vanity driven women who thought his sweat an aphrodisiac to their own failed men. It wasn't his choice to spy on women for an ego jealous Empress, was it any wonder he had no notion of love, of being loved for himself, and she Sage, who had struggled to understand his way of life, had hated him for it, had failed to heal his broken heart, broken soul, broken mind. Sage stopped walking. *How could I have not seen where I went wrong?* He was such a good showman, he had fooled her with his carefree attitude, his apparent love of a crowd. Now he was preparing for the last fight of his life, one that would kill him or free him, and he was doing it for her. All for a slave wife he never wanted, yet was giving everything he had for. She turned and ran back towards the city.

When she reached the arena, she sat on the stone bench that faced the large wooden gate in the high wooden wall that circled the training area. She was nervous, trying to think of what she might say, wringing her hands with how wretched she felt. Perhaps words were not what Sage needed, may be it was what she did rather than said, that would prove her feelings, but then how did she feel? She had always been afraid of Robaratus, he was taller than any other man, broader, stronger and without argument louder. If he wanted rid of her, could she just walk away? She needed him, was that the same as caring or love? Her hands twisted and she chewed her lip, how would she know if she loved him, or cared, it wasn't something she had thought about, since she had always known she wouldn't be the one who would want a husband. Yet when he'd been cut

124

so badly, hadn't she been afraid of losing him? Hadn't he wanted her more than his parents? Her stomach growled, and twisted, she hadn't eaten for over a day, the pickings from the picnics around the tombs hadn't been enough to sustain her, and now of all the bad timings, she was hungry. She pulled her shawl over and around herself, shivering despite the sunshine, she was tired as well, she wanted it over, but feared what road that led down. She jumped when the gate opened, she stood nervously. Robaratus was stooped over, his cheek bones more hollow than usual, his tan dirty, his eyes dark from lack of sleep. He stopped instinctively and looked up. He froze when he saw her, dropping his hands to his sides. Sage kept her eyes on those hands, if he so much as twitched a finger, she would run for her life. They stood neither moving, every nerve screamed for Sage to run, but her legs wouldn't move. In the end he said her name, softly, she shivered. *Oh Gods I don't deserve your kindness.* Tears welled in her eyes. He took a step closer to her, and she forced herself to stand still, to watch his hands, which remained at his sides, straight. He took another step, and she could almost feel the tension he was holding back, he was afraid she would bolt, so she took a step towards him, to show that she would not. She saw the way his abs tensed and she knew she had to make that first move, so she raised her head, shocked at the expression on his face, tiredness, and sorrow, without having to think, her hand rose to his cheek, instinctively he turned his face into her palm, he inhaled her scent still discernible under all the grime she wore. His hand slowly lifted to her waist and gently he pulled her to him, their eyes locked both filled with sorrow, both with hurt and then he lowered his head to hers and his lips brushed hers. Sage smothered a sob, and both his hands gripped her waist, pulled her closer, her hands snaked up and around his neck, his mouth pressed harder, his arms wrapped around her and they kissed deeply, both needing and for the first time Sage knew she more than wanted him, her heart was breaking at how he looked, she had done this to him. She had hurt him more deeply than any blade and it hurt her to know it, yet this was no act on his part, there were no crowds, a groan deep in his chest rumbled through her and her legs were lifted from the ground, his kiss growing more hungry, his tongue traced her lower lip, and she pressed herself closer to him, her skin on fire, her heart racing, her tears of joy flowing. Was this love? She hoped so.

Eventually he let the kiss fade, put her feet back on the ground and held her so close, she feared he would crush her. Still they didn't speak, though a thousand words raced through her mind. It had only been one night, yet he looked as miserable as she felt, so she clung to him, her arms around his massive chest, his head buried into her neck. Eventually she knew she had to say something. "I was safe. I slept at the memorial to those gladiators who died for you."

Without letting her go he replied. "I searched for you all day and night." His voice was raw, his emotions still too much, so she tightened her grip around him. "I owe you so much Robaratus, and those men reminded me of what you once were, what you've lost."

He said nothing and his hold did not change, so Sage pressed on. "I tried to understand your world and I just couldn't because it makes me ill." She shuddered. "Then I realised it wasn't your life at all. It was your punishment and that brings a madness with it you have had to live with for years."

His grip changed position, his arms running up her back, his thumbs caressing the nape of her neck.

"I cannot imagine how much guilt you carry, how much grief, but I do understand why you act like you don't care, like you love it all. You carry all those deaths even the ones you're not guilty of, you feel responsible for every life, and I understand that now. I wish I could've understood it before, because I wouldn't have acted so selfishly."

His arms crushed the air from her preventing her saying any more, he inhaled deeply. "Please." She wheezed and he loosened his hold.

"You are not to blame for my neglect." Robaratus said eventually, holding her just as tightly. "I could not let you come with me, there is a man in there so filled with hate for me, he would've taken you first chance he got and killed you to destroy me." He paused to place a kiss on her neck, to inhale the smell of her hair. "I knew about Victus, and I knew what he was doing. I trusted you. I had to, but when I found how many notes he'd sent you, it killed me." His words broke off, and Sage tried to pull away from him, but he held her tight. He took several ragged breaths before he carried on. "If I could be like that Sage." He paused, raised his head and she got her chance to pull back long enough to see the agony in his expression. "I would give you the world." The rawness of his voice had her hands flying to his face, cupping it gently. "I already have the world and more. I just didn't know it."

His own hands reached up to hers, taking them from his face he studied them as though seeing them for the first time then he kissed them. Sage sucked in a shuddering breath. She watched as his lips made a trail across her palms; she smiled as his teeth gently nipped the skin at her wrist. Her stomach grumbled and he lifted his head to look at her. "When did you last eat?"

She shrugged.

"Time to get home and feed you." He said, his eyes burning passion into

her own. Sage looked down at the ground. "What's wrong?" He asked.
"I. I'm not going back to your parents' home. I don't belong." She shook
her head fearing what his response would be. Instead he watched her
waiting. Sage sighed heavily. "It's not your fault or mine, but just as a
soldier won't touch me, nor will your parents ever accept me. You will
never be a slave in their eyes. I always will be." She looked up at him, her
eyes pleaded him to understand she'd never be anything more than a slave.
"Then we will stay at an Inn until I can find us a dwelling to call our own."
Her eyes widened, making him smile. Seeing how doing something
unexpected, something just for her had made him smile with a happiness
she had not seen before, Sage threw her arms around his neck, gushing a
thousand thank yous, which had his arms around her again, holding her
tight. Her stomach grumbled and he chuckled. "First you need food."
        "Why did you say a soldier wouldn't touch you?" Robaratus asked
as they ate. Sage paused, "You know why?"
"Yes I do, but you didn't. If you'd known Sage, you would never have
fallen for his tricks." On seeing her head drop, he added. "I am not
blaming you; I just wonder how you now know."
"I heard what he said. I also met the beggar woman again." Sage's voice
trailed away, remembering all the sorrow stole her breath and words.
Robaratus reached across the table and took her hand in his, stroking his
thumb over her skin. Sage sucked in a deep breath and tears filled her eyes.
"You don't have to tell me." He said with such utter kindness, it made Sage
strangle a sob. "I do, because you need to know her story too." So Sage
told him between gut wrenching sobs, she told of the two men who'd been
forced to murder each other, and what that had done to the woman who'd
loved them, what it had done to her again when Robaratus had wasted
their sacrifices by falling from grace. He listened, his face becoming darker
and darker. When Sage was done he bowed his head. It was Sage who
grabbed his hand in both of hers. "I'm sorry Robaratus." He squeezed her
hands. "I knew you'd want to know it all." Sage finished. He nodded, drew
a breath of his own and raised his head. "She had no right to say you were
a stain on their memories. I have to meet this woman."
"You won't hurt her." Sage said. He shook his head. "No. There may be
some women I'd like to knock into next week, but not her." A small smile
ticked at the corner of Sage's lips. "She has only ever tried to open my
eyes, to help me, to make me strong I suppose."
"She's got a fucking funny way of showing it." He mumbled.
"Are you done here?" The slave girl asked as she waited for their dishes.
Robaratus leaned back, allowing her to collect them.
"Do you have rooms here?" He asked. The girl nodded. "See the master"

She nodded over her shoulder at the barman. Robaratus got up, taking his wife's hand, they went to the bar. Robaratus booked them a room explaining it was just for the two of them indefinitely, while he sort a suitable home. Sage kept her head down; it was just too embarrassing for her. *Perhaps staying with his parents was the lesser of two humiliations after all.*

"Sage I need to see my parents at least to explain why we are not returning." Sage nodded. When he didn't move she realised he was reluctant to tell her he didn't trust her not to run away.

"You want me to come with you don't you?"

He nodded. She smiled at him softly. *Show him Sage.* She reminded herself, then took his arm and led him out of the Inn.

"Why do you think Atrox hates you so much?" Sage asked as they walked back through the south gate.

"It's in the beggars' story." He answered. "In the way Brutus trained those men. I think Atrox has a broken mind."

"Then how is my presence not going to make it any worse?"

"He is not as bad as he was when I first arrived so I can protect you better." When Sage didn't say anything, he loosed his arm and wrapped it about her. "I already told you I trusted you, but I am going to feel a lot happier if I can see when you're in danger."

You don't have eyes everywhere, but she didn't want to fight him, so she let it go. "Besides," he added, "I kept looking for you in the stands, and hated when you weren't there."

"Can Atrox be saved, or helped?"

"No. I think he is far too damaged now. I have got him to channel his hatred, by making him my chosen executioner, it has motivated him."

Sage ducked out from under his embrace and stood stock still. "You did *what?*" She gasped. Robaratus shrugged. "It worked; he is less likely to keep trying to stab me if he thinks he is eventually going to replace me."

"But Rob that's inviting the fates." She whispered loudly. He laughed and stepped back to her.

"You just called me Rob." He pointed out.

"So?"

"So you never have." He was grinning. Sage blushed. "You're trying to change the subject now."

"Am not, but Rob sounds good on *your* lips." He smirked. "There will come a time, likely sooner now I think, when I will offer Atrox the choice, me or Brutus. He hates that man as much as I do, but if he chooses me, it'll be bloody and I will win. I will win Sage, because I am still the better fighter and I will be the one who ends his torment. If he chooses Brutus, he will at least have the chance to get his revenge."

"Can he beat Brutus?"

"I wouldn't like to say. Either way whomever lives, faces me."

Sage's eyes widened. "Why you?"

"I am the one who trains him now, my responsibility, besides I owe Brutus for setting you up but more than that, I want to be the one who revenges Calclus and Ferox, and I want that woman close up when I do it, she needs peace in her life."

"That won't happen if Atrox kills Brutus."

Robaratus tilted his head to one side. "I think when the beggar hears Atrox's' story she will respect his right if he chooses it. She understands our honour."

They had almost reached his parent's home, when Robaratus stopped and sniffed, tilting his head up and turning around until he followed his nose to his wife. She looked at him alarmed. "You need a bath." He teased. "I think you could go to the baths while I visit my parents."

Sage grinned. "You don't smell so good yourself." She pointed out. "But a bath sounds like heaven to me." She admitted, so Robaratus diverted the journey by a few yards until they came to the Bath House. He entered with her taking her to the caldarium first. He introduced her to a slave woman, who greeted Sage with a warm smile. "This way mistress" She said. Robaratus leaned down and kissed his wife's cheek. I will come for you in a while he said quietly into her ear. "After my own bath" Then he was gone. Sage undressed and the slave wrapped her tunic up. "I need that." She exclaimed.

"Your husband has arranged for you to have some new things." The slave advised, "which includes removal of body hair."

Sage's jaw dropped, as a slave this was not done, not even as the wife of a gladiator, so she guessed it had cost Robaratus a small fortune.

"When did he arrange for me to have new things?" She asked. The slave girl smiled. "He did this some days back mistress, I thought he had forgot." *Something else he thought of without asking me!* Naked she stepped into the round bath, feeling the hot water seep into her aching joints, she sighed as she relaxed. The slave left the room, stepped outside and waved at Robaratus, who returned the wave and headed home.

Chapter 17

Robaratus arrived later in the day, he walked into the drying room and stopped at the sight of Sage, now dressed in a new tunic of light blue and matching shawl. She still wore the wooden sculponia sandals to save her feet from being burnt on the hot floors, but her hair shone from the oils in it and when she embraced him, she smelt of delicate perfume, which caused him to groan softly. Robaratus had himself benefited from the baths, also in a tunic of deeper blue, his face clean shaven, his tattoos more vivid, the swirling pattern that covered his eye, the snake that wrapped about his upper arm, Sage drank him in along with the aroma of oils, rosemary and lavender. He placed his hand against the lower part of her back and guided her out of the baths.

"Why does Julius Brutus hate you so much?"

"What brings this topic up again?"

"I was just curious. I mean he wouldn't care how many gladiators he lost when you became Optio, so what did you do to make him hate you?" Sage pondered.

"Apart from killing his trainer you mean?" Robaratus smiled, as he looked at the city.

"I was the youngest Optio. Jealousy is a powerful emotion."

Sage thought about that, indeed Decimus had been a jealous man when it came to business, and she knew from April that senators were always fighting each other over power, so she supposed it likely filtered into all aspects of life, add to that being expected to put on a show for some previously unknown soldier, who had made Optio at a young age, then there lay the recipe for a begrudging dislike.

They arrived at the Inn which was becoming crowded, already drunks were tottering around the monuments of the dead on the opposite side of the road. A group of young men hailed Robaratus cheerfully. "My sister is in love with you gladiator." One of the men shouted, his friends laughed. Some young women emerging from a late visit to a family member in the mausoleums, upon seeing Robaratus, ran over to him. "You really are as tall and handsome as they say." One of the women observed. They were pawing at him, wanting to feel his skin, his scars his tattoos. Sage tried to slip from his hold around her waist, but he refused to let her go. The other women were trying to push her away, but again Robaratus

130

hung onto her. "Give us space." He shouted, making the women stop in their tracks, then it was the gladiator who pushed his way past them, making ample way for Sage to walk beside him.

"Who is she?" asked one woman. Robaratus looked down at Sage and winked at her, she smiled back at him, taking a deep breath. "I am his wife." She presumed this was supposed to make her feel good, but it didn't, she trembled.

"Oh I have heard about her, the slave you were forced to marry, right? Why do you bother with her Robaratus? She is nothing to you."

Sage could feel him stiffen, he was annoyed, closer to angry, yet it seemed he'd never learn he was stuck with her as his *slave* wife, the reminder that he broke the rules his Empress Mistress set him. "Slave, Matron, Princess, Queen. I care nothing for the title, I care about the woman and the woman is my wife, so get used to it." He grinned at them and pushed himself and Sage by, entering the Inn where he steered them to the bar and ordered a meal. Glires was served a short time later, with a warning from Robaratus to be aware of possible mouse bones.

"Sage, you cannot spend the rest of our marriage hating the reason for which we were married. It's true that when I look at you I see a reminder, not that you are an inconvenience. I see the reminder of just how lucky I am to have a sage for a wife, with all the knowledge and wisdom of healing but who unfortunately faints at the sight of blood." His mouth twitched, as Sage suddenly choked on her glires, then he was giggling and laughing loudly. When he calmed down, he continued. "People are always going to play on the circumstances for our marriage, you have to rise above it. What we are shouldn't be the reason for our marriage, but *who* we are is what counts." He reached over the table and stroked her hand. She knew he was right, but she hated the way in which people always spoke so lowly about her, when he was of the same station.

*   *   *

The room he had booked was sufficient for a short stay. It had a bed big enough for them to sleep in, a wooden floor with a woven mat, plastered walls of deep red and a wooden ceiling. They were situated at the back of the Inn so less noise from the patrons below. Sage sat on the bed, no privacy here for undressing. Robaratus was already naked before he realised there was a problem. He climbed onto the bed behind Sage. Rubbing her shoulders, then tracing his lips over them, pushing her long

131

hair to one side to access her neck, which still wafted the scent of the perfume from the baths. He said nothing to her, keeping his attention focused on her responses. She was doing her best to relax, he could see that, so he kept working on her, gently trailing his fingers down her arms, followed by his kisses, lips tender upon her goose bumped skin.

"You taste so good Sage, but a dash more salt just here would improve things. You seem a little unflavoured."

She felt his smirk against her skin.

"Oh dear, you think me not sweet enough?"

"Well only just here." He picked out the point on her collar bone. She turned to face him.

Seeing for the first time he was naked, she kept her eyes above his waist line, less she blush deeper than a strawberry. He bent down and kissed her lips softly, his arm slipping about her waist. Sage wriggled to face him, wrapping her own arms around his neck, clutching at his jata locs, their kiss deepened as she ran her hands over his chest, a smooth and taught chest, which bore patterns over one side in tattoos. His face was also smooth and soft, which made her lean into him more and more. Her tongue tentatively traced his lips as they pulled away. She moved over his chin, tracing her tongue along his jaw. "Nice" She muttered as she slipped down his neck, feeling how his grip on her waist and back flexed with each sensitive sensation. She kissed his shoulder, and worked down to his chest, flicking her tongue over his taught nipples, loving his deep rumbled groan. "Sage" She bit him.

"Ow."

She kissed him better.

"The pain is here now." He touched his heart; she moved to the spot and kissed him softly. "Here." He said watching her obey. He closed his eyes and revelled in the evocative sensations she brought out in him, like a hundred women had not done this to him before, and it'd meant nothing, he'd felt nothing, yet now he ached for more of the feeling, he lay back allowing her emotions and touch to seep into his soul, to own him. Instinctively he pulled up her tunic dress, she didn't shrink away, but continued her exploration of his upper torso, he held back as long as he could before he pulled her up to his lips and kissed her deeply, flipping her over. He nipped at her neck making her squeak in response, his hands careful not to rush what his mind and body urged him to do, his fingers crept along her skin, making her arch her back yielding to him, wanting him, and when he touched her, how she gasped and groaned, fingers gripping his jata locs, raking over his back. Robaratus had seen this response all his adult life but now, he was feeling it, waves of heat that

132

engulfed him as he felt her every desire, he burned for her, as his fingers explored her, aroused her, he was lost in the emotion, drowning in the sensations he had never known before. He moved up her body until he faced her, her face flushed, eyes hooded. "Sage I want more." She could only nod. "It will hurt for a moment, you will bleed. Promise me you won't faint."

Sage burst out laughing. "I won't look." And then it was over. She had hardly finished her answer, and he had taken her, made her his. She gasped; eyes wide with surprise. He smiled at her and returned to his administrations, quickly distracting her from any questions that would kill this moment, a moment he wanted to last a lifetime, a moment he knew he wanted over and over, Sage. He showed her pleasure, brought her to exquisite climax, he kissed her over and over until he could not put off his own desires any longer, he moved atop her and asked, "do you want me?" Her answer was a gasp of yes. He took his time, as much torturing himself as her, but when he did finally take her they both gasped, he had to stay his movements, his head buried down to her neck as he breathed deeply, then slowly he showed her everything he could be, everything he wanted to be. *It is who he is, it is all that is left of the man I loved. You have his heart Sage; you just don't know it.* She knew it now. She knew it with every fibre of her being, he loved her, *was* loving her, and she knew it instinctively that this was the first time he had ever felt love, or given it.

*   *   *

It was chilly in the early dawn. Sage stood by the monument of the gladiators, Robaratus not far away hidden from view. As the sun touched the tallest monuments, the beggar woman arrived. She stopped dead when she saw Sage, wrapped in a new shawl, her hair shining from the oils. "What brings you here again? Did you forget you are a stain on this place?" She eyed Sage up and down, then moved past her to place her simple posy of wild flowers.

"No. I came to thank you. I realised what I had to do. I understand him now, because of you."

The beggar placed her steady gaze upon Sage, her rheumy eyes spilled old tears she nodded. "Am glad to know it."

"I owe you gratitude too." Robaratus stepped out from his hiding place. The beggar woman glared at them both. "What is this?" She snarled, stepping backwards. Robaratus dropped to his knees before her, lowering his head. Sage watched in undisguised surprise.

"I beseech you Sabia to take what is rightly yours to take, or allow me to take for you the one who is truly at fault."

Sage gasped; he hadn't mentioned this. The beggar apparently known to Robaratus, stepped back in horror. She looked down at the offering, Robaratus the most famous gladiator, was offering his life in honour of the brother and promised she had lost, in his name. "Nay." She said reaching forward and touching his head with trembling fingertips. "Nay. I'll not take from your wife what was taken from me, stand and be unburdened of that guilt." Robaratus did as bid, still with his head lowered. "And of the one who is truly at fault?" He lifted his head now, his eyes burned with hatred and anger.

"Aye that I would like to watch." Sabia said firmly, nodding.

"How do you know her?" Sage asked.

"Sabia and I were from different worlds but we grew up here. I knew she was fond of me, see she still is, she blushes beautifully."

The woman was a little pink in the cheeks, her eyes wide at his acknowledgment of her. Robaratus stepped forward and engulfed her in his arms, pulling her into him, holding her tight. Sage felt the emotion between them as though it were she he was embracing. She stepped back to allow them the moment. "What have I done? What have I done?" Robaratus repeated over and over as the beggar sobbed years of grief into his tunic. They remained like that for some long time, and Sage felt it was likely the only time Robaratus had hugged anyone with genuine emotion. "There is something I must tell you." Sabia said as she pulled away from him. "All them years ago, when you fell from grace, you was set up."

Robaratus looked down at her, his face set in a serious expression. "How do you know it?"

"I can't say as I can prove it, but the wealthy uns, they don't see slaves, but slaves hear all." She pointed to Sage. "She knows wot I mean, don't ya?" Sage nodded.

"One of me old friends works at the baths, she heard the wife bragging about the way they had cheated you. It's cos you was cocky, and rising so fast, her husband feared for his position, so they devised that he would catch you an er together."

"If you cannot prove it, what do you think my knowing about it will do?" Robaratus asked, annoyance in his tone.

"I dunno, but you should keep it in mind."

He shrugged, he'd often wondered at the timing himself, he had never been caught before, and the whole situation had stunk to his way of thinking, now he had another who had thought the same way, and frustratingly he could not do a thing about it.

He promised Sabia he would let her know when it was her time for retribution, then he and Sage left returning to the Inn. He had spoken about these plans, to give Atrox the opportunity to fight himself or Brutus, to beat Brutus himself if possible, yet now he was at the point when he would call Atrox to the arena to make his choice, Sage suddenly felt the reality of it all, the man she had just accepted as her husband in name and soul, was about to put his life on the line for the first step towards their future, and now it scared her to death. "Robaratus. I am scared."

Robaratus pulled her close to him resting his head on hers. "Every time I go into the arena, I am terrified I will die. I am terrified I will have to kill my opponent; many just don't deserve to die killing them is cold blooded murder. Now I have you I have a reason to live, to fight with more enthusiasm than I ever have. Sabia doesn't know *everything* about gladiators." He crooned. Sage pulled back astonished. "You never seem afraid."

He laughed softly. "The louder I roar the more fear I am venting."

"Won't I be a distraction?"

"Never. Motivation." He answered. "Shall we go and talk to Atrox?"

She didn't want to, she had cold terror running in her veins. She clung to her husband tightly. "I am terrified I will lose you, just when we have found each other." She whispered. Robaratus understood her completely, he felt the same way; it would be a cruel trick of the Gods if he were to be killed now. He hugged her tightly then let her go, taking her hand he led the way back to the arena.

In his absence the men were sparring, clashing heavy wooden swords against each other, smashing huge shields together pushing against each other to gain the better ground. Atrox sat on the benches watching with a bored expression on his face, on seeing Robaratus arrive he developed a sneer which grew deeper at the sight of Sage.

"Gladiator why are you not training?" Robaratus demanded, Atrox spat on the ground. Robaratus nodded. "It is time Atrox." The gladiator rose slowly and stood motionless, his eyes squinting as though assessing what that meant. "You wish to die in front of your wife?" he asked.

"I am offering you a choice. Julius Brutus made you mad with his idea of training. It is your right to have retribution against him. Would you choose to fight him or me?"

Everyone stopped what they were doing, to gather round this tense confrontation.

"You killed our trainer and you take his place, change the way we train, have always trained, and you think I want to kill Brutus?" The big dark-skinned man spat on the ground again, staring Robaratus straight in the eye. "I'd say the choice is obvious, old one."

Robaratus nodded. "It is dixi. We will meet here at dawn, you and me only. The rest of you can watch, but whomever wins, wins. Do we understand this?"

The gladiators stayed silent, they did not like what was happening. They had all come to accept Robaratus, a strict man but one who played fair, who had taught them honour and respect. He had improved their diet, their training methods, sleeping cells and medical assistance, he had earned their loyalty. Not one of them wanted to see Atrox win, but Robaratus would find them out if they cheated, and he'd never accept a cheat in his name, so as uncomfortable as it was they had no other choice but to accept the conditions and result. They mumbled their agreement. Robaratus accepted it knowing how they must feel. He nodded to Sage and then he left, wrapping his arm about her as she joined him.

"You know Brutus won't allow it." Sage said as the gate shut behind them.

"Oh he'll allow it, because he will be there." Robaratus grinned.

"Who's going to tell him?"

"I imagine they all will including Atrox." He chuckled.

"Why do I get the feeling you set that up?" Her answer was his continued chuckling. They ate at the Inn, enjoying fresh fish and salad, when a stranger approached them. Robaratus stopped eating and watched the man. "Is it true?" he asked.

Robaratus raised his eye brows questioningly.

"You fighting Atrox?" The man said.

"Well that has to be a record!" Robaratus laughed. "It is a private affair." He added. The man sloped away and soon the whole Inn was afire with the gossip, as people looked in their direction and nodded heads at Robaratus.

"Time to keep a low profile." He growled.

"Where in this city can you possibly keep a low profile?" Sage asked, quirking her own eyebrows at him. He grinned. She rolled her eyes, then smirking they slunk up the stairs to their room.

*   *   *

Robaratus traced kisses down her back, setting her skin afire with passion, his fingers traced lines as he indulged himself in learning every small fibre of her being. Sage stayed silent as she let him cover her line by line and kiss by kiss. Eventually she turned over and found herself looking

136

straight into his eyes, dark and filled with desire. His eyes drank in her freckles, her long lashes, her soft tanned skin, her smooth body ignited passion in him he'd never known. Not for the first time did he wonder why, why was she so very different from any other woman he had known. What was it about her, slight and fragile as she was that had won his heart, broken down all his resilience and given him a reason to hope, to want to live and to know what it was to be free again. "What are you thinking?" He rumbled to her.

"I am thinking how lucky I am to be the one who truly knows you." She smiled at him, as he planted a kiss on her nose. "Will you marry me?" He asked. Sage laughed. "We are already married silly."

"Our marriage was made on false grounds. I am asking you to be my wife because you want to be." He looked serious. *Because I want to be not because I love you.* Sage pulled away, her hurt showing before she could hide it, instantly his grip was on her arm. "What?"

"You never speak of." She couldn't say it, it felt childish.

"Sage. You know I am not good at this romance stuff, help me here if I am doing it wrong."

"I can't, I feel silly." She tried to turn away but he pulled her to him.

"What am I not speaking of?"

"I feel silly. You are so much more experienced than me, so it feels childish to speak of such things." Sage blushed. Robaratus frowned, he was lost.

"It's the flirting thing. When you flirted with other women what words did you use?"

Robaratus turned onto his back. "You *really* want to know what I said to other women? They were words Sage."

"Well did you ever mention anything about loving them?" She looked up into his puzzled expression.

"Why in Hades would I? I've never been in love Sage."

She pulled away from him, horror in her expression.

"Oh Shit." He realised too late his mistake, Sage was scrambling off the bed, tears in her eyes. Robaratus bounded off the bed himself catching her at the door, wrapping her to him, pressing her against the wall. "I am sorry." He breathed heavily, kissing her forehead. "I didn't mean to include you in that statement." The hurt in her eyes when she looked up at him near crippled his heart. "What man asks a woman to marry him without love?" He asked, looking into her eyes.

"All of them. That's why they have affairs. I don't want a man like that." She wriggled in his hold.

"Listen to me Sage. I have uttered meaningless words all my life to get what I want from a woman. If I said those words to you, I'd feel cheap,

I'd be lying to you, that's how it'd feel. I know you cannot understand that part of me, but I try." He lowered his head. "Gods but I try to *show* you what you mean to me. I honestly have no idea what love is, but if it is wanting to protect you, then I love you. If it is wanting to wake up beside you every day, then I love you. If it is watching you smile, hearing your laugh, seeing your expressions, holding you tight, then I love you. If it is being terrified of losing you because I was foolish or I didn't understand, then I am guilty a hundred times over of loving you. I ask myself a million times a day how did I get you, because I'm damn certain I don't deserve you, but would I betray you? Would I want another woman even for a moment, never Sage. I will never want anyone because all I want is you, all that I am is you, all that I can love is you." He sucked in a deep breath, swallowed hard and looked back into her eyes. She had no ability to speak, so she cupped his face in her hands, his vulnerable begging face and she kissed him, long and deep, her tongue tracing his lips, her fingers scrunching his locs. His arms held her tightly, his breathing ragged, when he pulled away, he looked at her. "Will you marry me Sage? I want you to be my wife because I love you"

"I will marry you because I love you." She replied. The kiss he planted on her lips was fierce and demanding, as was the stiffness in his groin, he picked her up and instinctively she wrapped her legs about him. He supported her with his powerful arms and watched her arch her back and moan with the pleasure of accepting him.

*   *   *

It was a chilly dawn, one that made Sage want to rub her arms to get some heat, but Robaratus provided that the moment he slipped an arm around her waist. "Do you have your smelling herbs?" He asked smirking. Sage gave him an unappreciative look. "Yes I have them."
They walked towards the arena, Sage hating every step, it felt for all the world like she was walking to her own death. *Is this how it feels for gladiators?* She wondered. *One step closer to my last breath.* Robaratus seemed unaffected by the mood. Though his expression was grim and his eyes fixed, she wondered if he was preparing himself for this fight. Atrox was almost as good as Robaratus, which was why he had chosen the man to be his executioner, because he was also over ambitious and he had not learned to stay that exuberance and turn it into tactics. She had to believe in Robaratus, had to believe he knew what he was doing, yet she still doubted,

still felt fear. "I will win." He said as though he'd read her mind. "I won't make it easy; he has to believe he is the better fighter."

Which translated in Sage's mind to a bloody fight, hence all her strong-smelling herbs, to prevent her from fainting. At the gate to the city the guards stood to attention, none spoke but most nodded to the couple. Robaratus smiled. "They know this is a private affair yet still they turn out." He mused, and the people had, all lining the way to the arena, all silent as they watched the greatest gladiator of the times walk past them. Sage had a million questions racing through her mind, not a one could she voice in such deadly silence, so she walked with her husband, a proud wife, head high. The gate opened as soon as they arrived and if outside had been impressive, inside was like a grave, empty and dead. Not a single gladiator in sight. "I don't like this." Sage whispered. Robaratus said nothing but his eyes were wary. The arena was cleared of training apparatus and the sand had been newly laid. Sage stood close to her husband as the tension stretched within the training grounds, then from one of the side entrances Atrox appeared. He strode into the arena wearing a leather tunic, large shield and sword, his head bare, helmet under his arm. He looked menacing with his shaven head and scars, his face sullen. Once onto the sand he stood facing Robaratus. "I half wondered if you might not show." He greeted, but again Robaratus made no response, his mind was wondering where all the other gladiators were, he needed witnesses for this. He removed his tunic revealing his bare chest, covered only by his shorts. His golden helmet sat on the bench waiting for him.

"Where are they all? Where is Brutus?" Sage whispered to him, her answer a shrug of the shoulders. Robaratus was wondering if he had read his men wrong, and that this would be the day he would die by mass murder. He looked up to the heavens and gave a short prayer to Mars, God of gladiators, then he turned and kissed his wife, who stifled sobs against his lips.

"Arh how touching." Came a sarcastic voice.

"At last Brutus at least is here." Robaratus whispered to Sage, relief evident in his tone. He turned slowly to face the owner.

"Explain what is going on here." Brutus demanded.

"Atrox has a desire to kill me, I don't wish to disappoint him, so I am giving him the opportunity."

"I see. And you think you do not need to ask my permission for this?" Brutus was keeping his temper in check, but he looked about ready to explode. Robaratus shrugged. "In sooth, I knew you'd be here."

"Lucky for you my men are loyal to me then." Brutus looked smug, and Atrox grinned for the first time. "If you intend to fight my best gladiator, then I am not about to make it a private affair. I have a notion the whole of Firenze should witness your death Robaratus." He waved his arm regally and the gates opened allowing a flood of humanity to pour in. *So that is why they were all waiting outside.* Sage felt betrayed by the people of the city. *They have all come to see my husband die.*

Robaratus looked about him as the steps were filled with enthusiastic men from the city, not what he had expected at all. *This could work in our favour so many witnesses, none can blame me for bribing every citizen of Firenze to speak in my favour. Brutus cannot lie about this fight.* He thought as he turned to Sage and winked at her. He picked up his golden helmet and faced the crowd opposite him letting out a huge deafening roar. He strode into the arena arms above his head, and he roared as he turned in a circle encouraging the crowd to roar back, which they did. Brutus walked towards him into the arena, and waited for Robaratus to stop his bear display.

"Citizens." He began, but was stopped by a shout and roar of other voices. Everyone looked puzzled as all the gladiators ran into the arena, weapons held high, and to the horror of everyone present, they all descended upon Brutus. Robaratus stood stunned, but he backed away all the same, distancing himself from the onslaught, he found Sage and buried her head into his chest, as blood fountained out of the middle of the crowd of angry vengeful gladiators. Atrox just stood unable to comprehend the scene before him, too stunned to move as larger spurts of blood covered his face and torso. The crowd cheered and raged along with the gladiators and then it was over. What emerged as the gladiators stepped away was a bloodied corpse, so many knife cuts had left hardly an ounce of flesh on it. Brutus' eyes stared in frozen horror, blood seeped into the sand and the smell of it filled the arena, enough for Sage to grab her herbs in between sobs of terror. The last person to stand was a ragged beggar woman holding a short blade that had once been owned by a gladiator. She was covered in blood, and her eyes were pure madness. Robaratus looked at her in horror, though he knew why, he still couldn't accept that the woman he had once known would do this. She stood and looked at him square on, her back straight; her eyes softer. "You think I'd let one such as you do for me? Twas my duty Rob. Now I can die in peace, they can rest in peace, we all have peace." She looked over her shoulder at the corpse that was Julius Brutus. Robaratus nodded to her, he understood, his men understood and they were *his* men now.

"What about Atrox?" Sage asked making sure she only made eye contact with her husband.

"He has disappeared. Perhaps he fears he would be next." Robaratus said looking around the arena for the other gladiator.

Chapter 18

The council chambers were an elaborately large building in the middle of the city. Large columns stood sentinel at the massive front entrance. Inside was a huge hall with a tall ceiling, several stone statues of various gods stood watching over the citizens of Firenze, and a few busts of previous Emperors were positioned between them. The paintings on the walls depicted the history of Rome. Robaratus entered the building and headed for the ornate marble stairs that took him to an upper floor, where again statues stood. He chanced a glance over the stone balustrade at the hall below, still filled with the busy passage of everyday business. He knocked at the door opposite him and entered when called. The room was large, and well-lit from open windows. The floor a mosaic of red tesserae tiles depicted various scenes of city life in separate rectangles, surrounded by a twisted rope pattern. In front of him was placed a long table behind which sat six senators of the council.

"Robaratus Ectorius, you understand why you have been summoned here?" The man at the end of the table asked.

"I do."

"Were you in any way involved in yesterday's assignation?" The same man asked.

"I was not."

"Explain what happened." The man opposite him said.

Robaratus took a deep breath. "I had spoken to Atrox the day before. He had become a liability, so I had offered him a fight, his life or mine."

"Did you clear that with Julius Brutus?"

"No."

"Why not?"

"Julius Brutus would've denied me."

"So you decided to go ahead without his permission?" Another senator asked.

"Yes."

"I don't recall that being part of your remit from Rome."

"It isn't."

"So what right do you think you had?"

Robaratus, sighed. "Atrox was damaged. He was and is mad, he had become a liability to the rest of the gladiators always undermining my

141

authority. I had to make a choice."

"Julius Brutus was still his owner; you had no authority to make that choice."

"I accept that, but I also knew Brutus would be there. Atrox would've told him, so I expected to see him. He was there, and to my surprise he said that a fight against me and his best fighter should not be a private affair, that the whole city should witness it, and he opened the gates."

"And why would that surprise you?"

"I thought he would've prevented it."

"Is that what you were secretly hoping for?"

Robaratus shrugged, he had not hoped for anything like it, he'd wanted the fight to get rid of Atrox, but he could hardly say so here.

"My intention was to give Atrox a good fight, in private, and win it, showing him he is not yet ready to take me on. Brutus changed the plan by inviting the city to witness."

"Arh but you just told us you had offered Atrox a fight to the death, your life or his. Was that a lie?"

"No. I was giving him a challenge. He had to believe it was a death fight or he wouldn't have accepted."

The men nodded. "So what happened when you arrived at the arena?"

"I thought it strange that the city had turned out so early to watch me walk to the arena. When I entered the gate, the place was empty. I had no idea what was going on, but the only people there were myself and my wife. After some time Atrox stepped out of the waiting area, He seemed oblivious to the fact we were alone. I had got to the stage where I thought I had misjudged the gladiators and that they would be waiting to kill me, but just as I got ready to start fighting, Brutus showed himself. He said that a fight as important as this was to be should not be kept behind closed doors, so he had the gates opened and all the people outside poured in. Only then did I get what they were doing there." He paused waiting for any questions, when none came he continued. "Brutus was about to give a speech but he'd hardly opened his mouth before all hades broke loose and gladiators poured into the arena and attacked him. I was stunned. I couldn't believe what I was seeing."

"You made no attempt to stop it?"

"There was no time. It was over so fast."

"Wherever you go trouble isn't far behind is it?"

Robaratus had no answer to that.

"We have spoken to many who were there, all of whom appear to back your story up. We don't think you were behind this, however given how Brutus trained gladiators it has been common knowledge you and he disagreed, you can see how things must look now? With so many witnesses to the event it is clear you were not party to the intentions of your gladiators, which reflects badly upon you. However, a report to Rome will be required and I have no doubt you will be recalled to give your version of events. I have no notion what Rome will do or say, but if you have the chance to return here, the training post will remain open for you."

Robaratus kept his face impartial, though he hadn't expected such generosity, truly Brutus must have been deeply disliked by more than just gladiators.

"Just one more thing Ectorius. Do you know where Atrox might be?"

Robaratus shook his head. I searched for him yesterday but found no clues as to where he ran to."

"Interesting. The gate guards swear he hasn't left the city." The man at the end of the table said, rubbing his chin.

"That means nothing, no one was looking for an escapee he could've left in a wagon." One of the other men pointed out.

"You may go."

*   *   *

The whole city had been alive with the gossip of what happened to Julius Brutus, very few seemed to be upset by it, and Robaratus hailed a hero for all he had no part in it. On a morning a week on he urged Sage to wear her best toga that they were going to the Temple of Mars to give thanks to the God, for his safe keeping of Robaratus during the murder of Julius Brutus. The Temple was a huge building of red columns with golden tops, and a giant statue of Mars on the roof in gold carrying a golden spear. Inside the Temple was dark, made darker by the deep red painted walls, marble pillars that supported an upper balcony had white sheets that hung from column to column. Fire sconces burned high up on hanging ceiling chains and groups of candles burned on the floor, which was a richly decorated marble affair. At the far end stood an enormous golden statue of Mars in the same attire as on the outside roof. Sage was awe struck as she and Robaratus walked towards the giant statue. A priest greeted them. "This is an unusual request." He commented. Sage looked bewildered.

"We were forced to marry by the Empress Aquilina. I understand I am legally allowed to remarry my wife of my own choice." Robaratus said in his deep bear like voice. The Priest nodded. "As I said unusual, but

143

perfectly legal."

"What is required for this marriage?" Robaratus asked, to which the Priest shook his head. "Only the signing of a contract. Did you have a contract last time?"

Robaratus shook his head. The Priest let out a long breath. "It wasn't legal then."

Sage stared in shock at the priest. All this time they had believed themselves married, and yet apparently they were not.

"Then we will make it legal." He said looking to Sage, who nodded carefully. Robaratus was the dominant person here, and normally a woman had no say in her own life, but Robaratus was a different kind of man she had come to learn, even so, in front of authoritative men, she was careful not to appear as an equal. They stood before the Priest, spoke the words they had spoken almost a year before, and this time when he invited them to kiss, Robaratus smiled and made no hesitation in sealing his marriage vows. The priest smiled, and presented them with a contract to sign.

"So we weren't really married." Sage said as they left.

"We were married, it just wasn't legally binding."

"Is that why you wanted to marry me again, to make it so?"

Robaratus smirked. "Partly, and partly because I want you know a contract is harder to break. Sage Ectorius, I own you!"

Sage watched his face as they left, his huge smug grin never leaving it, made her smile up at him.

*   *   *

The command to return to Rome arrived a few days later. Sage and Robaratus set off for the capital. If Robaratus had any misgivings, he didn't let them show, but Sage was a pent-up bag of nerves as to how things might be once they returned. The weather seemed to empathise with the mood, dark clouds often accompanied them with sporadic showers. Sage had to travel under the cover of the arcera in light showers, and when it poured Robaratus sought shelter, so that the horses might avoid too much of the rain and he would wait inside the wagon, in doing this, the journey back was a slow one. Once they joined the Appian way, the traffic became much heavier, Sage sat beside her husband in a rare show of sunshine, leaning her head on his shoulder, her heart getting heavier with each step the horses took. "What is wrong?" He asked quietly, she sighed heavily. "I fear what we face. I had thought coming back here would be a welcome thing, to see my friend, to see Rome again, but all I have is a sense of foreboding."

"Then I think I am about to make it better for you." He said softly smiling. Sage looked up at him with a curious expression.

"I have decided that I will ask the Emperor for my freedom. It is time for me to retire from killing. I want to return to Firenze and train the gladiators there, but as a plebeian because then I can join the council."

Sage squeezed his arm. "Won't that mean fighting for your life?"

"No. I have won many battles more than earned my freedom, so I see it as no problem." He planted a kiss upon her head.

"So why do I think there is a "but", in that?"

He laughed. "I have no idea. The Emperor owns me, his wife has used me, but I am still entitled to ask for my freedom." He paused for a moment. "I suppose the "but" side of it would mean we won't be living in Rome." Sage smiled. "I think I can live with that. I have at least one good friend in Firenze."

The tombs started to appear; huge monuments of extravagance dedicated to the dead. Sage stared in awe about her, just as she had the day she'd left. This time Robaratus slowed the horses to a walk, so that she could admire the huge buildings as they passed. "These are not the best examples." He told her. "You see that round tomb up ahead?"

She nodded. "It is thirty-six feet high." He smiled at her wide-eyed look. They continued at the slow and gentle pace, Sage gawping at the many shapes and sizes of tomb, some with columns some like towers, some with huge gods adorning the roofs. The smoke from the city's chimneys rose like a huge grey blanket, carrying the distant aroma of burning and food. As the breeze blew so became clear the vast aqueducts that fed the city with water, and even with the many big tombs blocking out the views, the villas on the hillsides could still be spotted, here and there. The sight of the greatest city of all, was indeed breath-taking and magnificent, yet Sage had no happiness in her heart at returning here, to the only home she had ever known, a home which had left her broken, married and unwanted.

"First things first, we need to find a place to stay." Robaratus said, breaking into her thoughts.

"We could go to our old home." Sage suggested, though it was not a place she wanted to be in, but it was theirs according to Aquilina.

"I think you would not be happy returning there." He said plainly. "I wish us to have our own place not a given dwelling from a spiteful Empress." He drove the arcera down many streets looking for property to rent, most came with shop space at street level, but eventually he found a dwelling which was spacious and affordable. It had a bed and table to eat at, cooking facilities, just enough to see them through, until things were sorted. Sage was glad to be in one place at last, she flopped down on the bed. "I could go a long soak in the baths now, just to wash the dust and weariness off me." Sage announced. Robaratus thought it a good idea, but first they needed to rest, at least he did. He joined her on the bed and pulled her into his arms, long muscular arms, arms that protected her, warmed her, and loved her. He kissed her hair, inhaling the soft scent of lemons, his arousal instant, and his emotions on fire. "Why do you affect me so?" He murmured into her hair. Sage wriggled round to face him, looking up into his green eyes, gone dark and sexual. "I am probably the longest relationship with a woman you have ever had." She smiled. "The longer you stay with me, the more I seem to affect you." She traced a finger down his tunic chest, blowing softly on the fabric. His growl was deep, a noise that Sage had come to love about him. She leaned on his chest and kissed him, it was meant to be tender but his need told her differently, and he made the kiss deeper, nipping her lip and tasting her flesh. He pulled her tunic dress up so she lay beside him naked, her whole-body aching for his touch. He traced his lips down her, planting soft kisses, and tasting her skin, he nipped her flesh making her sigh or wriggle, his fingers strong and expert as he explored her. He tasted her most intimate parts, making her moan with yearning. Words may not have been his way but he made up for it with his knowledge, that she was certain he never showed to anyone but her. Once he was on top of her, her hands ran over his back making him press against her, longing to be a greater part of her, he loved her with tenderness until she begged for release, and his own beast warred to be assertive. Robaratus roared, his passion so great his inner beast so protective of the woman he knew he loved down to his soul. "If this is love, then I am a man fulfilled." He whispered to her, as he held her so close, wrapping his body around her.

"If this is love, then I have found heaven." She whispered back, and his arms closed tighter, as his lips found the back of her ear, the line of her neck.

A loud banging on the door woke them up. Robaratus threw on his tunic, leaving Sage to get dressed. He opened the door and found soldiers pushing their way inside. "What is going on?" Robaratus ordered. Sage had made it to the top of the stairs.

"You are under arrest Robaratus Ectorius." One of the soldiers informed him.

"For what? I only just got here."

"The murder of Julius Brutus."

Robaratus was roughly turned around and had his hands bound. He looked up at Sage who stood with her hand over her mouth, eyes wide with horror. Robaratus made no effort to fight back or to argue, he had no argument with soldiers who were just doing their job they would not be the ones who would answer his questions. He was marched forcibly from their home. Some people stared at him as he passed by, but most ignored the procession. He was flung into a holding cell, which had no window, and stunk of piss and vomit, blood and shit. Chained to another prisoner and left in the dark, Robaratus had no notion of how long he would spend there.

"How the mighty fall." Grumbled the man he was chained to. "Guess you can't roar your way out of this then."

Robaratus remained silent, turning his thoughts to Sage, he focused only on his love for her, his fear as to what she was doing now.

"What crime did you commit this time that puts you here?" His companion asked, still met with silence. The man gave up trying to talk to his famous companion. Robaratus sat on the floor, yanking on the chain and pulling the man almost to the floor with him. "If you wanna sit in shit, that's yer choice, but I'm standing." The man complained. Robaratus was considering his situation, he had been recalled to Rome that had come from the Emperor, being chained in a cell had to have come from Aquilina, which meant she was not happy he was back, so something was going on he had no idea about and she had no intention of him finding out. It came as a shock that he'd hardly arrived and he'd been arrested, which meant she'd been waiting for him. He had considered this possibility at some point, and somehow forgotten about it. Time passed slowly when locked underground in darkness, with only the sound of water trickling by your ear, and other prisoners moaning, sobbing or shouting out. Guards came for people and new people arrived, but nobody came for Robaratus, all he could do was to sit and wait, and it would be a long wait if Aquilina was anything to do with it.

Eventually guards did come for him, and Robaratus was dragged significantly weakened into a bright day, making him close his eyes on instinct. He stank which he hated. Soft hands touched him, and he dared to squint open his eyes enough to see Sage crying as she ran alongside him. "The Emperor had no idea where you were, you are being taken to him now." She was back handed by a guard. "You were told not to tell him." The man snapped. Robaratus roared weakly, his voice hardly audible from his dry throat, he tried to pull away, but he was weak, his legs buckled. They dragged him along, Sage no longer following, she'd delivered her message he knew where he was going. He closed his eyes and allowed himself to be dragged along, memories of this treatment fresh in his mind.

When he had first been found out by his Centurion, he had been stuck in a hole in the ground for a week, half starved. He knew how cruel treatment of prisoners could be, back then he had no care if he lived or died, but now he had Sage, and death was not an experience he wanted when he loved her so much it hurt.

"Gods Robaratus, you stink." The Emperor stated, holding a cloth to his face. "Get this man some water."

Robaratus drank, the cold freshness chilled to his stomach.

"What in Hades were you doing in a cell?"

"I believe that might have been on your wife's orders." Robaratus croaked. The Emperor stared at his most famous gladiator, no one else would have been allowed to suggest his wife behave improperly, but where Robaratus was concerned, she was capable of just about anything, so he let the accusation go. "Your wife is quite sweet. Little Sage. She told me what had happened to you, clever girl that."

The warmth in Robaratus' heart was enough remedy for his worried soul, and he managed a smile, though it seemed the Emperor still viewed her as a child, which Robaratus thought odd, given how the man prided himself on knowing everything about everyone.

"I imagine you have been told you are being charged with murder?"

"I was."

The Emperor frowned. "Robaratus you are charged with the murder of both the previous trainer in Firenze and with the owner Julius Brutus. I cannot think you would behave in such a way, especially under the orders of my wife to train gladiators, not to kill indiscriminately. Yet, although I have spoken to the senators in Firenze, who acquit you of blame, and there are plenty of witnesses who also acquit you of blame, there is one who claims to have insider knowledge that you personally organised at least the death of Julius Brutus."

It didn't take more than a breath for Robaratus to know who that would be. "Atrox"

"I do not like the look of him, he looks more barbarian than gladiator, but I cannot so easily ignore his claims. So tell me Robaratus, why did you kill the trainer?"

"Julius Brutus insisted his gladiators be trained with hidden sharp knives and objects."

"That's cheating." The Emperor interrupted. Robaratus nodded. "It is also the reason why they don't pass the first stages of tournament here in Rome."

"Can you prove any of this?"

Robaratus lifted his dirty tunic up to reveal the scar across his stomach, and then he revealed his arm. "The trainer did this to me, which is why I killed him."

The Emperor looked at his gladiator, then nodded. "And Julius Brutus?" Robaratus sighed and then repeated his story.

"Atrox is right then. You didn't have control of the gladiators you trained." The Emperor cocked an eyebrow at Robaratus.

"I believed I had their trust. I had no idea what they were planning."

"Atrox claims you offered him a choice, to kill you or kill Brutus. Is that true?"

"I offered him a choice because Brutus had caused his madness and he had a right to have retribution."

"You had no right. You didn't even give Brutus the opportunity to accept or not."

"Because I knew Atrox wanted me more, Brutus wasn't really at risk in my view, it was really to ensure the man turned out to watch the fight and witness it."

The Emperor rubbed his chin, eyeing Robaratus over.

"Atrox claims when Brutus put in an appearance you changed your mind and had the gates opened so the people could witness the fight."

"Not true. The fight was to be private, I needed to show Atrox he wasn't ready."

The Emperor smiled. "Did you intend to kill Atrox?"

Robaratus closed his eyes, then took a deep breath. "If necessary."

"Bah Robaratus, gladiators do not *do* if necessary! You would have killed that barbarian, he is mad, *your* words." The Emperor shouted. Robaratus couldn't argue. Silence fell on the room. A long deafening silence. The Emperor got up from his large chair and ran his hand through his balding hair. "Atrox says the gladiators talked at night, of all the things you had said to them about seeking their revenge on Brutus for making them mad." He looked at Robaratus who frowned at him. "He says you told them to focus on killing Brutus when they fought in the arena." He turned his head to look at Robaratus, who shook his. "You understand this is a difficult situation for me. I cannot prove either of you right or wrong. I'd *like* to think I know you Robaratus, but I also know how you can get angry. I cannot reconcile myself to believing you capable of cold murder nor inciting it, however I have seen no evidence of madness in Atrox." The silence fell again like a suffocating blanket this time.

"I would only speak truth to you my Emperor." Robaratus said in a hopeful plea for things to fall his way.

"Your sweet wife tells me that you hope to have your freedom?"

Robaratus sighed. Sage had obviously pleaded on his behalf. "I had."

"Of course, I cannot deny that is long overdue, and the senate in Firenze have a vacancy for another councillor, and of course a Lanista for the gladiators."

Robaratus felt a twinge of hope ignite in his heart.

"I can't help but think Sage is right when she thinks you would be a good candidate for the roles. She informs me you have been instrumental in finding better ways to train men. I am impressed with her reports on your achievements."

Robaratus couldn't stop his lips from twitching a smirk, *typical Sage!* The Emperor studied him.

"It is a complete contradiction to the claims of Atrox. I don't doubt any of his accusations, they all apply to you."

Robaratus felt his heart sink.

"About five years ago." The Emperor smiled kindly. "I do believe you're a changed man, and that the life of a plebeian would suit you well, even a senator would be a deserving role."

Robaratus sighed deeply, the Emperor could have a cruel sense of humour. "My problem is my wife. She is furious with you; from her ranting it appears you have re-married your wife?"

Robaratus looked pleasantly surprised. "News travels fast." He grinned.

"Huh! Thing is Rob, she planned of relieving you of Sage once you officially returned from your time away, hence why your marriage wasn't legal."

Robaratus wasn't surprised, he had guessed Aquilina had something up her sleeve, what she hadn't considered was that he and Sage would make it work.

"I admire you for thwarting her plans, few manage to do that. Alas it comes at a high price, and I cannot deny her. You disobeyed her instructions when you caused trouble at Albus Juventus' place and you did not inform her of where you were going."

The hope died instantly.

"Then there is Atrox. He still wants to be your executioner. It is a matter of balance Robaratus." He paused to look out of his large window, seeing who knew what in his mind. Then he drew in a deep breath and let it out. "You know Rob, the times are changing. Soon gladiators will be a thing of the past. I imagine that pleases you." The Emperor turned to face his favourite gladiator. Robaratus kept his expression neutral. His Emperor studied him for a long moment. "I will be glad of the day when that arrives. It won't be me who decides it, but my successor, who will be Honorius. He is an ardent Christian believe it or not."

Robaratus still made no response, he wasn't certain why his Emperor was telling him all this, he did not know this man Honorius though he had heard of the new religion.

"People are tired of the killing. I am tired of ordering it." He sighed, suddenly looking older and more tired than Robaratus had ever seen him, he sat in his large chair behind his marble desk. "I am sixty years old Robaratus. Sixty and I want to retire." He looked at Robaratus, who looked back at him with a sadness.

"So how to please the senators here, who have listened and believe Atrox. My wife, who is ranting day and night now, making my blood pressure rise, and then Atrox, a gladiator who wants his chance to kill the most famous of Rome? What would you do?" The old man asked.

Robaratus knew what he would do, and so did his Emperor. He said nothing and the silence stretched.

"As I thought." The Emperor said sadly. "I sentence you to one more fight against Atrox. A fight to the death. It must be final. If you win, I will make you a free man." The Emperor sighed, even Robaratus could see the weight he carried on his aging shoulders; the wrinkles on his face seemed deeper with his decision. Robaratus felt sadness, Sage would cry, he had told her he only had to ask for his freedom and it would be granted. *Damn fucking Aquilina and her scheming.* He hung his head. If he lost what would happen to his Sage? Yet for him there could be no pleading for another outcome or sentence, so he nodded his acceptance.

"May Mars smile down on you." The Emperor said in a soft sad voice.

Robaratus was about to turn but realised he hadn't yet been dismissed. "Is there anything else your highness?"

The Emperor looked up. "Yes. Aquilina wants you held in prison, on half measures of food. I cannot prevent her wishes, she'll only have you arrested on some other trumped-up charge, at least in prison, you will be safe from further harm, and Sage can visit you. I suggest she does, with extra nutrients to help keep you fortified." He winked at Robaratus, who looked horrified. He would never survive without Sage, who would protect her if not him?

"It is the best I can do Rob."

Robaratus nodded, looking down to hide the tears that stung his eyes, and the murder that thumped in his heart.

"Now you're dismissed." The Emperor said softly.

Chapter 19

The cell was slightly better than the underground one he had previously occupied. This one had a slit in the brick that allowed a sliver of light to stream into the dark room. It was cold and moss grew on the walls, it still stank of all the human waste the other had suffered from, and he still shared the space, such as it was, with others. The food was a weak tasteless type of stew, which was guaranteed to keep him alive but not to nourish him in any way. When the door at the top of the stairs opened, the day light poured in, causing everyone to squint and groan, covering their eyes. Sage walked carefully down the steps which had water running down them from the walls. When she saw her husband she tried to stifle a sob, running to him she all but threw herself into him, crying openly. Robaratus couldn't even put his arms about her, because of the way his wrists were chained. He hurt deeply to see Sage so upset, to not be able to comfort her, protect her. All he could do was bury his head into her neck and plant those soft kisses upon her skin. He wouldn't lie to her by telling her it would be all right, when he knew too well this might well be his last fight and the end of his life.

"She is giving him an unfair advantage." Sage said when she'd finally got control over her emotions.

"Strength may be an important factor Sage, but it isn't the *most* important. Many a man has used strength in the wrong way, and Atrox is good at relying upon his strength to achieve his goals."

"If not strength then what?" She asked shivering from the cold.

"Strategy and intelligence. I was a soldier, an Optio. Atrox was a murderer. I have the advantage regardless of strength." He tried to sound optimistic, but he didn't fool Sage, who just wrapped her arms about his waist and hugged herself close to his chest. "I have brought you food. Nuts and fruits." She told him unloading her tunic to reveal apples and oranges, and a variety of nuts. He smiled down at her. "Thank you, my clever bright wife." He smiled, eating some of the food while she remained there. Sage knew well the diet of gladiators after the months with Albus and Octavia, she would bring for him as much as she could to help restore his strength. "Guess who has also arrived here?" She said with enthusiasm. Robaratus shook his head, he had no idea who might want to come to Rome. "Sabia" Sage said smiling.

152

"What is she doing here?"

"She decided to follow us."

"Well at least you have a friend here." He said.

"Two actually. When you were arrested I searched April out, and she helped me to see the Emperor. We pleaded your case, but he already knew most of what had passed. He likes you Robaratus, I think if he had his way you wouldn't be fighting."

"I think you might be right, however I promised Atrox this fight, and may be it is good that it is held here, then everyone can see me one last time." They stood in silence as Robaratus ate his food. "Atrox will have the advantage of light. I will be blind up there; my eyes will hurt badly when the sun shines off his blades." Sage looked pained, but could not find any words to comfort him. Robaratus continued to eat. "The Emperor told me something Sage, something I think he wanted me to know that would bring me some solace should I be killed." He looked down at her, at those beautiful wide eyes. "He says he is stepping down after this fight. Retiring."

"Why?"

"He is tired. He has ruled Rome and the Empire for twenty years, he wants to pass the responsibility on."

"Who would take his place? None of this sounds like solace to me." Sage said almost panic stricken. Robaratus smiled at her. "Have you heard of a man called Honorius?"

Sage frowned, thinking. "Is he the man who has taken up the new religion?" Robaratus nodded. "He is a devout Christian, who does not approve of gladiatorial games, he will ban them. It has been thought for some time that the appetite for killing in the arena has lost its momentum. Slaves who are gladiators will become free."

"That is a mercy."

The door at the top of the steps opened, and Sage was called out. She hugged her husband, who bent down and kissed her lips to the cheers of the other prisoners. He made sure his kiss lingered, as the others enjoyed the light and warmth that flooded the cell. The guard came stomping down the steps. "Time to go. You've a good enough time for all that stuff, now out!" He went to grab Sage but found himself staggering backwards. "The wife has a rights to a good passionate kiss you miserable bastard. The fucking man is facing death, where's yer compassion?" All the other prisoners agreed, and made to block the guard from interfering. Robaratus kept kissing his wife, who ran her hands through his hair, uncaring that it was filthy. Finally they parted and Sage thanked the prisoners for their kindness.

"When I work out which one of you punched me, you will pay." The guard sneered.

"We are all facing death, what can you do that is worse than that?" A man shouted. Sage slipped passed him and ran up the stairs, not looking back.

*   *   *

The weather turned colder, and Robaratus spent a week in the cell on half measures of food. If Sage had not brought him essentials, he would've been too weak to stand, Winds blew and showers came, winter was on its way, Robaratus wondered if these were the last days of his life, cold and dark and wet. Sage arrived as she always did loaded with as much nutrients as she could hide away. "This is my last visit." She told him, tears in her eyes and a tremble in her voice. He said nothing at first, only buried his head so that he could give her the last kisses she would ever know from him, her arms were warmth about his frozen torso. He was weak and she knew it. "Sage." He ventured.

"No don't." She begged. He sighed. "I must."

"No. I won't let you. You're going to win, you were an Optio." Tears poured from her eyes; her lip trembled uncontrollably. "*Please* don't say anything." They stood in silence both shivering some of it from the cold, some from fear. Robaratus had made his peace, thanked Mars for keeping him safe long enough to know love, peace and the knowledge that all this was coming to an end. When the guard called Sage, there was a sadness even in his tone. "Sage. You *must* listen to me. Don't come to the arena, don't watch." He begged his voice husky with emotion. Sage pulled away shaking her head violently. He had tears in his eyes, her husband was crying for her, how undignified it was going to be to die in front of her, hacked to death by Atrox. "NO, you will win." She pleaded with him. "Sage you have given me more than anyone I have ever known. I love you, but you'll only faint at the first cut." He tried to smile but tears fell from his eyes as he looked upon her desperate expressions of hope. "The people will choose." She whispered, hardly able to see him through the blur in her eyes. He shook his head. "This will be a quick affair. I am weak."

"Mistress, you gotta leave now." The guard reminded her. She clung to Robaratus reaching up to pull his head down, to taste his last kiss, feel his lips for the last time; hold him. "I am with you my love." She whispered. Then the guard was pulling her away. "Promise me Sage, you won't watch. Promise me." He yelled after her but she refused to answer him.

The rain poured down; it bounced off the sand in spiteful pellets.

The Colosseum seemed to have the entire populace of Rome crammed into it, they were dry thanks to the great covers that hung above the seats, only the arena was soaked. Atrox paced with increasing agitation, he was nervous and eager to be done with this spectacle. He had never fought in the great arena, never been in front of so many people, he felt the anticipation heavily bearing down on him and he smacked his fist into his other palm, pacing, pacing. "Calm down my love." The Empress soothed, but Atrox had no interest in her now, his focus was on Robaratus. "It isn't a fair fight." He grumbled. He had wanted it as Robaratus had intended, just the two of them, but here there were so many eyes watching him, how could he sneak an extra blade in, or trip where it was not allowed.

"I did it for you, and don't you dare forget it." The Empress warned him. He glared at her; it had all gotten out of hand as far as he was concerned. She had seen an opportunity to get rid of her most famous gladiator and had promised Atrox fame and women in return for him killing Robaratus. It had all seemed so easy at the time, but she'd omitted to mention the fight would be made public, or that she'd have Robaratus half starved. Atrox looked out of the tunnel at the masses, all of them fans and lovers of Robaratus Ectorius, he would be the bad gladiator, he would not be cheered when he killed their hero, then he would be spending the rest of his life looking over his shoulder. Atrox spat into the dirt, his temper rising with his agitation. Suddenly a huge roar erupted in the seats, the earth shook from the shear vibration of noise, as every voice shouted at full capacity. Atrox stopped moving, seeing the cause of that reaction. Robaratus was being dragged into the arena in chains. The rain fell on him, running down his face, dripping off his locs. His skin was pale beneath the grime of dirt, he wore just his shorts. He was denied his golden helmet, disgrace would do that Atrox supposed. Still he had not expected the pathetic man that leaned on guards for support. He wasn't even a challenge. When Robaratus dropped his shield, Atrox turned in fury upon Aquilina. "That is not worth fighting." He raged. Even the crowd were deadly silent at the sight of their hero so weak. Aquilina turned to her husband with a glare so fierce it would've struck lesser men down. The Emperor just shrugged. "Your orders my love." He smiled softly at her; the pity so obvious it cut deeper than her own anger ever could. Robaratus staggered to hold his sword, as rain poured over his face half blinding him. Atrox entered the arena, and the crowd hissed and booed so loudly it sounded like thunder. He wore a black leather tunic, black helmet, bare legs. He knew he would not gain fame from this easy win, and he was being judged because the stupid Empress had kept the prisoner half starved. Atrox roared back at them but his voice was drowned out so easily. Robaratus watched emotionless, his eyes squinting against the rain. The Editor called them together, he laid out the rules especially about cheating, his eyes on Atrox as he did so. The big man just sneered at Robaratus, whose expression remained blank, though his eyes were focused and sharp, they were the only sign left of the man he had once been. "Begin."

Immediately Atrox kicked the sword Robaratus was leaning on, away making him fall over. It could've all been over at that point, but Atrox felt robbed, his anger overwhelming him, he kicked at his opponent viciously, his sharp toenails cutting flesh, from his open sandals. Robaratus rolled away, lifting his leg to kick Atrox back forcing the man off him as he tried to stand. Atrox waited as his opponent struggled to his feet, holding his sword in both hands Robaratus made a huge effort to lift it but Atrox, impatient for a hit brought his own sword down, so that Robaratus fell again at having too much weight put on him. The crowd booed, another sound like thunder as they voiced their disapproval of the fight. Atrox struck again in fury, Robaratus rolled to avoid the blade, the sand stuck to his skin momentarily, thick and wet and cloggy, then the rain washed it off, the cold made him shudder but he had always trained with cold water, even in Firenze the well had refreshed him with its shuddering ice, here the rain reminded him of that feeling, and he licked his lips for the fresh water. He rolled onto his knees forcing himself to stand again as Atrox roared his rage and ran towards Robaratus' back, but as he reached the weakened man, Robaratus turned and swiped his sword for all he was worth, cutting into the shield that Atrox carried, in return Atrox swung his own sword, slicing deeply into the thigh of Robaratus. Blood poured from his leg and the man fell over, gritting his teeth in agony. He thought he heard a distant scream but it could've just been the wind in the covers. Atrox smashed his fist into Robaratus' face, cutting his eyebrow open, so now he had blood and rain to contend with. He felt so weak now he was losing blood, the rain washing it away as fast as it escaped him. He put his arm up to shield against another blade cut, only to discover that of course he had no shield, so his arm was cut to the bone. He lashed out with his foot, tripping Atrox causing the crowd to roar with enthusiasm, but he was too slow to make anything of the move. Atrox was on his feet in moments, shaking his head to clear himself of rain. Robaratus got himself up and hopped on one leg, as blood seeped down his other. Atrox looked like he was having fun at last, he grinned at Robaratus. Lunging forward to strike again, Robaratus turned aside stabbing Atrox as he passed him, blood began to seep from the black gladiators wound, a deep hole in his side. The crowd roared again, screaming and cheering. Atrox staggered, the wound had been deeper than it should've been; he'd left himself open.

156

His anger returned tenfold, he roared as he leapt at Robaratus, spraying blood as he did so, he kicked towards the other's head but Robaratus leaned back avoiding the blow, but losing his balance, staggering before getting control. Atrox was on one knee as he breathed hard, his lung had been nicked in the stab, he could feel it filling with blood. His murderous look told Robaratus he had hit true, and the man was really pissed now. Atrox forced himself to standing and walked over to Robaratus, he lashed out with his sword, kicking and punching and landing several cuts and blows on his opponent's torso and head, Robaratus doing his best to avoid the worst, but he fell, face bleeding eyes swollen, rain blinding him. Atrox was above him now sword raised. Robaratus looked up at the killing blow, and as the sword came down, so Robaratus threw sand in his opponents face. Atrox yelled as the grains of sand scratched his eyes, though the rain quickly washed them clean, Robaratus had taken his moment to focus, grunting he planted his short sword into Atrox's' gut, then rolled out of his way, but the gladiator stumbled backwards, clutching the sword, his brown eyes searched out Robaratus, who was trying to stand still but staggered about in the rain. Atrox staggered toward Robaratus, his madness evident as the crowd yelled with enthusiasm, chanting Robaratus' name over and over, the rain ran over his skin like a waterfall but its coldness invigorated him. The two men fell to each other, Robaratus wrapped his arms about Atrox's' waist squeezing the wounds he had inflicted, Atrox tried to strangle him, but he was losing too much blood. His lung was filled with it, and his ability to breathe getting less as Robaratus maintained his bear hug. Robaratus hung on though his vision was blurring, his strength slipping away. The crowd had fallen silent, only the rain deafened them, it had become a fight of wills.

"Robaratus." Sage screamed from the tunnels. His eyes moved to see her and Sabia standing at the entranceway. Tears filled his eyes, why had she not listened. "I love you." she screamed. "I am with child."

The words were slow to enter his brain, slow to connect but with certain clarity he was sure she had said she was with child. He focused on her words, and used every ounce of strength he had left to squeeze until Atrox suddenly coughed blood all over him. Robaratus let him fall to the ground. The Editor was at his side, he turned to the Emperor, who stood up and faced the crowd, who all screamed and shouted Die. Die."

Robaratus looked at Atrox, Coughing blood onto the ground, he turned his head to the Emperor, who waited for the crowd to hush. Aquilina was on her feet, looking as savage as Atrox once had. Robaratus and the Emperor looked at each other for a mere moment, then he turned his thumb down. The crowd screamed in triumph. Atrox rolled to his knees

157

and placed his hands on Robaratus' thighs. His dark eyes sought out Robaratus'. "Find peace Atrox." Robaratus said kindly. The dark gladiator lowered his head in his last act of submission, blood dribbled from his mouth, thick and dark. Robaratus then raised his long sword with his last vestiges of energy and plunged it between the other man's shoulder blades, at a slight angle that it would go through his heart. He withdrew the blade, letting Atrox fall sideways. While the crowd screamed victory, Robaratus looked sadly at the deceased gladiator. Some said he cried that day, but others said it was the rain running down his face. The most famous gladiator of Rome stood motionless, as washed out as the rain that drenched him. Another name, another death, but this time at least, came a sense of relief. His wife and child were safe. He dropped his sword and raised his head to the sky and roared his grief to the Gods. Sage ran out to him, clutching him tightly afraid he would fall down if she didn't. His arms wrapped about her; his head lowered to her. For the first time in ten long years, Robaratus was not alone with his grief. He clung to his wife even as slaves came out to help him limp away.

In the medical room, the doctors attended Robaratus, trying to staunch the bleeding, while Sage wiped his swollen face from diluted blood and rain. She sobbed endlessly as she worked, planting kisses whenever she could, telling him to be strong, to live; it was over. He didn't move, he hardly breathed, but he listened and knew she was there right by his side where she had always been. Stitches were put in and eventually the blood was stopped, burning brands had been used on his sliced arm to stop the bleeding, the stench of burning flesh made Sage gag. She packed his leg wound and arm wound with sage to help with the pain, and prevent infections, she fed him a sage drink to help him internally then he was covered up.

"How is he?" Asked a deep and worried voice. Sage turned to see the Emperor standing at the doorway. "I think he will live." She said. The older man entered the room and stood beside his favourite gladiator. "You did well Rob. You did well." He patted his arm and smiled softly. Sage looked at him oddly but the old man just winked at her and left the room.

Robaratus was watched with an armed guard, Sage never leaving his side. He drifted in and out of consciousness for a week, the sage working to keep his pain at bay, the Emperor asking for regular updates. Eventually Robaratus woke up, hardly able to see through swollen eyes, he could smell Sage, her scent wrapping itself around him like a comfort blanket. He was moved to a room at the Emperors villa, with extra guards. Aquilina banned from going anywhere near him, less she be exiled.

"You are over the worst of your injuries; we just have to work on your strength now." Sage told him, once he could sit up in his bed.

"Why did you disobey me?" He growled at her. Sage smiled. "I had a secret weapon." She rubbed her stomach fondly.

"It wasn't a dream then?" He asked.

"Nope."

Robaratus used his good arm to wrap about her and pull her to him, saying nothing he held her close, his head to her chest. "You could've lost him Sage, had I been killed, or if you fainted." He let her go, "why didn't you faint?" He tried to frown but his swollen eyes wouldn't allow it.

"It was easier with the rain; I couldn't see so much blood it was all so quickly diluted."

"I am to be a father." He grinned through swollen lips. Sage smiled for them both. "We need to get back to Firenze and soon. I have a lot to organise." Robaratus thought loudly.

"You will stay here until your face looks respectable." A deep voice ordered.

"My Emperor?" Robaratus asked, trying to squint at the doorway.

"Yes. I am here. We have a contract to complete Rob, and for that you need to be visually capable." The older man was smiling kindly. "You are staying here as my guest for now, once you can move and see I will grant you your freedom."

Sage looked stunned.

"Forgive me little Sage, it was an idea Rob and I shared. My wife thinks herself clever, but she has yet to really outsmart me. I gave her what she wanted with a little deception from my once Optio." He smiled warmly at Robaratus. "Strategy has always been his strongest asset. I shall miss that Robaratus Ectorius, for you have always been far more soldier than gladiator."

"What does he mean?" Sage asked.

"He means being a gladiator is about being a good showman." Robaratus said and waited for the *as* to drop.

"You acted it?" Sage said, unbelievingly. The Emperor chuckled.

"Robaratus Ectorius! You put me through Hades." She was about to thump him but couldn't decide on a place that wasn't already injured. The Emperor laughed.

"It had to be believable Sage. That was partly why I didn't want you there. I had to get badly beaten up to give Atrox and Aquilina some satisfaction, and fool them into thinking I was losing."

"By the Gods, you took it too far." Sabia said softly. "You could've lost your arm and leg Rob."

159

"That was unfortunate, but I think you and the doctors have saved me from that scenario."

"Keep your anger little Sage, you will both have many years together, think now how you might make him suffer! Rob, I envy you." The Emperor laughed and left them to it.

"He wants me back in Firenze to be a plebeian, so I can own the gladiators and prepare them for a life outside of the arena. He also wants me to take up a position as a senator on the council there." Rob told them. "We have a good future for our children." He tried to smile, but split his lip open again. Sage leaned over the bed and hugged him so hard he winced from the pain, but at no point would he ask her to stop. The love he felt for his wife was worth all the agony in the world, *his* Sage carrying *his* child. His heart filled with emotion and pride.

Chapter 20

Once again the arena was filled with a population of devoted fans to the historically greatest gladiator Rome had ever known. The yells, cheers and screams of the population were indeed far louder than the famous roar of Robaratus Ectorius. It was fitting too, that the day was dry and sunny for this tribute. A platform had been erected in the centre of the colosseum, where the Emperor now stood. He raised his arm for silence, and the place hushed.

"I have ruled Rome and its Empire for twenty years, and never in that time have I witnessed the popularity of any gladiator, as much as Robaratus." The crowd cheered, and the Emperor allowed it to carry on for quite a while. "He came to me a month or two back and asked for his freedom." The crowd booed and cheered. "All gladiators have that choice after three years' service. Do not begrudge this man his right after ten years." Again the crowd roared and cheered. The Emperor put up his arm for silence. "Robaratus has served us all well, entertained us all with his unique performances, has a wife and is soon to be a father." Again the crowds cheered, chanting his name before the Emperor raised his arm for silence. "I call Robaratus to the arena for the last time."

Everyone stood up. Everyone cheered and waved. Robaratus walked into the great arena of the biggest Colosseum in Rome. His arena, his stage. He wore a toga of red and white, his hair even longer in locs, now down to his shoulders. He walked around the perimeter of the arena, where people threw flowers at him, covering the floor in a carpet of white, a request he had made to honour the men, who had given their lives in blood for the entertainment of the populace. He raised his arms to embrace his audience and he roared, to the sheer delight of the crowd he bellowed at them, and they roared back at him. This honorary walk took several long moments but the Emperor was happy to allow it. He understood the fame of this gladiator, understood better than anyone the sacrifices he had made. If any man had earned this moment it was Robaratus Ectorius, though the Emperor also had a feeling that whilst this chapter was closing, it was far from the end of such a powerful man. Robaratus would make his name worth something no matter what he did. So when the walk ended, Robaratus stood a respectful distance from his Emperor, with a bowed head, he waited.

"Robaratus gladiator of Rome, I formally release you and make you a freeman. Step forward."

Robaratus obeyed, and was given his laurel of leaves and wooden sword of freedom. "From now on you are a plebeian of Roman society and entitled to re-own your name. May the fates smile upon you Robaratus Ectorius." The crowd went wild, then one of the canopies was tipped up and millions of white petals floated down to the floor. Robaratus turned in a circle of amazed wonder, opening his arms to feel the soft petals, tears in his eyes for the men who would never know this day had come. He stood alone as the citizens of Rome honoured him, over and over and over.

* * *

During their stay in Rome Sage had not seen her mistress Heva, only her friend April, who stood beside her at the ceremony for Robaratus, tears pouring down her face. "Who would've thought it Sage, that you would be the one to win that big man's heart."

Sage wondered that as well, it had been a long journey for both of them. "Do you ever hear of Heva and Decimus?"

April looked at her a moment. "I believe their marriage is as best as it could be, but it never recovered really."

"And you? What happened to that man you fancied?" Sage enquired.

"Oh he up and married some senators' daughter or something. I am biding my time. Although I fancy I could become his mistress." She waggled her eyebrows up and down, making Sage laugh. She felt sad that April would always be a slave to Aquilina, out of the two of them it was Sage who had found good fortune.

The journey back to Firenze was uneventful, and as they passed the village where Albus lived, Sage had wondered if Robaratus would call in, now he was a plebeian and free, but he did not. Perhaps a new beginning meant just that, leaving all things past in the past. They arrived back in Firenze without ceremony, and Robaratus put them back in the Inn they had stayed at before. Sabia insisted on returning to her beggars' way of life, though Robaratus had other ideas for her. His first port of call was the council building where he sought out the man who was responsible for suggesting he might return and take over the gladiators training. Vitus Quirinus wore a long white Toga, he greeted Robaratus with a warm smile and open arms. They did not go to an office, but walked the long corridors of power.

162

"It is good to see you returned Robaratus." The man said with warmth in his voice. "How does it feel to be liberated?"

Robaratus laughed lightly. "Still getting used to it." His deep voice rumbled. "I had a message from the Emperor, regarding a possible job for you. I take it you must be aware of his suggestions?" Vitus asked. Robaratus nodded. "It is the reason for which I am here." He affirmed.

"Good. The council would like to see you take over the training of gladiators that would make you the lanista as well. The position comes with the villa Julius Brutus owned. It would be yours in its entirety."

"Are you aware that the Emperor intends to step down and retire?" Robaratus asked. They stopped walking, as Vitus looked at him. "Really? That is news indeed. Who will take his place?"

"Honorius."

"The Christian?"

Robaratus nodded. Vitus rubbed his chin. "He despises gladiatorial fights." Then the senators' eyes widened. "He is going to ban them isn't he?"

"That is what the Emperor currently thinks. He says gladiators will need to be prepared for freedom."

Vitus nodded. "The popularity for blood has diminished, and continues not to draw as much public interest. Changing times indeed. Seems you got your freedom at just the right time." He smiled at Robaratus.

"Have you heard of a man called Cassius Tatius?" Robaratus asked

"We have such a man here, he used to be a Centurion a few years back, but he has had ambition and risen well to become our tax officer. Do you know of him?"

Robaratus smiled. "I do indeed. How is his wife these days?"

"Which one? He has had three so far." Vitus confirmed with humour.

"His first wife."

"Arh she is married to the senator for public relations."

Robaratus nodded "Thank you. I need to reacquaint myself with both, it has been some years."

Vitus pointed him in the direction of the tax senator's office.

The office of Cassius Tatius was on the top floor of the large building, and had good views over Firenze, but Robaratus was only interested in the man's response to him, which was gratifyingly full of surprise. "By the Gods, it's true! You have your freedom." Cassius had aged far more than Robaratus had, which came as a shock to him, given his had been the harder lot of the two of them. Cassius was bald now, gone his blond head of hair, he had gained severe lines around his brow and eyes, and his mouth sagged in a sour downturned way. "I am glad you remember me." Robaratus said without any hint of emotion.

"I could hardly forget or ignore you, even as a gladiator you managed to do well for yourself." Cassius put on a strained smile.

"I expect you hoped I would be killed." Robaratus looked the man straight in the eye, Cassius met his glare but soon looked away. "What do you expect? You ruined my marriage."

"Am I to blame for the ruination of the second marriage as well?"

Cassius blushed a little. "Not unless you are responsible for her death, but you certainly killed the first marriage. She had your bastard you know. I had it killed."

Robaratus laughed. "What an arrogant prick you are Cassius. We had not got that far when you burst in! You killed your own child or someone else's." He chuckled at the thought some more. Cassius looked angry.

"So what are you doing in my office?" He asked bitterly.

"Oh I just popped by to say hello. I own the gladiators now and I train them."

"So what?" Atticus looked confused.

"So I am a senator by appointment of the Emperor."

Cassius paled. "I am not sure there are any available appointments at the present time, so you maybe a senator, but a senator of nothing as it stands." He grinned unkindly.

"I will be here to vote, to walk the corridors and my ears will be open. A senator of the people for the people." Robaratus told him. Cassius shrugged, "We have a public relations senator he's married to Roxan."

"I wonder how much of the peoples' issues he is sympathetic about; I dare say I will find out given I am planning to pay your ex-wife a visit, I am sure she will be glad to reacquaint herself with me." Robaratus smiled warmly, watching how Cassius reddened.

"Leave her alone, she is happily married now."

"That shouldn't make any difference to old lovers saying hello."

"It shouldn't but her husband might wonder what your connection is, it wouldn't be difficult for him to join the dots, why ruin her life for a second time?" Cassius had a note of desperation in his voice.

"Between the two of you, my life was ruined hundreds of times over, think I care if I spoil your lives anymore?" Robaratus growled.

"Arrh, so this about revenge?" Cassius said as though the *as* had just dropped.

"What need I of revenge unless you and your dear wife set me up?"

"Resentment is a good cause for revenge Ectorius." Cassius replied smoothly.

"Look over your shoulder Cassius, I am always going to be behind you."

Cassius laughed. "You want my job? I would've expected you'd prefer my

life! This is a job you couldn't do Robaratus. I have no fear of you."
Robaratus smiled and chuckled, "who says I want your job?", then headed
for the door, leaving Cassius looking bewildered.

Sage looked up at the big villa. "This is really ours?" She asked her
husband, he nodded and smiled. "There is a room for Sabia if she wants
it and a room for our child, he looked down at her slightly round belly.
They walked through a main archway into the tiled meeting area, where a
gap in the roof let rain in to stock up a pool that held fresh water for
drinking and washing. Straight ahead of them was an open eating area with
the long couches that allowed for eating lying down. Above the eating area
were the slaves sleeping rooms, and to the right was a sheltered area with
a room above, stone stairs led to the bedroom door. Beside the stairs was
a path into the garden, with bushes and statues which could all be viewed
at different angles from the sheltered walk way, or from the large bedroom
that opened onto the garden. "There is plenty of scope for adding onto
the building as needs arise." Robaratus explained, grinning as he looked
again at Sage's growing belly. All the furnishings were lavish and spoke of
wealth, and they even had their own private baths which Robaratus had
organised to be built onto their bedroom. All the floors were warm from
the heating system, which made it a pleasure to walk on. A long path led
through another garden to the high wall of the training school, and the
cells for the thirty gladiators that lived there. When Robaratus and Sage
entered the training school, all the men stopped training and hailed them
with cheers. Never in her life had Sage ever imagined being the wife of
one so loved and so famous.

*   *   *

Roxan Ran her fingers through the fine silk shawl on the market
vendors stall. "I always thought you looked much better naked." A deep
sexy voice spoke so close to her ear as to make her jump, turning to face
the solid torso of a man she never thought she'd see again. "By the Gods
what are you doing here?" She spat in a quietly urgent voice. Robaratus
smiled and laughed softly at her discomfort. "I am a lanista now, owner of
the gladiators." He told her as she blinked up at him with surprise. "I had
heard about Julius Brutus, but replacing him with *you* of all people." She
hissed utterly annoyed at his rise in fortunes. "Leave me alone Robaratus,

I am not married to Cassius anymore." She looked about her warily.

"Let us walk." Robaratus said, kindly taking her elbow, ensuring she had no choice in the matter. "I have often wondered about how your husband timed his arrival so very well, although from what he told me, he was somewhat premature." Robaratus laughed.

"What do you mean?" She asked.

"He said he killed your child; he thought it was my bastard. Didn't you tell him we had only just begun our fun?" His deep voice rolled over her thumping against her heart, reminding her of a time, she had tried to bury. "Obviously he didn't spend much time on you in bed, if he thought I was done with you. No wonder you wanted me Roxan." His voice was silk against her ear again. Roxan sniffed. "How dare you." She turned and hit him, but Robaratus hardly felt her, he just laughed more. "You think your fists can hurt me, when I have faced blades and death for ten years because of you."

Roxan was pale and tears filled her eyes. "He killed my new born son, not even a day old, you have no notion of what loss is."

"Whose fault is it that he made such a mistake Roxan?" Now Robaratus' voice was harsh. Roxan looked away, tears streaming down her face. "What good is dragging up the past now, you cannot get back the years you lost." She spoke bitterly "Let it go, I beg you." She added.

"I shall be glad to, but there is a problem here, one of imbalance. I lost ten years of my life and you lost a child. Tell me what did Cassius lose?" Roxan looked up at him, his features were not angry, but curious.

"What do you mean?" Her tone was suspicious.

"I lost something. You lost something. What did your ex-husband lose?" Roxan had no answer to that. "It was a long time ago."

"Whose idea was it?" Robaratus asked. Roxan threw her arms up. " Damn you drop it; it was too long ago. What can you gain now?"

Robaratus gripped her arm enough to make her wince.

"I want to know."

"His mainly. I mean I agreed to it, I wanted his promotions as much as he did."

So Sabia had been right, and Robaratus felt sick at the admission.

"So you ruined my life so that your husband could gain promotions?"

Robaratus wondered at his own calm response to the realisation of what this woman and her husband had cost him.

"Robaratus, I am sorry for what happened to you, Cassius said you'd just be thrown out of the army, he was going to suggest it was all he desired, but he lied about that."

Robaratus looked at her, he didn't really know what to feel.

"I have killed friends, good men because of you, and because of you I have lost ten years of my life being punished for a crime you and your sad husband set me up for. Never think a gladiator has no notion of grief. I have cried tears for those men, I will continue to cry tears for their lost lives, lives you and your husband made me take. You have no memory of their names, but I remember them all." He turned, and left her staring after him, tears streaming down her face.

Robaratus walked towards home, lost in his thoughts, when he walked into a hand cart filled with furniture. "Woe Centurion, watch where you're going!" Called the annoyed owner.

"Felix?" Robaratus asked.

"Robaratus! I didn't recognise you! So now you have become one of the elite?" The man called Felix joked. Robaratus mock bowed before him. "Why are you packing up your home?"

"The taxes are too high for us to stay here. Have you not heard yet senator, that the taxes have risen again this year, it makes living in the city impossible for many of us."

Robaratus frowned. "What reason has been given for such an increase?" Felix shrugged, making his face wobble and his larger stomach wobble. "What reason does the tax man need?" He joked. Robaratus felt annoyed that his friend was having to move out. "Is it just you who is moving out?"

"Nay. Plenty have gone. Look around you senator. If you live in the main street, the taxes are much higher than those in side streets or outside the city. We are moving out to the countryside." Felix told him.

"I shall miss you, so will Sage."

"Then be sure to come and visit us." Felix smiled, but Robaratus could see the sorrow in his eyes, instead of going home, he turned around and headed back to the council building.

It was lucky for Robaratus that his friend Vitus was in his office, and was welcomed with his usual smiling face and enthusiasm. "Robaratus what brings you to my office with such a worried frown?"

"Forgive me, it is something that I have been thinking about for many months."

Vitus was not alone; he had another man sitting at one end of a desk. "Let me introduce you to Julius Decimus, he is the assistant to Cassius."

Robaratus smiled warmly at the man, who was young and rather skinny.

"What is this thing you have been thinking of?" Vitus asked, his eyes bright with interest.

"I want to erect a monument to the gladiators." Robaratus said, watching Julius' response. The thin man frowned.

"What a gallant idea!" Vitus enthused. "It would be a good way to remember the heroic sacrifices such men have made."

"I would also like to propose a day of memorial, to be known as Gladiatorial Day, whereby gladiators could still demonstrate their skills without drawing blood. Where the citizens can donate coin to the upkeep of the monument, and to those gladiators who are aging or disfigured by battles."

Julius Decimus had paled throughout Robaratus' speech, and whilst Robaratus noticed, Victus did not. "I suggest you raise this at tomorrow's meeting of the senators."

Robaratus smiled and nodded to both men. "Give my regards to Cassius." He smiled at the young man, and left.

*   *   *

In the eating area of the villa, Robaratus told Sage and Sabia about his findings. Sabia hissed with anger. "Serves that Roxana right to have lost her first born. The Gods dislike schemers."

"Then I must be certain to pay homage to Dolos, for I am about to begin my own schemes!" Robaratus laughed.

"What schemes?" Sage asked.

"There is something not right with the taxes in this city." Robaratus explained about Felix leaving.

"I shall miss them." Sage said sadly.

"I have seen a few vendors leaving, and heard rumours about the tax rises." Sabia confirmed.

"Have you heard any rumours as to why?"

"No. Plenty of theories but nothing that explains it really, though you might want to look at Cassius's young wife. She seems to dress above her station and wears much jewellery." Sabia tapped her lips thoughtfully. "Not such a difficult step to take, after all he is much older than she, he could be spoiling her to keep her in his bed."

"I rather think you could have a point there. Cassius never was very good in the bedroom; he walked in on me and Roxana way too soon!" Robaratus laughed loudly. Sage and Sabia couldn't help but join in. "I hadn't even got to the interesting part."

"Tomorrow I will be putting my thoughts to the senators; it will be interesting to see what reactions Cassius has to my ideas."

"What you are doing isn't going to be dangerous to you is it?" Sage asked once they were alone in their room. Robaratus stroked her arm, standing behind her, with his free arm wrapped about her holding her newly formed bump. "I am always aware of dangers Sage, it has been my life for too many years, but for you and our unborn child, I will always be extra careful." His lips caressed her neck making her sigh and relax into his body. She turned to face him, slipping her arms around his neck, feeling his body react to her immediately, his arms wrapped about her protecting her, giving her his strength. His lips brushed against her and she moaned deeply, aching for his hands to do more than just hold her. "I owe you so much." He whispered against her neck. Sage pulled back from him. "You owe me nothing Rob."

He smiled. "That is only the second time you have ever called me that. I like it." His eyes looked into hers intently. "But for you, I would still be a slave and a gladiator."

"Robaratus Ectorius, but for you I would never have known any loyal men existed!" Sage stuck her tongue out and he nipped at it, his teeth working their way down her neck to her shoulder, then he swept her into his arms and carried her to the bed, laying her down with so much care and gentleness. He soon removed her tunic and lay beside her admiring her form, running his large hand over her bump, words could not have expressed more completely just how much he loved Sage and her bump, his tender kisses that trailed down her skin, the way he cupped her breasts and let his fingertips torment her, until she begged him to do more, he always took his time, always so tender, she would gasp and moan and he would bring her to climax just to see the emotions she would go through. Sage could ignite his passion like no other woman he had ever known, and when he claimed her, he would make her tell him what she wanted, until they both shared the exquisite release together.

Morning saw Robaratus in his white robes, kissing his wife farewell, as he left for the council meeting room. Sunshine poured down into the garden and the drinking pool, warming it up. He strode down the cobbled streets, a man with a purpose, head high and jata locs dancing around his shoulders. He entered the council building nodding to a few other senators who were standing about the steps, enjoying the sunshine and conversation. Beyond the giant pillars were the huge wooden doors, that entered into the foyer, a vast marble floored area with small alcoves for statues, and fresco's on the walls. Robaratus headed straight for the round room in the middle of the building, divided in half with a wide corridor, he took the left double doors into a semi-circular room, where several senators sat about debating water supply to the city. Robaratus found Vitus Quirinus sitting alone watching the debate whilst fanning his face with a parchment, the room was warm and had no windows for

169

ventilation. "Robaratus. Join me, it is a most unwelcome day for debates."
Vitus explained. "I shall enjoy the baths much more after this!" He smiled.
Robaratus sat and caught up on the debate thus far.

"The aqueduct on the Eastern side of the city was in need of repairs, this
was ordered but it seems the repairs were done badly. The argument we
are seeing is that the builder, that man who looks fairly annoyed, named
Magnus Orca, claims he didn't receive the full amount of the costs he
submitted. That man, the very tall one with hair around the side of his
head, is Consus Rufus who is in charge of the repair department, he claims
he gave Orca all the funds *he* was allocated for the repair work. So Rufus
has asked the treasurer, the man now standing, rather large and short, what
happened to the full funds." Vitus explained pointing out the relevant
senators.

"Those *were* the full funds. I gave the allotted fees to you." The treasurer
replied huffily.

"Who gave the funds to you Consus?" A stooped older man asked.

"Who is he?" Robaratus whispered, recognising the older man seemed
important.

"He is Cato Martinus, Speaker for the house." Vitus informed him.

"Cassius dropped them in to me as a favour for Appius." Consus Rufus
replied. Robaratus' ears pricked up and he leaned forward in his seat.

"In my defence senator, I picked up the coin bag and dropped it off."
Cassius declared.

"There was a significant shortfall from my original quote." The builder
complained.

"So who is responsible for the misinformation?" Cato Martinus asked.
Thus the debate dragged on, so that even Robaratus began to lose interest.
When they finally decided to drop the whole matter and ask the builder to
re-do the repairs, it was getting close to the hora sexta, and mid-day meal.

"We have time for one more request." Cato Martinus announced. "May I
welcome our new senator Robaratus Ectorius." The men in the chamber
all stood and applauded Robaratus.

"Thank you senators. I would like to propose a memorial to the Gladiators
who have given their lives for the entertainment of the citizens of this city.
I am also proposing a day of memorial whereby gladiators can
demonstrate their skills without bloodshed, but as a reminder of the way
in which we train and fight." There was much response to that, some
nodding enthusiastic agreement, others frowning and murmuring loudly
their displeasure.

"Does the new senator have any idea of the cost of such a memorial?"
Appius the treasurer asked, his face trying to maintain a friendly

expression.

"I don't imagine it will be cheap, and I am happy to contribute funds towards it." Robaratus explained.

"Very commendable senator." Vitus stood and said loudly, giving opportunity for those in favour to shout backing.

"It is commendable but unfortunately unfundable." Appius said, shaking his head and trying to look regretful.

"How so? The man is putting up his own funds towards this." Vitus reminded them.

"Pardon me senator Quirinus, but the taxes have had to be raised to fund the repairs this city needs, and frankly such extravagant expense would not go down with the populace very well. We are unpopular as it is."

"Perhaps if I fund it myself?" Robaratus asked smiling. The whole chamber began to mumble. Appius looked confused and turned to Cassius who shrugged.

"Why have the taxes been raised? We should have ample funds in the treasury." Vitus asked, a clear note of concern in his tone.

"We do have funds senator, it's just that to build a memorial to thieves and murderers is extravagant and needless to say, the citizens would not want a reminder of such people, heroic or not." Appius explained boldly.

"Do you mark me as a common criminal?" Robaratus growled, his eyes hard as he stared at the treasurer who turned red, and seemed to shrivel in size compared to Robaratus.

"Forgive me, but you *did* break the law." Appius pointed out.

"With my wife." Cassius added. The whole chamber looked appalled and loud mutterings broke out. Robaratus smiled broadly.

"Arh yes! I wondered when you'd bring that up. Seemingly unable to satisfy your wife in bed, you arranged with her to walk in on us, sadly it was somewhat too early as I had hardly begun." The chamber broke out in raucous laughter. Cassius went puce. Robaratus actually considered that he might burst a blood vessel, the whole chamber was now hanging on every word.

"How dare you show such disrespect to me in front of my colleagues" Cassius snarled, his eyes blazing bloody fury at the ex-gladiator. Robaratus shrugged. "You brought it up."

"Say what you will Ectorius, you were sent to the arena as a common slave." Cassius reminded him.

Robaratus bowed to the man. "And thanks to you I gave ten years of my life to killing good men for your entertainment, and now I am a free man, a lanista of the very law breakers you despise. Men who often paid with their lives for their crimes, and others who became good fighters and

171

lovers of your wives. You should honour them. You should bow down before them, for they have served you loyally. What greater sacrifice is there than your own life? Would you be so willing to die for the cheers of an audience Cassius? I was."

The chamber fell silent. Vitus allowed the silence to hang heavy before he rose slowly. "I support the proposal for a monument to the heroes of this city, and a day of holiday to celebrate the skills these men aspire to."

"I second it." Atticus Italus spoke out, standing. Robaratus turned to look at him, he bowed to Roxana's husband who smiled back warmly, he had forgotten about the man not being supposed to know about her marriage to Cassius, but Atticus didn't seemed surprised by the revelations, which was a relief for Robaratus.

Chapter 21

As Robaratus left the debate chamber, he was hurried after by Atticus Italus. "Senator Ectorius, may I have a word?"

Robaratus stopped. "My apologies back there senator." He offered, expecting Atticus to start making accusations, but the man just smiled. "Honestly I have been wanting to stab Cassius in the back for a long time now, but that isn't the sole reason for my backing you. I really do admire you Robaratus, if any man could be an example of good coming from bad, you're it."

"Mind if I ask you why it is you dislike Cassius so much?"

"Because of what he did to Roxana. Did you know he beat her half to death before divorcing her?"

Robaratus stiffened, anger flared in his eyes. "I didn't know. Why did he do that?"

"Punishment for sleeping with you. Husbands are allowed in law to punish wives who cheat. He needed to be rid of her, so he beat her. I am certain it was his intention she would not survive, thus allowing him to marry his second wife, however she lived so he had to divorce her stating infidelity." Atticus paused to gauge Robaratus' responses. "You did know she had a child, Cassius killed. He said it was yours, now because of what he did to Roxana, she cannot have children."

"She told me you knew nothing of her past, how is it you do?"

Atticus smiled sadly. "Roxana is a fighter, and I admired her for that. I made some discrete enquiries about her marriage to Cassius, and found him wanting. We have never talked about it because she has never wanted to, so I never asked."

Robaratus felt overwhelming sympathy for Atticus, who clearly loved Roxana very much, she deserved that. "The child wasn't mine; it was his." Atticus nodded. "I had hoped as much."

"Seems odd that he hasn't had offspring with either his second or third wife." Robaratus remarked thoughtfully. Atticus grinned. "Rumour has it he is infertile, or just not man enough in the bed, take your pick!" It was Robaratus who grinned now, as a thought popped into his mind, one he tucked away for later. "What did you want to speak with me about?"

"Oh yes! I almost forgot. Cassius has quite a controlling way with the senators, the treasury is bleeding coin, and some of us think the records

173

are being fixed. Anyone who has tried to raise this issue has met with accidents, some ending in death. I warn you to watch your back if you choose to take this man on, he is lethal."

"I never heard of a council anywhere that didn't have its fair share of back handers!" Robaratus smiled, "but I thank you for the warning."

The two parted company and Robaratus left the building, only to be met by Vitus. "I am going to conduct an investigation into the funds of the treasury, it seems we have little to spend on the things we once had plenty to spend on. How are you at sums Rob?"

Robaratus smiled. "I do better than most imagine. I had an education."

Vitus nodded. "Then perhaps you could poke the vipers nest a bit, see what you can discover?"

Robaratus nodded and they parted company, he knew Sage would be annoyed at him for getting involved in this, but he wanted Cassius to pay for the things he had done wrong.

Sage wasn't pleased. "You've been there hardly a heartbeat and already you're up to your neck in trouble."

Robaratus wrapped his arms around her, it was the one thing that calmed her and that he loved to do most. "Sabia can you do some spying for me? Cassius has no offspring from either his second or current marriage, is there a reason for it? I need to know."

Sabia smiled. "My pleasure."

"I also need to know anything about his current child bride."

"She is a woman in law and of marriageable age Robaratus." Sabia reminded him.

"Compared to Cassius, she is a child. He is old enough to be her father." Robaratus growled.

"You're supposed to making friends from the senators, not enemies." Sage complained, as Robaratus nuzzled his face into her hair and neck.

"I don't need corrupt friends, nobody does."

Sage sighed, it was difficult to be annoyed with her husband when he held her so close, planted soft kisses on her skin, and let his tongue tickle her neck.

"I might well become senator for internal investigations!" Robaratus mused as his arms wrapped tighter around his wife, Sage smiled and turned her head just enough to nip his neck, making him growl.

"Before you two get carried away, I think I shall take my leave, I have friends to visit." Sabia made her excuses and left.

"I feel a bath is required wife." Robaratus lifted Sage into his arms and walked purposefully towards their bedroom and their private bath beyond it. The water reflected patterns onto the ceiling, and the warm mosaic tiles offered a luxury Sage still marvelled at. The walls had fresco's on of gladiators posing or fighting, never would Robaratus forget the long years of his hard fights for survival.

"I look forward to the day we bathe our children in here and they learn of the might of gladiators." He said as he undressed and watched his wife disrobe. His eyes roamed over her resting on her slight bump, he stepped into the water, holding out his hand for Sage to guide her in without slipping. They sunk into the warmth, Robaratus pulling her close to him, kissing her lips gently, trailing his tongue over the soft flesh, before letting his fingers drift lightly down her arms. "You are beautiful Sage." He murmured against her lips. Then let his tongue lick the water from her skin as he travelled down her body. Sage sighed, hands holding his hair, pulling on his long locs as he aroused her, always taking his time, always enjoying her reactions. His fingers found their way lower, gently slipping inside her making her moan in ecstasy. Sage met his rhythm and soon found herself clutching at his locs and shouting his name. Then he wrapped her legs about him and teased her with his own arousal until she begged for him to enter her, even then he took his time torturing himself as much as her, until they found release together "I love you Sage." He growled covering her in more kisses. "I love you Robaratus." She whispered back.

*   *   *

As Robaratus had no room to call his own, he visited his new friend Atticus Italus, who had already anticipated having to share his small space, and had placed a desk in the corner that Robaratus could use. "Julius Decimus dropped in the treasury ledger early this morning. I have been giving it the once over, and I have to confess, it is a lot worse than we suspected." He told Robaratus, as he watched the tall ex gladiator engulf the room. "How so?" Robaratus asked, as he squeezed into his chair.

"I have only had a quick glance, but it seems that the builder was right, he wasn't paid his full fee, thing is the treasury records the quote as being 21 Aureus, yet the builder quoted 20. There is no record of where the extra Aureus went, however the ledger records that the builder was paid 20 Aureus."

"So what is the problem?" Robaratus asked, "apart from 1 Aureus."

"The man who counts out the coin recalls the fee being 10 Aureus, so the question is, where is the missing 11 Aureus?"

Robaratus looked confused. "How does the coin counter have a lesser amount?"

"That is what we have to find out." Atticus said. "I also discovered from a quick glance that numbers have been changed in the ledger, and that has been going on for some time."

Robaratus grinned, and opened the ledger. "How in Hades does anyone read this mess?" He groaned trying to fathom the endless scribble of changed numbers. "I think Appius Sextus needs to explain this sloppy record keeping." Though he didn't immediately do anything about that, he sat quietly reading the ledger and turning the pages backwards realising the mistakes, if that is what they were, went back more than one job, and to his surprise more than a year. "We need past ledgers Atticus; this has been going on longer than a year."

Atticus got and looked over Robaratus' shoulder. "I'll make the request. How far do you want to go back?"

"Let us try five years, it is bound to be within that amount of time."

Atticus left the room and Robaratus got stuck into the ledger.

It was well into the afternoon when Cassius knocked on the door. "Mind if I come in?" He asked in a smooth tone. Robaratus watched him walk into the room without being invited. "What do you want? I'm a busy man." He told Cassius.

"Yes, so I see." Cassius walked over to look at what Robaratus was doing, but his way was halted when Robaratus slammed shut the ledger making the other man jump. "I am curious to know what keeps you such a busy man, I mean can you even read that?" Cassius smarmed.

"I was expecting you sooner to be honest." Robaratus remained impassive in expression.

"Really? Why would you be expecting me?" Cassius asked, his voice honeyed innocence.

"As the tax collector, you have to work closely with the treasurer, so you know why you would be here." Robaratus made himself sound bored, and the game was boring as far as he was concerned.

"I know the treasurer has been making me put the taxes up each year and now twice a year."

"Have you reported this?"

"Not yet." Cassius looked uncomfortable.

"Why not?" Robaratus tilted his head to one side, curiously wondering what lie Cassius would give him. "Perhaps I don't read into small errors imagined things, like other's do." He smiled graciously.

"Indeed? I wouldn't say the errors are at all small, but then you know that. So let's not play this game. How about you tell me why the ledgers are being fixed?"

"Be careful Robaratus, it is unwise to make hasty accusations, fixing ledgers is a serious accusation." Cassius was talking softly now but the threat in his voice was unmistakable. Robaratus leaned forward equally quiet in tone, he looked up at Cassius. "I hope I don't find you in any way a part of this conspiracy to rob the city of vital funds. It won't end well if I do." The two men stared at each other for long moments.

"You once said you weren't after my job; seems you were lying." Cassius growled in a low tone. Robaratus leaned back in his chair and smiled broadly. "I am not after your job. I also told you to look over your shoulder, I would always be there." He waved his fingers at Cassius, still grinning.

"Maybe it is Atticus who is filling your head with vengeful thoughts. I can hardly imagine you being able to read ledgers."

Robaratus laughed lightly. "I didn't make youngest Optio without a sound education Cassius, you keep making the mistake of thinking me an uneducated thug!"

"You are. All fucking gladiators are ignorant thugs."

"And yet here I am, and here you are, and the ledgers are being fixed. Odd how our paths keep crossing."

"If you had any sense you'd leave well alone." Cassius warned, his face undisguised fury.

"And if you had any sense you'd come clean and explain your part in this."

"You *dare* to accuse me?" Cassius was furious.

"I am looking forward to seeing how many lies you can tell to try and cover for yourself, but involved you most definitely are."

Cassius looked bloody murder at Robaratus, then left the room, almost crashing into Atticus on his way in laden with past ledgers. "Did I miss something interesting?" He asked humorously, leaning out the door watching Cassius stride away at speed.

"You might say that." Robaratus grinned. "Seems our tax collector has ruffled feathers."

Atticus nodded, then deposited a pile of books on the table where Robaratus sat, burying the ledger he had been looking at.

"He's not the only one. Treasurer is almost having a heart attack!"

"Not in the least bit surprised." Robaratus said half-heartedly, as he ran his fingers down the side of the pile of ledgers. "It will be interesting to see which idiot will cave first."

When the day was done, Robaratus was met by Sabia. "Is Sage alright?" Were his first words, fear suddenly gripping his heart.

"She is fine. I came to catch you on the way home. Did you know Cassius' second wife is dead?"

177

Robaratus nodded. "He told me, but I wondered why she had not had children with him."

"We will never know." Sabia said sadly.

"So what of the latest wife?" He asked as they walked easily down the main street.

"Her name is Hester and it seems you were right about him being no good in the bedroom." She paused as they wove in and out of a crowd of shoppers. "According to my friend at the baths, she was complaining to another wealthy woman, that he drinks too much, is sweaty, has bad breath and takes no time with her."

Robaratus burst out laughing, causing some nearby citizens to turn and stare at him. "There has to be some exaggeration in that!" He managed to say when he could hold off the giggles long enough. Sabia had been smiling with him, but now became serious. "I think not. She is the granddaughter of a cousin of the Emperor, according to my friend, she hasn't learnt not to talk about married life, so she pours her exasperations out at the baths."

Robaratus rose his eyebrows and looked genuinely surprised. "I guessed she had to come from a high-ranking family to be married to him to start with, but one related to the Emperor?" He let out a long breath. "Impressive even for Cassius."

"The rumour goes that Cassius has ambitions for promotion to Rome. He heard about Hester who had quite the reputation at thirteen by all accounts, and he set about finding a way to meet her. I have no idea how he met her Grandfather but turns out the man was quite a dice player."

Robaratus stopped walking at the amphitheatre. "Let me guess, he got lucky at dice and the old man owed him a debt?"

Sabia shrugged. "My friend says that Hester made him court her with expensive gifts, or she wouldn't flirt with him."

"Wait. Why would he care? He was owed her to pay the debt, he didn't need to court her." Robaratus looked confused.

"The old man begged him to make it look good. He obliged."

Robaratus started to walk again but slowly. "So why is he still pampering her? A married man can force his wife to have sex, he doesn't need to spoil her."

"Well firstly he still needs to impress Vitus Quirinus that he is suitable to be recommended to Rome, and for that his marriage to Hester is vital. Secondly, Hester is an unhappy wife, and he needs to keep her on side if he is to get his promotion, he promised her he would be in Rome within a year, and that hasn't happened. I think she stays because of the gifts he buys her, though even those are not winning her interest so much these

178

days." Sabia said.

"So do we assume Cassius is getting into debt with all his expensive gifts?"
"That my dear Robaratus is for you to find out." Sabia and Robaratus walked into the training yard, where the evening meal was being consumed, they were both greeted noisily by the gladiators. Sabia carried on to the villa while Robaratus stayed and talked to his men and their trainer.

As soon as Robaratus approached his villa, he knew something was wrong, it seemed altogether too quiet. His hand crept to his dagger which was hidden within the folds of his robes, then he stepped into his home a smile on his face and called for his wife. Sage walked into the greeting area, her face pale. Robaratus ignored her and opened his arms to her. "Hello Sage, where is my hug?" He grinned at her and she moved towards him. "That's far enough."
Robaratus knew that voice, and both he and Sage stilled, as Cassius emerged from the shadows with Sabia in front of him, a knife to her throat. "If you wanted an invite to eat with me, you only had to ask." Robaratus joked, keeping his rage in check.
"I am not hungry for food. I have plans Ectorius, and you are about to piss all over them, so I am giving you a subtle warning, leave well alone, and persuade your friend Vitus to promote me to Rome."
"Or what?" Robaratus asked knowing pretty much what the answer would be. Cassius looked at the two women.
"I am not in a position to influence Vitus." He expelled a laugh, "hell I don't even have a room!"
"You don't need a room to be up his arse. Perhaps your friend here has no importance in your lives, maybe I should focus on your wife. That is *your* child she is carrying?"
Robaratus smiled, though it didn't reach his eyes which were cold as steel, though his tone when he spoke was business like, as if he wasn't staring at a man with a knife. "I cannot think you intend anyone here any real harm, especially as you want a promotion so badly, however, I might remind you that if anything happens to any one of us, or my unborn child, it is you who will find no place on this earth to hide."
Cassius laughed lightly. "You think death scares me Gladiator?"
"Not a quick death no." Robaratus said casually. "However Gladiators are trained to draw blood and I can cut you Cassius and still you will live. Then again a slow death on the cross might be more compelling, I hear it can take up to four days to die, what then for your plans?"
"Drop your investigation Robaratus and no harm will come to you and yours, but understand how mishaps can occur so easily." Cassius threw

179

Sabia forward, Sage reached out for her, and Robaratus let his intruder go. Sage looked up at him, he stood like a giant, tall and straight, his expression cold and murderous, she noted the dagger in his hand; he had been ready to kill for his family. She might want to rage at him for bringing trouble to their home, but she knew shouting at him and crying wouldn't make things any better. Robaratus defended his own with his life, it was what his life was meant to be about, soldier and gladiator, now husband and senator. Sage knew he was planning against Cassius, the man had just signed his own death warrant, the question for Sage was could she survive until Robaratus carried it out?

The morning brought the usual bustle of senators into the debating chamber. Atticus intercepted Robaratus in the front foyer, telling him he would be asking questions of Cassius about the missing coin. Robaratus nodded excluding himself, saying he preferred to get stuck into the pile of ledgers he had on his desk. He headed up the stairs at a leisurely pace, whilst he wanted to get on, he was in no hurry, and he had no desire to catch the eyes of anyone who may be watching him. He had been at his desk for some time before a knock on his door gave him a break.

"Is it convenient to interrupt you?" Vitus asked, poking his head around the door.

"Please do come in." Robaratus tried to get up, but his bulk had him squashed towards the desk too much. Vitus entered and sat in the chair Atticus normally occupied. "How can I help you?" Robaratus asked.

"Oh I am not here for favours, just to keep you company. Cassius failed to attend chambers this morning, so I wanted to be here in case he paid you a visit instead. I hear he can be quite persuasive when he sets his mind to it."

"I have already had the pleasure of those persuasions. I had some advice of my own for him."

Vitus raised his eyebrows, then smiled. "I figured you could handle him."

"I dislike cowards who threaten my family." Robaratus growled, not looking at Vitus.

"I can provide you with guards." Vitus offered, though he knew what the answer to that would be.

"I have gladiators. Guards can be brought off, bribed. My men cannot."

"I have to assume you have upset him already if he is paying you visits so soon?"

"Atticus was intending to ask him about the missing coin from the aqueduct repair. From what I am seeing, these books are the worst kind of book keeping I have ever seen, and Cassius seems to have been fleecing the Council for some time, more than a year, from the books I am looking at." Robaratus paused tapping his lips, then he turned to Vitus. "Is there a requirement for senators to keep records of their spending?"

"Alas no. Senators are expected to fund the council from their own pocket. Taxes are for general repairs and monuments to gladiators." He smiled indulgently.

"Well that explains a lot then." Robaratus washed his face with his hands. "I cannot yet provide proof, but I am told his wife has many trinkets, expensive silks, perfumes. If Cassius is keeping her happy by spoiling her, it seems he has gone through his own funds, and is now spending the cities."

"How do we prove it?" Vitus asked frowning.

"We need witnesses."

"They tend to meet with accidents." Vitus said tapping his lips with his finger. "We have never been able to prove Cassius was involved, even if he likely was."

"I'll start with the treasurer; he is obviously involved; I'd like to know by how much." Robaratus struggled out from behind his desk as Vitus stood from his chair easily, he chuckled. "We need to get you a room of your own!"

Robaratus gave him a pained look.

Appius Sextus sat hunched over at his desk, squinting as he wrote carefully in a ledger. He was a short man, who ate well and whose head lacked hair, though he sported a beard, which was grey and curly. He had become a nervous man since Cassius had suggested a little sleight of hand here and there, and these days he knew his days were numbered, it was only a matter of time before he was accused, or met with one of Cassius' famous accidents, so when Robaratus knocked on his door more loudly than he needed to, the little man near jumped out of his skin, splattered ink everywhere and discovered a number of new swear words. Robaratus, for his part, fought to keep the smirk off his face, as he stood politely in the doorway. "Are you busy?" He asked innocently. Appius gave him a sour look. "Apparently not anymore." He complained, dabbing his clothes and beard with a rag, to mop up the spilled ink. "Why are you here?" He added suspiciously, even though he had a good idea.

"It's your ledger keeping, it is the messiest I have ever seen; how have you managed to keep your job here?" Robaratus kept his voice friendly.

"I am not as good at seeing as I used to be." Appius said shrugging and trying not to look guilty.

"I can see why the taxes need to be raised so much. I had no idea the aqueducts were so badly constructed." Robaratus folded his massive arms.

"What?" Appius looked bewildered, then the *as* dropped and he smiled.

"Arh yes, they are showing their age, certainly."

"I think we should start recording who does the repairs, as that work is also bad, given the amount of times some parts are being re-repaired within months of being repaired." Robaratus frowned pretending to work out if he had said his last sentence correctly. Appius fidgeted. "I have nothing to do with who carries out the repairs."

"Oh, who does? I shall need to speak to them."

"I erm, I think Cassius uses some merchant he knows, though I could be wrong." Appius blinked nervously, fluttering his dark lashes.

"Why would Cassius do that? Isn't he just a tax collector?" Robaratus made his voice sound curious. Appius shrugged, not looking at him for fear he would give himself away. "I, I really don't know. Perhaps you should ask him?"

"I can't. I'm told he is shopping or something." Robaratus lied.

"Huh!" The disgust in that sound told Robaratus just how much Appius disliked the man. "Is there anything else you want?" Appius asked snappily.

"As a matter of fact, there is. I was sort of wondering why it is that you record the price of a job as being much higher than it actually is?"

Appius looked offended. "I assure you I record what I am told is being charged."

Robaratus nodded. "So as Cassius is providing the workers, logic assumes he is also the one who is telling you what a job costs?"

Appius opened his mouth then closed it. He had been had. He shrugged helplessly.

"I need an answer." Robaratus pushed.

"Cassius gives me the builder's price. I have told him many times the prices are far too high, but he insists, so I have to adjust the books to fit the new prices and he puts the taxes up to cover it all."

"What about other tenders?"

Appius laughed a bitter laugh. "There *are* no other tenders."

Robaratus frowned. "So you're telling me that Cassius gives work to his own builders?"

"No. He has no builders, well sometimes he does."

Then the *as* dropped on Robaratus. Cassius was creating fictitious jobs to cover his stealing of coin, other times he gave the work to men who had no knowledge of the job, so that it had to be done again.

"You know this is going on and you say nothing?" Robaratus pushed.

"I want to live." Appius moaned.

Robaratus thought for a moment, then suggested, "when did you last have a holiday?"

Appius looked at him as though he were mad.

"You are worn out Appius. I shall recommend you take your family on a break, you look ill, then you can take your family to my training school, and stay there. You will be protected."

Appius looked nervous. "What about my work?"

"I'll be doing it."

Appius nodded.

Chapter 22

Robaratus stood in the greeting area of his villa reading a note. "Good news I hope?" Sage asked as she entered the area.
"The Emperor has announced his retirement and named Honorius as his successor. This will be public news tomorrow." Robaratus read.
"Does this news help your cause?" She asked frowning up at him.
"Not sure yet. Cassius wants his promotion to Rome, but with a new Emperor whom Vitus is not familiar with, I wonder how Cassius can be promoted."
"Won't a new Emperor want new staff?"
"Not if he already has his own."
"You say Cassius won't learn of this until tomorrow?"
Robaratus nodded. "What are you scheming up my wife?" He looked at her earnestly. Sage smiled and tapped her nose. "I am off to the baths husband; I have a hunch and that is all you need to know for now." She quickly kissed his cheek and hurried out of the villa before Robaratus could stop her.

Sage found the baths unusually devoid of patrons, but it was still early by Roman standards, so there was time for an indulgent soak. Sage was helped by the slaves that served, and she stood in the baths admiring the frescos on the walls, the statues that stood evenly spaced of naked men and women, some with serious expressions, others with seductive smiles. She inhaled the strong aroma of the mineralised water, and splashed some of its sliminess over her skin. Then from behind a large white marble column emerged a young girl, naked, who slipped into the baths and walked towards Sage. "Greetings." She said as she approached. Sage returned the words with a smile.
"I am Hesta Tatius, wife of Cassius." She announced boldly.
"Sage, wife of Robaratus."
Hesta's eyes grew wide. "Oh you're the wife of the horrible Gladiator." She blurted before covering her mouth and blushing a bright red. "Apologies. I didn't mean to say that." She rushed. Sage laughed, hiding her anger at having her husband judged so. "To what does my poor husband earn the title of horrible for?"
Hesta shrugged. "Honestly I am not sure, except my husband seems to dislike your husband a whole lot."

184

Sage tilted her head to one side and nodded. "Yes. I can agree with that!"

"I expect you know why they hate each other don't you?" Hesta pressed, sensing a good bit of gossip.

"It isn't my story to tell." Sage said kindly. "I'm sure Rob would be happy to tell his side of it, should you really want to know."

Hesta shrunk away. "I'd be too scared to ask." She admitted. "Your husband has a reputation of being a lion. I heard it said he can out shout thousands in the great Colosseum in Rome. That he has great strength even when he is visibly weak. A man isn't called a lion for nothing."

Sage smiled. "Yes, he has that reputation, he is ruthless, but then he had to be to survive ten years as Rome's most famous and most popular gladiator."

Hesta sighed. "How lucky you are to have such a hero for a husband."

Sage smiled. "Cassius is quite famous isn't he?"

Hesta rolled her eyes. "Yea famous for being drunk. Famous for being limp, you know in the bedroom way, and Gods forgive me, he *so* boring."

Sage let out a light laugh. "Surely he isn't all that bad?"

"Oh but he is. He works late, like he did last night, comes home and wakes me up, he starts fondling me and all I wanted to do was go to sleep, but oh no! "You're my wife." He says, "It's your duty." He says." She rolled her eyes again. "I told him if he could get it up for long enough it might be worth waking up for it, then he called me a rich spoilt brat and went off to sleep in his own room."

"I am sorry to hear that." Sage said, not feeling it in the slightest.

"Don't be. You know he promised me we would be back in Rome within the year, yet we are still here in this God-forsaken hole. I probably shouldn't say this but .." Hesta chewed her lips for a moment. "I am planning to leave him." She nodded with conviction.

"Gracious can you do that?" Sage asked looking worried.

"Yes I can. I checked with my father, who is the second cousin of the Emperor. Cassius made me a promise and he hasn't kept it, it was part of the marriage deal, they said Dixi on it, sealed it, so I can leave any time I like as the year is up."

"I think Cassius might be a bit upset at losing you." Sage sought her words carefully.

Hesta hmphed. "He told me that if we got married it would guarantee him a promotion to Rome, except he lied. He keeps buying me things to keep me happy, but I am not as silly as he thinks. He's been getting rid of furniture and other things, I asked him about it and he just said we were refurnishing, but he hasn't ever replaced anything."

"That does seem like strange behaviour." Sage replied. "Do you think he might be in debt?"

Hesta smiled. "Oh! I never thought of that. It makes sense now you mention it."

"I had heard he is a very ambitious man, does that require funding?"

"I don't think so, but he does buy me very expensive things. I admit I have often wondered how he affords it."

"Well that's a good reason to stay isn't it? A man who showers you in gifts must care for you a lot." Though Sage wouldn't have liked it herself.

"A wife needs more than presents. He ought to know, I'm his third! Besides a contract is a contract." Hesta insisted.

"Be careful Hesta. I think Cassius is a very possessive man." Sage cautioned.

"I know he is. I know what happened to his first wife, but she deserved her fate, she was unfaithful. Do you know he caught her in bed with your husband?"

Sage smiled. "He was a reckless young man back then. Did you know he was Empress Aquilina's most favourite bed mate too?" by the wide-eyed look on the young girls face she hadn't known, which made Sage feel smug. If Hesta were trying to incite trouble she had failed spectacularly, at Sages disclosure of her own knowledge of her husband's past.

"Time for me to depart. I'm starting to wrinkle." Sage excused herself and got out of the bath. "I'm not sure how this might affect anything your planning, but tomorrow it will be public knowledge. The Emperor has resigned, naming Honorius as his successor." She knew Hesta would spread that bit of gossip like wild fire, which meant Cassius would need to re-think his plans quickly. The shock on Hesta's face was worth the bombshell.

On the way home, Sage met Robaratus walking to work, his face lit up when he saw her, and he embraced her as if he hadn't just seen her a couple of hours before. "I have some news for you." Sage said once she was freed. "Walk with me." Robaratus took her arm and Sage told him what she had learned. "That makes his situation far worse than even I imagined." He said seriously. He thanked his wife and they parted company on the steps to the Council building. Robaratus watched her walk away, his mind a whirlwind of thoughts. Inside the debating chamber another argument was going on. Robaratus looked to Vitus who shrugged. "In these times of higher taxation, I have to raise my prices. How else do I cover the tax?" A man argued. "By raising your prices, we have to raise tax." Cassius argued back.

"If you raise taxes any higher you'll cripple this city." The man shouted back.

186

"Then lower your prices." Cassius said calmly, to the cheers of other senators. "I cannot lower my price. How do I pay for the materials if I can't afford them?"

Cassius shrugged, opened his arms which made his white toga look like a sail on a ship. "I will seek a cheaper quote. Business is done, you may leave." The man stood opened mouthed, then stormed out.

"Cassius. How are these higher taxes affecting your own purse?" Robaratus asked loudly. Cassius stopped preening and turned to face him. "What business is that of yours?" He replied louder than necessary. Robaratus shrugged. "It's an innocent question. I am certain every senator here is having to tighten their belts given the hike in taxes." Everyone fell silent. In truth the higher taxes had not reached the purses of senators, just the citizens of Firenze. "I manage well enough." Cassius replied disinterested. He moved to retake his seat.

"Then why was your slave selling your furniture?" The whole chamber broke out into a loud murmur. Cassius stopped and turned looking murderously at Robaratus. "I am restyling my home." He growled, his face reddening up to his bald scalp. Robaratus smiled kindly. "You see, the tax raises are affecting you!. That man was right, the cost of materials is rocketing, is that why the restyling requires a cut in your slave labour?" More mumbling broke out. "What in Hades are you suggesting Ectorius?" Robaratus shrugged again. "May be you have a debt senator, one that requires a hike in taxes to cover?"

"What requires a tax increase, are the exorbitant prices our builders are putting in for work in the city, especially for work on pointless monuments to dead gladiators." Cassius snapped.

Robaratus smiled at him, then turned to address the chamber. "I am taking over the treasury for a few weeks while poor Appius has a much-needed break."

"Absurd!" Cassius spat. "You have no experience regardless of the education you claim to have had."

"From the ledgers I have already seen, you appear to be the only person in Firenze who is providing any workers for work."

The chamber mumbled with discontent. "Furthermore these workers seem to have to re-do their work far more often than they actually do. Can you explain all this?"

The grumbling grew louder and Cassius glared at Robaratus.

"Then there is your wife, who seems to have a very definite opinion of you." This time there was laughter. Robaratus drew the conclusion most of the senators were aware of what Hesta thought and said.

"Is it not true that your contract with her father is now overdue? Isn't that why you are so desperate to get your promotion? Why you broke into my home and demanded I get you promoted?" Cassius made to lash out at Robaratus but the ex-gladiator was much faster. Catching his arm, twisting it behind his back and as he did so, Vitus called the guards and had Cassius arrested. The senators exploded into a riot of shouts and arm waving, of furious faces and promised threats. Robaratus watched his revenge play out, feeling a sense of closure to years of his life lost to this self-righteous, overly ambitious man.

"Well played senator." Vitus said in his ear. "I believe we will have a room vacant for you soon enough!." Robaratus nodded. "You should be proud Rob. You have done a fine job."

*   *   *

Robaratus sat in the room Appius used to do the ledgers, he was trying to start anew, work out what was left in the treasury that might be used for repairs and the such; when the door burst open and Cassius barged in. "So how does it feel to finally get your own back on me?."

"I thought you'd been arrested." Robaratus said in a distracted tone, as he checked figures in the ledger, not looking up.

"Arrested doesn't always mean imprisoned." Cassius sneered. Robaratus gave him a tired look. Cassius grabbed a lighted torch from the corridor and stepped inside the room, closing the door. Robaratus looked nervously at the torch. "Have you considered the consequences of what you're doing?" His voice was low, and calm, but his eyes surveyed the waste papyrus on the floor.

"It's good to see you paying attention to me at last. Did I not warn you accidents happen?" He dropped the torch onto the floor. Immediately Robaratus jumped from his chair and pushed Cassius out of the way, trying to stamp on the flames that had found food in the papyrus. Cassius had stumbled to one side laughing maniacally. "My wife left me this morning; I expect you know why." He shouted over the crackling of fire. Robaratus made no response, being too busy to stamp out the flames, but realising he was losing the battle he sort to escape by the door while he could still see it. Cassius was upon him, grabbing his toga and bellowing in his face as the heat rose. "There is a new fucking Emperor, that's why." Robaratus punched him, knocking him sideways, flames were dancing all around him and he coughed in desperation to re-find the door. A vicious punch in Robaratus' gut winded him, he doubled over gasping for air to refill his lungs, but all he got was smoke. His eyes watered as he tried to locate Cassius in the increasing heat, another punch from behind him had him on his knees, Robaratus flung his arms around widely trying to locate Cassius, he caught a leg and pulled at it, Cassius yelled from the pain, though his screams were hard to hear over the roar of flames, snapping and crackling at ledgers that surrendered to the heat on shelves along the walls. Cassius laughed, a mad man's laugh. "We will die together gladiator." He screamed over the noise. Robaratus felt his strength wither, robbed of his ability to breathe, he began to succumb to the heat and smoke, he felt his skin bubble from burns, and he sobbed though his eyes were dry as bone, to think he would never see his child born nor hold his adored wife ever again. He dragged himself along the floor, memories flooding his mind in a confused state, of bloody battles, of almost dying, of his last ever fight, half-starved and weak, and Sage. Sage who had saved him with the news of her pregnancy. Robaratus made one last effort to reach the door, he pulled himself along on raw arms but just as he made it to the door; he found it closed, of course. He had no strength to stand, had nothing left to give. Softly he called her name "Sage." *I'm so sorry.*

*   *   *

     Sage paced restlessly around the room; she rubbed her arms with her hands as she waited for the doctors to finish their work on her husband. Sabia had tried to keep her calm, reminding her she needed to keep her pregnancy, Vitus had held her comforting her as she cried at the news of the fire.

"I should've insisted he be imprisoned." Vitus moaned. "He was truly mad."

Sage just eyed him. The doctors entered the greeting area and Sage rushed over to them. "He will live." Was the verdict of both, "but he will have burns. He won't be growing those locs any more, his head will be scarred. His face is raw, but will recover. He has lost the top part of one ear, due to his metal clips melting the flesh. His back is raw so we have placed him on his stomach which did not get burnt at all, miraculously. His legs will be scarred and he may not be able to walk again, likewise his hands are burned and we shall have to see how they heal." The doctor looked tired; they had been with Robaratus for quite some time. Vitus thanked both for their efforts.

"He will live. Nothing else matters." Sage breathed with relief, unconsciously rubbing her belly as if to reassure her babe as well.

"We will help him." Sabia said with determination.

"He will not take kindly to being a cripple, nor will he allow himself to be treated as such." Sage shook her head, she knew she would be dealing with a stubborn, angry man when he did start his recovery.

"We have the best doctors to deal with him, even Rome has had to borrow our doctors before now!" Vitus tried to sound reassuring, but Sage wasn't listening, instead she walked to the bedroom where the light was blocked from the room to protect Robaratus' eyes, just a small candle flickered at the far side of the room, allowing attendees to see their way around. Sage stifled a sob at the sight of her husband, raw and bloody with watery wounds. Softly she approached his side. "Rob. My dearest and most adorable man I am here, and we will all help you become the best you can possibly be. Please come back to me. I would hear your frustrations a hundred times a day rather than this terrible silence." She placed the softest of kisses on his cheek and let silent tears slip down her face.

*   *   *

Robaratus lay on his side. The rain tapped out a tune on the roof, the coolness in the air was a blessed relief from the itching his wounds caused him. Sage sat at his side telling him the latest gossip, her belly large now, her baby due any time. Robaratus' eyes watched her intently, a vivid green that often flashed with anger. Every day he worked his fingers and facial muscles, determined not to become the cripple he dreaded being. Sage gently worked his legs, though now Sabia had taken over that job because of the pregnancy. "Your parents want to visit you. Do you want that?"

His sharp eyes flashed upwards to her, his voice was still hoarse, but he looked keenly at his wife. Sage smiled. "I will stay out of the way."

Robaratus gave his twisted snarl, the closest he could get to a smile; he moved his arm slowly, holding it out of the bed for Sage to grasp. "You're welcome" She said. "Vitus and some of the gladiators want to annoy you later."

He rolled his eyes and snarled again.

"Hesta sent me a note, she has got a huge amount of coin from the sale of the things Cassius brought her; she has offered it to us." Sage knew

190

exactly what her husband would say to that, and judging from his screwed-up eyes, she was right. "I'll ask her to return it to the treasury, or better still donate it to the gladiators monument." She leaned over and softly kissed his lips. "Good thing I know you so well, my husband." His fingers squeezed hers and his eyes watered. Sage pretended not to notice it was tears, but if they rolled onto his cheek as they often did, she would lightly brush them away, and say it was good his tear ducts worked, even if it was involuntarily. The baby kicked, so she placed his hand on her stomach so he could feel the life he had created with her, again his snarl came back and his eyes watered. "He is as strong as his father already." She told him. "Sabia said we are having a boy; I am carrying all at the front." Sage laughed lightly. He nodded carefully. The sound of feet had her turning towards the door. "Robaratus! You'd better be behaving yourself; you have guests."

"Vitus Quirinus, I shall be talking to your wife about that!" Sage called back, but she was grinning. "Later my love." She said and waddled her way from the room.

As usual Robaratus had a steady stream of visitors, including his parents, who declared their pride in him once more. Sage couldn't help but notice how some words made a difference to how Robaratus healed, his parents' approval of him of was something he had yearned for since he and Sage had returned, though he never said a word about them, she knew he missed not seeing them. Perhaps when the child was born, it might provide an opportunity for him and his parents to see each other more, she could use those visits as an excuse to catch up on her own time, the idea made her smile. The stone mason was doing well with the memorial column, and it had been decided that Robaratus would be the crowning gladiator, standing on the top. Sage longed to see the finished thing, longed to see what her husband would make of his own image as the crowning glory, but all were agreed it would never be revealed until Robaratus was well enough to stand before it. Since the fire several months before, businesses were returning to the city. Vitus had lowered the taxes to encourage traders back, and now the city was a thriving, busy place again. Robaratus had grimaced at this news, he was still unable to smile properly, but he was determined to keep trying. Sage had hardly noticed the winter months, as all her time had been in the darkened room nursing her husband, but now the spring was coming, and her child would be another kind of new beginning.

*   *   *

Their son was born in their private bath, quite by accident. Sage had thought the waters would help Robaratus to move more easily, she'd been right, but in her excitement her waters had broken and she could not be moved, so Robaratus ended up being a rare witness to the birth of his first born. It both shocked him and left him in awe. He had refused to look in the early stages, but as Sage's cries grew louder, he offered his own hand for her to hold and was shocked at the amount of strength a woman could discover during contractions. Sabia had encouraged him to move to her end of his wife, and watch the birthing process, he had caught his son as he was born, his eyes so wide with joy, and filled with tears. Sabia dealt with the rest of the birth, as Robaratus could not be parted from the baby, all he could mutter was "Mirus, Mirus, Mirus."

Sage shed tears of joy to see the proud father, at least she wouldn't be laying him down before her husband and waiting to see if he would be accepted. "I think he has named the boy!" Sabia whispered to her. Sage laughed, then the baby began to cry.

"I did nothing." Robaratus insisted, looking worried. Sage laughed louder. "The greatest gladiator of all time is completely helpless against a new born." She laughed. "He needs a feed husband."

Robaratus almost handed his son over, but couldn't let go of him completely, he supported his head and stroked his mass of dark hair, still muttering "Amazing, Amazing."

"I think you have named him." Sage said looking adoringly at her husband. Robaratus managed to tear his eyes off his son for a confused look at his wife. "Mirus." She said, he beamed. "I like that for a name. Do you?" He looked worried again, making Sage smile at him. "Rob, if it gives you pleasure, it gives me joy. I think he is amazing, so the name suits perfectly well." Robaratus leaned over and kissed his wife in a slightly lopsided way. "Thank you." He whispered in his new husky voice.

*   *   *

If having his parents' approval again had helped Robaratus in his recovery, then having been witness to the birth of his son had pushed him to work harder, and it paid off. He boasted endlessly about being at the birth, and educated most every man he could on how wondrous the event was, he was seldom seen away from his son, and at times almost forgot he had a wife. Sage had marvelled at the change in him, and two years ago would never have imagined he could be as sensitive and gentle around something as fragile and beautiful as a new born. He took Mirus everywhere, showing him off. He had fallen over so many times in his determination to use his legs again, to be the father he imagined his son would need. He had made up his own exercises for his hands and fingers, using stones to squeeze as gladiators did, to make their grip stronger. He and Mirus had crawled across the floor together, both laughing, but all these things made Robaratus walk, gave him the need to find a voice and finally came the day when he would unveil the monument to gladiators. He stood beside the column, several feet wide, his face had hardly a mark on it now, but his head was bald and scarred. He now wore ear cuffs as decoration, adding to his fierce look, which his son seemed to like, as his ears with their pretty metal sparkles were a constant attraction to small chubby fingers. His back was deeply scarred but he seldom allowed the pain to stop him doing what he wanted. He stood on a platform facing the population of Firenze.

"Citizens of Firenze. Today we honour the valiant men who have given their lives in the name of entertainment. Once being a gladiator was supposed to mean death, the ultimate fate for being a criminal. Then it became a sport, when people loved the brutality of it, the sportsmanship of acting, of surviving raw combat. To those of us condemned to this fate, it was a madness. I have known men who took their own lives, because it was preferable to the taking of another's. Good friends have been made to murder each other, and good men have died for entertainment. Today we hail a new era under Emperor Honorius, whereby the gladiators will no longer kill each other, yet it is not enough to just forget. Good men have died. You do not recall their names, but I do. This monument is made in their memory and each year upon this day, we shall gather to honour their memories again."

The crowd cheered loudly and white petals fell from nets high in the sky. Robaratus pulled the covers free. A tall wide column stood in the middle of Firenze, engraved with every gladiators name in the records, even from Rome. It reached up into the sky, and atop it stood a huge gladiator, wearing shorts and a leather tunic. In front of him rested a large shield. One fist clenched at his side, a short sword in his leather straps across his chest, a long sword stuck into the sand beside him. His head was tilted back with one arm in the air holding a golden helmet, his mouth was open as he roared to the crowd. Around his feet was inscribed.

ROBARATUS ECTORIUS MOST FAMOUS GLADAITOR UNDER ROMAN SKIES.

Historical Notes

As: Roman coin

Arcera: Type of cart for travelling, normally open if carrying goods, can be covered with material or wooden roof.

DM: Rest in Peace

Firenze: Now Florence Italy.

Glires: Edible dormouse (and hamster) a favourite Roman meal.

Hora sexta: Noon, the 6th hour. Roman day was 12 hours long. From dawn to dusk was 12 hours, and called day. From dusk till dawn was 12 hours called night.

Mitte: Let him go.

Mars: God of gladiators.

Optio: Centurion's second in command, supporting him in organising 80 men.

Ovid: One of Rome's most popular poets.

Puer Decimus: Slaves had the owners name, therefore Puer who was owned by Decimus, is known as Puer Decimus.

Urbs: city.

The way in which gladiators trained is actual archive. The abnormalities in bone development comes from archaeologists comparing skeletal remains.

It is quite possible that the slight differences could have been detected, therefore it became a small stretch to have Sage observe such a difference.

The historical inclusions were researched by me, including the importance of a gladiators sweat.

Printed in Great Britain
by Amazon